THE ISLAND QUINTET

A SEQUENCE

ACKNOWLEDGEMENTS

Wayne Brown taught me the rudiments of good prose writing, the Corporation of Yaddo in Saratoga Springs, New York, gave me the time and space to practice in 1994-5, Nathan Hazel's, and Tom and Susan Montvel-Cohen's generosity made sure I did not starve while I was working through the difficult part of the education that allowed me to produce these stories, and Ken Jaikaransingh, of Lexicon Publishers in Trinidad, for no reason at all, humbled me with his belief in my work. Without all these people, this book, and its author, would not exist.

THE ISLAND QUINTET

A SEQUENCE

RAYMOND RAMCHARITAR

PEEPAL TREE

First published in Great Britain in 2009
Peepal Tree Press Ltd
17 King's Avenue
Leeds LS6 1QS
England

ISBN13: 9781845230753

Supported by
ARTS COUNCIL
ENGLAND

CONTENTS

...it's Karl Marx, that sly old racist skipping away with his teeth together and his eyebrows up, trying to make believe it's nothing but Cheap Labour and Overseas Markets... Oh, no. Colonies are much, much more. Colonies are the outhouse of the European soul, where a fellow can let his pants down and relax, enjoy the smell of his own shit. Where he can fall on his slender prey roaring as loud as he feels like, and guzzle her blood with open joy. Eh? Where he can wallow and rut and let himself go in a softness, a receptive darkness of limbs, of hair as wooly as the hair on his own forbidden genitals [...]

Out and down in the colonies, life can be indulged, life and sensuality in all its forms, with no harm done to the Metropolis, nothing to soil those cathedrals, white marble statues, noble thoughts... No word ever gets back. The silences down here are vast enough to absorb all behaviour, no matter how dirty, how animal it gets...

Thomas Pynchon

For Aurora

Who outshines any Sun

THE ARTIST DIES

Trying to remember the moments leading up to this occasion, I stand here, staring out over the disembodied faces: Babs, rosy and content, her face's angles just beginning to curve into motherly roundness; Bain, upright and grey, protectively close to her; Balthazar, restless eyes constantly moving in search of the perspective that eludes the rest of us; the girl's furious, helpless red eyes; the Artist's parents, featureless and bewildered; Aixman's flat, rapacious face retaining its ruddiness even in the gravity of the occasion, unfazed by the Gothic scale and slant of the roof, the stained-glass windows, the marble pillars of the nave. These faces shine up at me, picked out from the crowd as I stand here, gripping the gilt edge of the lectern, peering down at the tired-looking sheets of paper I'd been scribbling on for most of the night.

The journey back begins with my eyes moving out over the faces, moving slowly, following the sliver of pale light through the doors into the grimy grey yard, over the spiked fence, outside into the pale slate bowl of the sky.

My mind caresses these moments, stroking each one that still holds its shape, that hasn't been deformed by the stretching of the years, or by the weight of other moments. The movement is a kind of sleep, and I suppose that's all right, because as it unfolds, I find myself thinking that none of this is suited to reality, nor appropriate to the furiousness that dictates action. *I will enjoy this more in retrospect*, I think.

It all began in sleep.

I keep the phone near the bed for just such an occasion – even though my life breathes quietly and regularly these days. The only thing that could disturb the pleasant stasis is the Artist. *Was* the artist. It takes getting used to. He was the only thing that could disturb me. Everything else – deaths, a crisis at the bank, any general incident of undirected misfortune – had already happened, or could not possibly happen now.

"Hello?"

"He's dead." Her voice was perfect for the moment; it was the suffering she'd been rehearsing for, all her life.

"What?"

"He… he's dead." The pause, the timing of it, was perfect. I was almost in awe. "I thought I should call you. You're the only one I could think of."

"Where are you?"

"At the hospital in the city," she said.

It was very early in the morning, cold in the hills where I live. The heat of my breath on the windscreen glazed the moon's irisless eye. She was waiting for me at the gate, under the narrow awning of the guard's hut. As she saw me, she leaned into the booth and the barrier rose – the kind with alternating black and luminous white lines snaking around it – admitting me into the nearly empty courtyard. A few other cars, a police car among them, sat there, painted in the silver light.

She looked like a child in a dark dream walking toward me: small, her wild, curly hair bobbing softly, its tendrils dissolving into the night. As she came closer, the outlines of her breasts under the surface of her thin white shirt became apparent. The nipples were large and stiff.

"You're here," she said, stopping very close to me.

The dark red eyes brimmed with the desperation and rage they still have.

"Come on." She took my hand. It was the first time she had ever touched me; unfamiliarly, awkwardly, as if she were holding a piece of wood. But the heat of her palm in the coldness of the night gave the moment a strange intensity. We were two people walking across a deserted plain, towards one of our number who was now dead. No doubt from as early as people have had the luxury of mourning their dead, such journeys have been made. I looked at her again: the hair, the large brown eyes, the gentle curve of her hips, her enigmatic smile (fixed in the picture of her the Artist had taped onto a wall of his studio).

I followed her silently. The hospital, like the church, had been built more than a hundred years ago by the British in the Victorian Gothic style. I followed her through the arched passageway into the building, into the elevator and along a maze of identical corridors – square white passages with discs of fluorescent light every few yards along the ceiling.

The room was like those you see in the movies, only more sordid; the Artist would have loved it. A battery of naked examination lights stared down at him on the gurney. The stains on the sheet draped across his chest were mildew, not blood. The bullet wound didn't look so deadly against his dark skin as they do against the white skin of corpses in the movies. The purplish wrinkled protuberance a few inches above his sternum looked almost decorative, like one of his tattoos – black lines along the lengths of his fingers; little diamonds around his neck; small, Maori-like symbols below his ears, partially hidden.

Now, with the eyes closed, his lips ashy and white, his face seemed resolved into its essential parts: a mouth, a nose, dark cheeks, eyebrows, the light stubble blending into the dark brown skin. I'd never seen his features so stable, so uninteresting. In life, depending on the direction from which you looked, you saw sometimes completely different people. From the front, you saw a youngish looking burnt-brown man with shiny black hair, firm, fleshy lips, piercing eyes. The brownness weakened the handsomeness; the face could be that of a labourer, but the slim body, slouching or coiled, made him striking. From the side, with the tattoos, with the face twisted into a sneer, the body louche and lazy, its curves inartistic, the eyes slitted, he could look like a petty thief – and he revelled in the languages that went with such poses.

She'd stood quietly as I stared at him, but as I began to smile, I felt her stiffen.

"They were in here before," she said. "They just leave him like that. They didn't even cover him up."

The tremor in her voice shook me awake. But now I realise it wasn't into wakefulness; not awake like I am now. I woke into another layer of life, where his death was negotiable, where I was playing along with another one of his games.

"Look," I said, turning to her. But her face was outside the Artist's game. A humourless pain deformed it, borrowing its gestures from suffering women in any one of a thousand movies, soaps, cheap novels. I sighed mutely. For her it was real and terrible.

"Look, there's nothing more here tonight. I'll take you home," I said.

No one appeared as we walked out; no policeman, no nurse, no doctor. She followed me and sat tensely in the car. We drove out of the hospital through grey and deserted streets and onto the King's Field, then around to St James, where she and the Artist lived.

Their apartment was at the end of a long street of houses, which tapered from respectability at the top – painted low walls, thick green hedges leading up brownstone paths to doors with shiny knockers – to dingy and poor at the bottom. He had settled on the border between comfort and misery, just where the high flaking walls, the staccato of barking mongrels, the carelessly repainted gates with the rust sores began.

A volley of barks greeted the car as it stopped in front of the gate, and she looked up the short path to the small apartment and tensed. She reached for the handle and pulled it back slowly, hearing the soft crack as the lock released and the door opened.

She turned to me and whispered, "Thank you." There was now just misery and tiredness in the smooth dark cheeks, the pulpy lips, the dark Spanish eyes. This was as much as I'd had to do with her in all the time she and the Artist had been together.

"Look," I said. "Pack a bag. Stay at my house. You shouldn't be alone tonight. We'll talk tomorrow after you've slept."

"Alright," she said simply.

I put her in the white room. As I shut the door behind her, I drifted into the cocoon – a small space at the back of the house that had inexplicably appeared because of some incompleteness in the Artist's and the architect's collaboration. The space was about ten feet wide, a gap between two converging walls. I'd glassed it around, since it looked down the hillside out over the sea, and put in two old leather chairs, each with an ottoman, and a small shelf with a few books, and the brandy I had saved for a special occasion.

The heat from my palm set off a slight trembling in the dark liquid in the bulbous glass; apart from the girl's breasts rising and falling in the white room, the surface of brandy was the only thing moving in the house and the night outside the window. The sea was still; in the half-moonlight even the ripples seemed fixed, making the expanse a vast, solid plain. There was no disturbance, no agitation. I grinned to myself as I settled into the thick moans of the leather chair, and willed myself to drift between sleep and half-wakefulness. The Artist's passing had not excited the elements.

I owe the Artist everything. That's one truth. One of his many alternative truths. I worked, I studied, I passed exams, I hewed raw wood into planks. But if it had not been for the Artist, my labours would have blushed unseen, wasted on the desert air, unhonoured in a country churchyard. It started about six years before. I was a teacher in the village where I'd lived all my life. I was just at that stage when torrential youth meanders into a silty middle course – in my late twenties. I'd been to the training college, gotten my teacher's diploma and settled into the regularity of the mapped-out life. I wasn't dissatisfied. I didn't know enough to be dissatisfied. There was a girl about my age in the village; she would have been my wife. We had spoken a few times. She had given herself to me on the understanding that the price was a lifetime of provision and mutual effacement. A date had been set.

Then I saw the advertisement in the staff room: teachers wanted in Great Britain. A few of the others were talking about it, talking about going for a few years – for the money. I'd sat with them, looking at the cheap cotton shirts, the resoled shoes, the fading trousers and skirts in that squalid room; the splintered tables, the sweat-worn brown chairs. They weren't going anywhere. They'd already fulfilled their compacts with the island's earth: the special-rate mortgages, the new car every fifteen years, the too-expensive miserable children.

I remember the slight stir as my protesting, indignant youth prodded me. Then nothing. Then came another circular from the

Education ministry: salaries would not be raised again for another three years. I told the girl we'd have to wait a year. She nodded. *What did she look like?* I remember the dark skin, straight black hair, the old floral print dress – sunflowers – as she said: "Wait."

She left me on the porch in the patched rattan chair looking out over the lonely, uncared-for road which ran from the central town into the old cocoa and sugar cane estates our people had been brought from India and Africa to tend. In the past few decades, the island had industrialised and the cocoa and sugar estates were being abandoned. The people had been forgotten, but remained quietly in the villages, breeding, merging into the land and the tangled, disordered vegetation – the thick, stifling quiet of the countryside.

My new shoes were filthy; it had been raining that day and the path up to the house was muddy. They were a poor family. The marriage would have taken her out of the faded white wooden estate house, a memory of the past which did not exist in any registry. It had been patched and nailed and worn from the traffic of successive families. Its jalousied windows stared mournfully over a rough-edged square of lawn, and a few crotons and ixoras struggled to provide a semblance of order.

It had seen births, deaths, a few joys, a few moments of real pain, the regular state of waiting. This was the house she would be leaving – the house she shared with parents, three brothers and two sisters – to enter mine, bought with the special teacher's mortgage. The land it stood on was in another village along the road, closer to the central town; it would be like starting another life.

She returned with the newspaper, folded to the page. A neat red box had been drawn round the advertisement.

"You could go for a few years," she said. She didn't say, "I'll wait."

I was mulling that over on the plane as I looked at the small photograph she had given me on our last evening – her face powdered in an unnaturally light shade, against a backdrop of a painted Taj Mahal in the photo studio in the central town.

From my first sight of the airport, a small rage had begun to grow in me. Our group had been herded to the counter by our contact, a red-faced Englishman dressed in shirtsleeves and khaki trousers. Outside our group were people whose existence I had never suspected: happy, busy, opulent. I saw I was poorly dressed. It was mid-August; the British teaching authority had felt it might be better to have us up before the autumn term began.

I can remember only the hair and the darkness of her skin from the photo headshot. I sat in a row of seats by myself. The plane held nine seats from wall to wall; nine of my colleagues filled the row. I was the tenth man; I sat by myself behind them.

Call it fate, but that moment marked my severance from the country, school and future I had accepted. He sat right next to me, looking just as he would always look – as ever, outrageously dressed. His hair was dyed blond, and he wore earrings, gold hoops, in both ears. The tattoos weren't there yet, but there were dark, make-up circles around his eyes. He wore leather pants and sneakers.

He turned to me as soon as he'd squeezed past to his seat.

"First time on a plane, pal?" He grinned crassly, his teeth white and uneven.

"Whoa, buddy," he sniggered, as I clenched my jaw and pursed my lips. "Relax, man. You're going to England. That's called taking the piss."

"You mean the piss they put in your hair to get it that colour?" I asked. I'd never said anything like that before, but then I'd never been confronted like that before.

He laughed loudly. "That's the ticket," he said. "This is a 13-hour flight, wouldn't want to be stuck with someone boring."

He was not interested in anything about me except my presence and my willingness to listen. He was a few years older than me, and an artist. I'd never met anyone before who had the audacity to introduce himself as an artist. I was more bemused than interested, and raised my eyebrows a little. He didn't seem to notice.

He had been to art school in the States, then come back to the island. He had tried to drag them into the 20th century, but for the island, modernity was still an unfinished idea: people clung to their ideas about beauty and transcendence. Perhaps it couldn't be otherwise when the ugly wounds of the past had not been healed – or even acknowledged. We needed art only to anaesthetize us from the pain of experience, and that was only when we realized that pain and ugliness were not our natural state, he said to me earnestly in the darkened cabin. We could not appreciate his vision; the ugliness of the world was its beauty; the clean Romantic ideas of beauty were merely bourgeois devices to cover our own inadequacies and hypocrisy.

"Um hm," I said, half-asleep.

I was dozing when he excused himself to go to the bathroom.

"Ah boy," he'd said, "I feel a good shit coming on. You know what I mean, Bhagwansingh? Nothing like sitting down and letting a nice wet, fat load plop into the Atlantic."

"What?" I was sleepy but still disgusted. Once he saw he'd been able to revulse me, he left with a smile on his face. He returned a half-hour later, still grinning.

"Nothing like a good bamsy-dig to get you settled, you know what I mean, pal?"

This was one of his less than intriguing traits I would come to know over the years. He was anally obsessed; talk of defecation, flatus, or his anus could occupy him for hours.

When I woke a few hours later, my neck was stuck in the unnatural angle it had settled in. The cabin was in darkness except for the ring of light next to me. He was reading. I twisted my neck to the side, bringing my ear towards my shoulder, and was rewarded by a sharp crack as the bones realigned.

"Jesus!" he said. "What the fuck was that?"

"Nothing," I said. "My neck."

"My father does that," he said. "Do they teach you that at coolie cane-cutting school or something?"

"What?" I was vaguely offended.

"You know, coolie cane-cutting school. My father came at me with a cutlass one time, and that's exactly what he did with his neck." He mimicked my twist, his blond head with the dark-ringed eyes looking absurd as he tilted it to the side.

"Your father came at you with a cutlass?" I vacillated between offence and morbid curiosity.

"Yeah. Didn't yours?" he said, looking surprised. "I thought it was a coolie rite of passage. You know: you become a man; your pa comes after you with a cutlass."

14

He was laughing. The blond hair bobbed surreally in the near dark of the cabin. Another of his jokes. I leaned back and closed my eyes and pursed my lips.

"Hey, now," he said, touching my arm. There was almost a tenderness in his touch – nothing that his words or face would have suggested; the fingers were hesitant, almost childlike and seeking. I looked over at him.

"Hey. Don't be like that," his brown face relaxed into something gentle. "I'm only joking."

"Alright." I said.

Once he saw I was calm again, he continued talking, telling me about his life, what he hoped to do, the names of the exhibitions he hoped to be included in, the critics he hoped to meet and impress. My own life seemed too inane to talk about; he never asked me about it and I never volunteered.

He was on his way to Goldsmiths College. He had managed to get a grant for a masters degree, and he hoped from there to launch himself into Europe: that was a continent that appealed to him, he said, the dark eyes squinting and intense, but still unable to outshine the blond hair.

The latest theorists in his field were writing in France: Stuger, Charlat, Epi. The names meant nothing to me, but they stayed with me like small outcrops on the smooth-faced slope I was sliding down. At the bottom waited drudgery, boredom, malaise.

I was given a two-year contract and a subsidized apartment in Clapham. The school was in Brixton, where many West Indians had settled, and British teachers were unable to penetrate the dense accents and angry resistance their mere presence seemed to provoke among the children.

The school, with its red wood and glass doors, its ancient rusted fire extinguishers, its dark grey walls and white-lit corridors, the enormous, dingy classrooms we had *all to ourselves*; the children all dressed and fed, if miserable and sullen – it was all infinitely *more* than anything I had ever seen, although I would later find out that it was extremely poor.

The British had struck a perfect match: their most insulting offers were better than anything we had ever dreamed of. The trains, the crazy order of the streets, the endless queues, the regal lions guarding Trafalgar Square, the redness of the buses against the drabness of the buildings, the monuments: it all fascinated me for months before becoming commonplace. But most wondrous were the people: everywhere and all the time, the endless stream of humanity of every shape, size, colour and description moving in all directions at once.

We were instructed how to use the Underground, encouraged to visit the museums and the theatres, shown where to get the necessaries. I fell into a routine after the first month, but I'd been changed. The Artist's intervention, as I think of it now, had brought me close to the world that confronted me at the airport. I bought some men's fashion magazines and spent most of the clothing allowance they gave me on new clothes. The others bought second-hand coats and sweaters; they'd decided that the flimsy trousers, the cheap leather shoes, thin merino undershirts they'd brought with them were going to make do, and hoarded the money they'd been given for the purpose.

I resolved to send £100 home to the girl every month, and to save as much as I could. I hadn't given much thought to the Artist, but the virus he'd planted in me began to multiply. At the weekends and in the afternoons I found myself restless. I wandered around the city, I went to the theatres and couldn't understand the plays. I went to the galleries and couldn't understand the paintings. I stopped after a month.

By Christmas, I'd fallen into a comfortable routine. Amnesia had begun to set in. I knew the way to school so well it required no thought. I went through the days easily, and made my way back home. I watched the telly, listened to the radio and began reading the London papers. I wrote the girl little notes about the school with the money orders I sent.

But when the school broke up for Christmas, and the routine broke, the desire returned. I found myself venturing into central London and wandering around, invariably ending up at the Nelson Monument, staring at the lions for a long time before I took the train home. The rage returned, the impossible desire to know and possess everything I saw. But the desire never lasted very long.

A few days before Christmas, as I turned to walk away, I bumped into the Artist.

"You," he said. "Sundar, Bachasingh, Potoolal, from the plane. I knew it was you. You got new clothes."

I didn't point out that my name wasn't close to any of the ones he'd uttered; I just stood there in the early London evening, smiling at him. The hair had changed colour, was now jet black and longish. He wore an old army officer's black coat, black jeans and boots with chrome embellishments. He looked like an alien; but I suppose I was the alien. It never occurred to me that we had been born on the same island, barely a hundred miles across.

"How are you?" I asked.

"How am I? How are you?" he asked. His voice tapered slightly at the ends, where the British accent was beginning to curl it. My own was flat and dry and unchanged from the island. The children I spoke to every day expected me to speak as if I, too, was a perpetual foreigner, the way their immigrant parents spoke.

"I'm doing some research at the National Portrait Gallery," he said, "and I just leaned over to dig my bottom and I saw you outside the window. I thought I'd seen you before, just staring at the damned lions. I thought I'd come out and see if it was you."

He took me to the bar he frequented. The place was old and dingy, with failed paintings and sculptures of metal, old televisions, electric irons and potbellied stoves, donated by several of the many artists who frequented it, placed haphazardly around. There were the remains of multicoloured burnt-out candles in tall, slender candle holders. That night it was packed with people whose appearance made his look tame; green lipstick, noserings, ruby-studded chokers and chrome-pointed dog collars. At the far end was a small dance floor with a few weak strobelights; a few bodies were dancing, some gyrating, some pairs pressed together and standing stock still in the bass-throbbing miasma of smoke and laughter.

He dragged me along, strangely at home, yet not quite belonging here, nodding to people, slapping some on the back, kissing one or two women on the lips. I followed mutely, and allowed myself to be plonked on a zinc stool by the long metal bar.

"Got money, Haridas?" he asked.

"A little," I said cautiously.

"Buy us a drink then," he grinned.

17

I passed out sometime after the eighth tequila. When I woke, my eyes fell on a small, helmeted knight on a white charger, surrounded by an army of identical knights. I was lying on an old green velour couch; my face burned. I automatically reached for my wallet; it was there, but slipping my finger along the groove where it closed, I felt nothing. No notes. I groaned and closed my eyes.

"Will you fucking shut up!" The couch faced a wall, and the voice came from behind me. I unsteadily pulled myself up and winced as I moved my head.

He lay face down on an untidy bed, dressed in the same clothes he'd worn the night before. I made my way past him through a door I thought must lead to the bathroom. The toilet had been vomited in and left unflushed. The cold water from the tap shocked me back to life. Sobriety came almost instantly, and brought with it sickness. My coat had disappeared. I wore only a shirt. I stumbled out of the bathroom and back into the bedroom and sat on the bed. He was still asleep. I contemplated walking out the door and forgetting about him, but remembered my empty wallet.

I lay down on the bed and closed my eyes again. When I was wakened by light slaps on my face, the pain in my head was less intense. I looked up into the Artist's eyes; his body was lying diagonally across the bed, intersecting with mine at the shoulders. He was propped on one elbow, the other arm still patting my face, his own face wearing a worried look.

"Oh fuck," he said. "We didn't do it did we?"

"Do what?" I asked.

"Oh thank… what indeed," he said pulling himself back, and flopping down, face up, muttering "what indeed."

It was late evening by the time we revived completely. The apartment was very small: a bed, a couch, a desk and a bookcase – all looking grey in the fluorescent light – and the bathroom.

After that we became friendly – or as close to friendship as the Artist got. He would invite me to parties, and would come to my school for days in a row to take me on outings, then disappear for weeks, not returning my phone calls.

It was the very alienness of it all that let me accept it so easily; but still, it changed me, in more ways than the obvious. It was because of the Artist that I left everything that had been given to me – the certainty of everything around me – and came to the unreal place in the hills from which you had to descend to find the world.

It was at the club he took me to that the journey to this church, looking down on this sea of faces, really began. The Artist had introduced me to a few of his friends when I'd visited him. These were mostly people he knew from college; young women with outrageously coloured hair and noserings wearing army trousers and see-through shirts; young men, bald headed and sullen, wearing T-shirts showing Margaret Thatcher pedalling a bicycle which powered a dildo that came up under the saddle with the legend "Self Reliance". I never had much to say around them; nor around the Artist for that matter. Mostly, I listened. Even after months of reading the reviews in the papers, going to shows and having their jargon begin to make the barest sense to me, I realised that I had nothing in common with them.

Close to the end of my first year, around the Easter break, I had not heard from him for almost six weeks. I found out later that during the periods he disappeared, it would usually mean that the Artist was pursuing other people, those with money or influence, or sometimes women about whom he became insanely possessive – and soon lost. Most of the time, though, he would just be by himself, in grimy solitude. Years later, back in the island, when I had not seen him for months, when he had refused to return my calls, I found out that all he was doing for weeks was sitting, staring at a field under an old, mossy tree.

But in London, I had no other friends. I was lonely. The girl at home was not a great writer. Her letters were dry and practical. The money was being placed in the bank. The rates had improved slightly. She hoped I was doing well. She might try to get a job in a new shop that was opening in the town. Nothing intimate or personal. She didn't ask if I was eating, was I warm for the winter.

I was so lonely I'd tried to gather some of the teachers to go out with me for an evening, somewhere in Piccadilly Circus, somewhere they'd never been. But they wouldn't go. It was too cold. They all stayed in under blankets or compressed into small bundles of desire and meanness before their electric fires.

So, on a cold March night, I wandered into a bar alone, and sat at the table looking out into the street with a single candle and a bottle of wine with my dinner. I reflected ruefully on how romantic it all seemed. I thought of the girl at home. She would never see this place, not as I was seeing it, with the dry cold outside, the hint of snow that would be my first snowfall. She would never see it with the detached pleasure of someone whose orbit had shifted irrevocably, into one charged with a longing for something I could not name.

His reflection stared at me from the window. I spun around. He sat with two people on the far side of the room. I could see them only in profile. He now had longish sideburns and the beginnings of a goatee. He and a man sat facing each other. Next to the man and diagonal from the Artist was a woman. The couple seemed – from their gestures and bearing – to be wealthy; this much of the local language I had learned, how to distinguish between the privileged and the low in Britain.

I got up and walked over.

"Hello," I said, from over the shoulder of the man, looking down at the Artist. "Now where have you been?"

"Choonilal," he said, the brown face split by uneven white teeth, but in a low, mellifluous voice I had never heard him use; his greetings were usually loud and vulgar and involved his anal fetish. His eyes flicked between me and his guests. I looked down at the craggy-faced balding man, and the woman with the red hair and powder-blue eyes. They were both unusually dressed, even in a place that thrived on the unusual; he wore a battered khaki field jacket with puffy ammunition pockets over a white flannel shirt; she wore a flaming red Nehru jacket whose line of buttons was interrupted by an oval of milky flesh around her bosom, and which then resumed and continued up to her neck.

"Meet Sir Robert and Niamh," he said in the same low, smooth voice.

The man smiled, showing yellow teeth, and Niamh angled her body slightly towards me and nodded.

I introduced myself.

"But that's noh wha' he called ya," Niamh said, brushing away tendrils of red hair from her face with long, white fingers adorned with several silver rings studded with turquoise, red and green stones.

20

"You don't think I told him my real name do you? It was just a one night stand," I said.

They both laughed. I excused myself after shaking hands. As I stood at my table wrapping myself into my coat and scarf, he came up behind me.

"They want you to join us," he said, in something closer to his regular voice. "I told them you were leaving and have to work in the morning." The smile and the too-light tone of his voice signalled an intriguing tension beneath. But I'd drunk a bottle of wine by myself and I was lonely.

"Why not?" I said waving past him. "A couple of drinks won't hurt."

"A couple of drinks never hurt anyone." He smiled weakly. "But look," he said as I began to unwrap myself from my scarf and coat. "These people aren't used to the way we do things, you know..."

"Uh huh," I said, smiling over at them.

"Remember not to raise your voice and try not to use any threatening arm gestures..."

"Right," I said, turning to face him. "No arms." I searched for the laughter burbling beneath, but it wasn't there. He was completely serious.

"Well, you folks are sure neighbourly," I said loudly, waving my hands crazily in front of me as I sat.

They both laughed. The woman was a curator and the man a collector. The Artist had managed to get a piece of his work shown at a gallery, and had met the pair; there was talk of a grant for him. Sir Robert, it turned out, was a philanthropist, but of an undirected kind. He funded things arbitrarily and erratically. He had once heard that a particular scholarship offered to the whole of Africa could only fund five applicants out of a thousand. That year, all applicants received grants.

Niamh told the story much later in the night, after we'd drunk three more bottles of wine.

"Yeah, he's loaded arncha, Roburrrt?" She elbowed him, as he smiled weakly. He had remained quiet most of the time, regarding Niamh indulgently. The Artist had remained aloof, smiling politely, willing around himself an aura of muted decadence, descending only to give a honey-voiced explication of anything connected to art that emerged from the conversation.

At the end of one of the Artist's stories, Sir Robert suddenly flashed his yellow teeth at me.

"But what about you? Where are you from?"

"Well," I said, "therein lies a story. He and I," I elbowed the Artist, "are actually fraternal twins separated at birth..."

"Naaaah... go on," said Niamh.

"Nah," I said. "I'm just some sod he hangs about with. I'm a school teacher in Brixton."

"Is that so," said Sir Robert. "And how are things in Brixton?"

"It is a place of great romance," I said. I had no idea where the words were coming from, but I was quite drunk.

"Really?" he said "Romance? In Brixton?"

"In Brixton," I said. "Romance." I peered out of the corner of my eyes at the Artist. He was looking at me blankly, but I could sense the resentment beneath the placid brown face. It was the first and last time I would ever upstage him.

"They're all so angry," I said. "The parents, the children, the teachers, all so miserable. But look where they live. All this," I gestured round, "the library, the museums, everything, *everything*, is so near to them. All they have to do is reach for it."

"But there's racism, discrimination, those things that prevent them from coming to these things," Sir Robert said, suddenly intent upon me.

"My ass." I said. "Where I live, the people who control the wealth look like me, but I will never be rich or happy. Unless you're born one of them, the means are just not there for someone who's not either completely devoid of all humanity, or so overwhelmingly imbued with genius that they cannot be ignored.

"In both those respects, I am unremarkable. The only way I could ever attain that life is by working myself into meanness, and then I would be too damaged by the effort of getting it to enjoy it, and then, what would be the point? So I was never going to win the one scholarship to Oxford open to the whole island, because there are so many more brilliant than I. But then, when the scholars come here, the brilliance shines briefly, and then fades, undone by the hugeness of the effort to escape. My friend here," I reached over and touched the artist's hand, "is the exception. Here, life is unjust, unfair, racist. But the means are here. Knowledge is within reach. That rage, that sadness can be focused. Channelled."

"Really?" said Sir Robert. "Is that right?"

The redhead's eyes were locked onto me.

"Yeah," I said, looking at him cynically. "That's right."

"Tell me," Niamh said. "Are any of ya relatives Irish?"

"Sure," I said. "Oscar Wilde fucked my great-great-grandfather once."

The night ended soon after that. I refused the offer of a lift in Sir Robert's car, and crumpled the slip of paper Niamh had slipped into my hand without looking at it.

Three weeks later, on the first Friday after school had reopened, the Artist showed up at my apartment, laughing.

"Sundar Dedalus," he said, smirking. "The redhead pined after you for a whole week. You jammy bastard. Look at this."

I took the envelope he offered. It was addressed to "The Romantic School Master" in a flourishing script. Inside was an official letter from the Home Office releasing me from my contract, and allowing me leave to proceed to Oxford to take up the fellowship granted by the Sir Robert Older Foundation. The Artist told me he had been awarded a substantial sum as well.

I never told the girl what happened. I kept sending off the cheques for another year. But then, as I was nearing the end of my first year at Oxford, I sat down and wrote to her, telling her that it was unfair of me to have held her to her word this long, that I would probably not return to the island for a long time, and she should get on with her life. Of course, I said, all the money I had sent was hers to do with as she pleased, and that I would continue sending cheques and would she please accept them.

The Artist remained in England for another two years, but we didn't see one another. He remained in London when I went up to Oxford. When I returned to the island five years later, he had been there for three years, and his life had taken several strange turnings, which I would encounter piece by piece over the years.

My new credentials took me far away from the old village. I was taken in by one of the large international banks, and my life set on a new path. It was as invariant and I was as invisible as before; but now my invisibility was one of lightness because it soared above the world, not because it lay buried beneath.

Meanwhile, the Artist had been everything but invisible. Upon his return he had been greeted with great enthusiasm by the artistic and government community, which good will he quickly squandered. He took up an appointment at the island's university campus, where he ran foul of the establishment in the art department, some of whom had been at the university since its inauguration thirty years before. They were painters and water-colourists of the island's flora and of 'characters', or sculptors of long-limbed dancing native women, and they all regarded anything not contained on a canvas with suspicion. Dr Dhabu, the head of the department had been on the panel which judged a competition the Artist had entered; he had written on the Artist's submission: "This is not a house-painting or pornography competition." In his first week's teaching, the Artist showed up dressed like the rapper Flavour Flav, complete with a clip-on gold tooth and wrote on the board: "The body is a site". He told the students the painting and illustration they were being taught was meaningless and useless and they should get out of the island before the old fossils squeezed them into a load of Dhabu.

One of the students taped the lecture. The Artist was fired after a year; it took that long only because of the university's constipated bureaucracy. The Artist thereafter announced he would be staging an exhibition of contemporary works at the best private gallery in the capital. The dealer, Marcel Aixman, a transplanted Frenchman, was the most ruthless businessman in the city. His gallery sold to the island's richest and most illustrious citizens, and he delighted in taking advantage of them. Selling them fourth-rate pieces for hundreds of thousands of dollars and bullying them into admitting the vilest pieces were beautiful.

Aixman's stable of artists included Nofobu, the island's leading African artist; Kassissa, the island's leading Indian artist; and Balthazar Bouvier, a contemporary of the Artist's who had been trained in America. There were others, of course, but these were the foundations upon which Aixman's practice rested: the work they produced was reliable and authoritative. They provided beautiful confirmations of the Africans' mythic struggles and their noble origins; of the intense spirituality and beautiful colours of the Indians' millennia-old culture; and finally, through Bouvier, a record of the origination of the culture of the island, and its heroic struggles against colonialism. Each had his appropriate rhetoric and style; each fetched considerable prices.

For a week before the opening of the show, the Artist would not let Aixman into the gallery, an old house in a fashionable part of the city, in a neighbourhood of wide streets with white stone sidewalks and leafy trees back-dropped by the mountains. By the time Aixman was let in, it was too late. The floor space was transformed, covered in cardboard with paths marked out in duct tape and labelled "the easy road". The white walls were painted with shacks and biological drawings of dismembered animals, and smeared with what looked like traces of excrement. The duct-tape paths led into the back room where, behind glass frames, were three human hands dismembered a few inches above the wrist, on pure white matte. A brown hand was cut clean from the wrist and stuck with a knife; a white one was nailed through the centre of the palm by a heavy iron spike, and a black one dangled from a chain. The piece was titled "The Hand That Feeds You".

But there was more. When the guests arrived – they included Goldy Abouko Singer, the island's semi-insane minister of culture, a poetess who wrote long, graphic poems about her menstrual cycles – they were met by a sign in the foyer instructing them to take off their shoes. Once inside and unshod, another sign instructed them that they could either take the easy road or walk through real life.

Everyone chose the easy road, and the evening ended abruptly with the first twenty or so most important people having to get medical attention to have the invisible glass shards the Artist had spread on "the easy road" removed from their soles.

Singer, a tall, black woman, who wore what she had been told was traditional African garb by a visiting Nigerian con-artist posing as a poet, probably saved the Artist from certain death, by pronouncing the show a success.

"A lesson we should all remember. The easy road is almost never that," she was quoted in the papers the next day from a private clinic in the city. Most of the other patrons, though, knew better. Had the Artist been present he would probably have been shot.

When he surfaced the next day, Aixman's rage was met only by a vicious smirk. He would never show in his gallery again, said Aixman, but by then the Artist was laughing so hard, Aixman could only threaten him.

"Some day, you little coolie bastard..." Aixman had said. "I do not forget this."

Whatever else the Artist was, he was lucky. One of the guests was a German diplomat, Dreich Friellur, who had kept his shoes on and actually seen the pieces on the back wall. He visited the Artist in the following week, paid an obscene amount for the three hands (in the confusion nobody had bothered to ask if they were real – they were – or where the Artist had gotten them) and commissioned him to reproduce the installation the following year in Germany. Aixman, on receiving his percentage, forgave and forgot.

Friellur took the Artist to the expatriate and diplomatic parties, and introduced him as a talent on the scale of genius, which the decadent transnational bourgeoisie, on the evidence of the patron's status, were happily prepared to accept, and paraded their gritted teeth as smiles. Within a few months, the incident at Aixman's gallery had become a minor legend – it became quite fashionable to claim that one had been cut by the Artist's shards.

It was at one of Friellur's parties that the Artist first met Babs Jones. The name her mother had given her was Barbara, after the author of popular romances, Barbara Cartland. In the London circles Babs yearned to orbit, she was what would be called a "sociable girl". This meant she would sleep with anybody – ushers, stagehands or gopher boys – to get into the theatre, or films, or modelling, or television commercials, or anything even vaguely related to the "world of glamour" as her mother called it. After four years in London, Barbara was rechristened Babs, short for "Blowjob Barbie", because of her blonde hair, blue eyes, and her reputed alacrity for fellating all comers.

Babs had drifted into the island to shoot a commercial with a British film crew a year before the Artist returned, and had been struck almost at once by the difference thrust upon her. As she walked off the plane into the stultifying heat, and down the stained terrazzoed floors, following the ill-printed plexi-glass signs along the corridors of wilted palm trees in cracked pots, out of the corners of her sunglasses she saw the stares, and felt the desperation of the men around her to impress. The immigration officer in the ugly blue Havana jacket uniform caressed her passport as he stared at her from behind the pockmarked wooden counter.

"How long you want to stay?" he asked, gently.

"Just a few days," she'd replied.

"I'll put a month," he said, showing tobacco-stained teeth and adjusting his Malcolm X glasses, "in case you see something you like here, and decide to stay with us a little longer."

From there, it only got better. The head of the local agency her crew was working with invited her out to dinner the first night and offered her a job at the agency for an obscene amount of money. Later that night, as he took her to her door, as Babs fished her key out and prepared to look vulnerable and invite him in, the ad man, a white islander, stopped short and said: "Well Miss Jones, it was an honour to be in your company. May I call on you tomorrow?"

Babs was flabbergasted, but she was no fool. She saw it clearly; from the attentiveness of the waiters, the naked desire in the furtive glances of the taxi drivers, even the grudging deference of the women in the agency, she quickly realised that what had been given away in London was worth several times its weight in gold in the colonies. The crew left without her.

Babs had worked at the agency for a few months, eventually rewarding the white islander, who presented her with a car in return, and finally decided it would suit her purposes to be an independent consultant. She had heard this term in London several times, but was never sure what it meant. Now she knew: it meant teasing the animals, and making them beg for what she'd been giving away in the mother country.

She worked as a design consultant, advertising consultant and a production consultant. That she knew nothing about any of these things did not seem to matter to anyone, and eventually,

Babs forgot that Babs really meant Blowjob Barbie and believed about herself what everyone else in the island seemed to. But she still missed a good shag, and every now and then, when it got too bad, some lucky bastard would get a night in heaven (as she had begun to refer to it) and was then sent on his way the following morning. His calls were only taken if he had anything really worth something.

It was in such a state that she happened upon the Artist at one of the German's parties at his house in the hills to the north of the island. That he was famous, even within the confines of the island, meant something to Babs. It appealed to her new sense of worth.

She talked to the Artist all night, drank with him looking out over the dark, discontented waters of the bay, and was quite seduced by the beauty of the scene which she had never noticed before. She recklessly offered to take him home, and was shocked when he refused.

"I don't like doing it on the first night," the Artist said. "It makes me feel cheap."

And Babs did something she hadn't done in all the time she'd been in the island. She laughed.

"You mean to say you're expensive? Come on luv, I'll show you the most expensive piece of real estate in the Lesser Antilles," she said.

And so they began an on-and-off affair. This all happened before I returned, but when the Artist spoke to me about it, I could see his feelings had been hurt. In a rare moment of clarity, he told me he had known what she was, but he thought there was something beneath it all.

For the first few weeks, apparently, everything had proceeded wonderfully. Babs added to the Artist's status and he fell in deeply with her and Dreich's crowd. He was hired as consultant on many large projects and his face began to appear in the papers. I think he enjoyed all this, though later, he would say it meant nothing to him. But it was the status that brought Babs to Vincent Bain.

Bain had been the Artist's first mentor. He was an artist in the schools of Johns and Freud. His huge neo-realist paintings never went out of fashion throughout what the Artist would call the endless inversions of postmodernism. On the rare occasions the Artist deigned to draw, it was clear his style came from Bain.

Bain had stood by the Artist throughout the vagaries of his career. He was from one of the country's oldest families, and very wealthy. His family had owned many sugar plantations in the early part of the century. They had never adapted to the toppling of King Sugar, and never diversified their holdings. The older members of the family had lived to see their estates reclaimed by the wildness of the island, and see the coolies they had once almost owned take up residence in their properties without so much as a nod in their direction.

Bain was the last of his line, and though all his holdings in sugar were now defunct plantations in the island's south – where I had been born – he still retained sizeable landholdings in the north, which made him a wealthy man, living a life of luxury off his rents. He had two daughters by a Scotswoman, an architect he had met in his youth in London, who had no need of his money and who left him and took away her daughters when she discovered Bain was accustomed to exercising his feudal rights over his female servants.

Now, at 60, he lived with an island woman in a refurbished estate house in the French quarter of the city. I found an early picture of them both, Bain and the Artist, splattered in paint, surveying one of Bain's huge canvases, "The Eternal Struggle of Man for Impossible Glory".

It was Bain who had arranged for the Artist to go to New York on scholarship for his first degree. And beneath all the Artist's *enfant terrible* behaviour, he always sought Bain's advice. Bain regarded his protégé's flirtations with modern art as a child's waywardness, which he was prepared to suffer, if with some bemusement.

They had kept in touch since the Artist had returned from England, and the meeting was inevitable. It happened after Babs had known the Artist for a few weeks, and they were at one of Dreich's parties, when Bain made a rare appearance.

The appearance was at the Artist's request. The party was to celebrate a piece of his work being accepted at a prestigious European exhibition, and to announce a new show of his which would be launched three months hence.

Bain was a tall man; he dressed in rich linen suits which fell perfectly off his trim, still-vital frame. His skin was a dark burnished brown, and his grey hair fell luxuriously back. It was reported that at Bain's birth, the doctor went into a panic and began to search every inch of his still slimy body with a magnifying glass. The colour of the child was so far from his pale mother and father, and the African component of their common ancestry had been so carefully expunged from their history, that his paternity immediately came into question. But for the birthmark which appeared high on his left shoulderblade, which marked several male members of the family, something terrible might have befallen Bain's mother that night.

But at Dreich's party, another, quieter variety of danger was in the air as Bain and the Artist greeted each other. They embraced each other, as Babs looked on with amusement. Then the Artist introduced Bain to her, and there the end began.

"Hello, my dear," said Bain in his stirring bass.

"And who might you be?" Babs grinned at him, elbowing the Artist whose normally cynical features were twisted into a look of almost reverence. "This one doesn't hug anyone, much less smile."

They shook hands, and Bain introduced himself. And then it was all over. Everything bad grew out of the seed of that moment. Once Babs heard the name, the Artist told me, all the softness he'd seen gathering about her in the weeks they'd been together dissipated.

"It was like watching someone become possessed," he said. "The lights went on in her eyes, and at that moment, I knew. I knew. And I knew what she was. And what he was. But still, I wouldn't have done anything if they'd been discreet."

But they weren't. The Artist left the party early as he and Babs had planned, but she refused. She left with Bain.

Bain changed from that day. He sent away the black woman he'd lived with for ten years. I must admit I don't understand why. I didn't know Bain, but I didn't and still cannot see how any man could sacrifice years of affection with so little thought. Perhaps the Artist's account of him is imperfect, as so many of his accounts were. Bain never spoke to the Artist again. He became obsessed with Babs, and proposed marriage and wanted her to bear his children. Initially, Babs did not return his depth of feeling. She called the Artist the next day, telling him nothing had changed, but to give her some time. She did not mention Bain. A month later, Babs showed up at the Artist's house, and asked to stay the night. He let her in.

Three months later, the Artist's show opened at the German embassy's cultural centre. As before he had locked himself in the space and allowed no one to enter. On the night of the exhibition, the guests entered to the sounds of moaning from loudspeakers placed at the bottom of four huge paintings, done in Bain's neo-realist style. The Artist must have begun them the night Bain and Babs had met.

The central painting was of a muscular black man kneeling before a woman-sized barbie doll, his head bowed and his arm reaching up, caressing a single strand of her blonde hair. The man's genital region was flat, in the manner of a doll's pubic region, while the doll's genitals were realistically displayed. The other paintings depicted scenes of the man in sexual positions with the doll, but with the limbs switched: the doll's left leg switched with the man's, in another the head and so on, with different moaning sounds coming from the speakers below the paintings. The edges of the paintings were lined with small prints of an ape dressed in a tuxedo with a collar made of blonde hair.

The moans were primal, but Babs recognised them, as Bain recognised the small birthmark high on the left shoulder of the black giant in the paintings.

No words were exchanged between them at the opening reception. All the paintings sold, but the following day, three of the buyers retracted their offers. Only Dreich's offer stayed firm.

Three days later, a review of the work appeared in the *Standard*, written by Bain.

> ...it would seem the preoccupation with morbidity has given way to an effeminate hysteria. He has delved deep into his low, barbarian soul to come up with these images of his deepest fear and desire. To admit his longing for whiteness, and his impotence before the power of true manhood.

After that, Dreich continued to patronise the Artist, but the invitations to the parties dwindled to nothing. When Dreich's tour of duty ended a few months later, it seemed that it was only the Artist's magnificent luck that provided another place of refuge.

That refuge was Balthazar Bouvier.

Bouvier belonged to the island's small Anglo-African middle class which had persisted from the earliest days of the colonies. His father had been the headmaster of the oldest boys' school in the island, and Balthazar had deeply disappointed him by becoming an artist, since he had been prepared from childhood for professional life as a lawyer, to be followed by a political career.

Bouvier's work was obsessed with nationalism and he, too, had had his work shown outside the island; his pieces had travelled to some reputable biennales in the Americas and he was well-respected. But Bouvier's art bore the marks of great effort; the lines of his thought were traceable, and the finished ideas lacked the effortless ease the Artist – they were roughly the same age – brought to his own work. Everywhere there were signs of order in Bouvier: his lines of flags, his carefully plotted canvases, his thoughtful essays on cultural isolationism – but they were all cathexised, like his class, in a moment in history and could see nothing that came after. In the Artist's work, there was an instinctual awareness of the moving and expanding present which was removing depth from human experience – complexity was virtual and human, not horizontal or vertical, he wrote in one of his catalogues.

This was the secret Bouvier wanted from the Artist, and was prepared to pay for it. He proposed a collaboration and introduced the Artist to Emily O'Malley, the daughter of one of the island's most successful industrialists, Colin O'Malley, an Irishman who had come to the island as a minor functionary during the last years of colonialism, whose perspicacity in realising the gaps in the stultified ruling class's vision of the island made him an unimaginably rich man in the short space of 35 years. He had more money than Bain's family, even in their heyday, could ever have dreamed of. He was reputed to be a generous man, but he would never have the ease and style of Bain, and always secretly lusted after them. He had married the coloured daughter of one of his subordinates in the colonial service, and had produced one daughter, Emily, but could never penetrate the island's aristocracy.

Emily had been sent to the best finishing schools in Europe and bore all the marks and accents of her shaping – including its most fashionable vices. Emily and Bouvier had seen in the other precisely what each lacked: he needed her money and patronage; she needed his intellect and legitimacy. Emily had recently announced her intention to open a gallery in the capital – she had not announced that she intended to drive Aixman out of business, but this was understood by all who knew.

So the Artist flitted from the Bain's camp to Emily's camp. He was hired by Emily to help in the setting up of the gallery, which was to be a grand affair, hosting artists from various parts of the world, and taking local artists to the outside world.

I don't know how much the Artist believed in Emily's integrity. I don't know what transpired between them, but I do know she had a profound effect on the Artist's idea of his life. Emily was raven-haired, dark-eyed and her pink skin was imbued with a softness only a lifetime of sensuality could impart. It covered an instinctive ruthlessness which her father had, from early on, attempted to cultivate, along with the cultured worldliness he could never possess.

Unfamiliar with art and culture, O'Malley had copied what he felt were the mechanics of acquiring them. He bought expensive paintings and hung them in his home, which he hired foreign architects and decorators to design and embellish. Everything in the house had to bear a visible stamp of quality, without which he would not have been able to distinguish them from the ordinary.

Emily, however, grew up with a tactile instinct for quality – the rich grains of the fabrics she sat on, wore, and had been bundled in from birth became second nature to her, as did the expensive machinery which saw to her wellbeing – the hum of the cars which transported her, the practised regularity of the servants who made the food she ate, laid out the clothes she wore, and realized the desires she entertained. Her finishing school tutors taught her the correct wines for the correct courses; she had been taken to see the paintings of Monet and Cézanne and had learned the appropriate responses to them – but understood that they were mere objects given a value. These qualities, and her colour – her mother's brown had been completely dissolved by O'Malley's fierce pinkness – served her well in London, and these combined with her money and her utter disregard for it, assured her membership in the circles of which her father had always dreamed. Some of the flimsier strands of the European aristocracy adopted her for a time, instructing her in the arts of detachment, exotic drugs, and related varieties of sexual experience. She had returned home when her affair with a brother and sister had been complicated by the near strangulation of the brother in a three-way tryst.

She was sensible enough to understand the limitations of the island. There were only so many clubs. She soon became bored with driving around from beach to beach in the new Mercedes her father had given her as a welcome present. So it wasn't entirely unexpected that one day, after meeting Balthazar Bouvier who had come to her father's office to hang a painting, Emily decided she was interested in art, and proposed her vision to him. A new art establishment in the island: bigger, better, and more cosmopolitan than anything the island had seen to date.

Bouvier, smelling great fickleness hinged on great wealth, saw a potential use for the Artist. He would invite the Artist into the circle – a sign of his own largesse, a demonstration that the Artist was not his equal and therefore posed no threat to him – and it would also leave the Artist to take the blame should anything go wrong. Besides, Bouvier needed time to work; let the Artist do all the running around, minding Emily.

The closeness had the expected effect, and a little more. All his life, the Artist had seen himself as an alien deposited in a life he was fated to overcome. His parents were school teachers who lived in the southern plains of the island that their ancestors had been brought to plant and harvest for Bain's ancestors one hundred and fifty years before. So far as I could ascertain, with each passing year, the Artist became ever more of a stranger to them. At eighteen, after arrangements had been made for him to study medicine at Kings College in Dublin, the Artist, out of nowhere, had announced to his parents one night that he had changed his mind. He wished to be an artist. Three weeks later, he left home and, using the money his mother had given him unknown to his father, went to the city and lived in a small room while he worked in an advertising agency as an illustrator. He was welcome back home once he went to medical school. Until then, his father said, he was on his own. Artists had to starve, and he was allowing his son to do that.

Once free, the young Artist had sought the society of other artists. His talent was apparent to all who saw it, none moreso than Bain, who was selected to judge the first young artists show the Artist entered. They had met, and there, concluded the Artist, began the defeat of his history.

Emily disrupted all that: she had ridden her own history of parasitism to a position above the Artist and everything he held important and real. He was fascinated by her glibness and sophistication, and confounded by the fact that, behind her seeming admiration for his own knowledge and talent, was her unshakeable belief that it could be bought – so there was no need for her to strive for it as he had done.

In the course of working for her, the Artist became involved with her, though his involvement was not common knowledge. Emily was involved with another man, a foreign executive, and the Artist's attentions were received in the social penumbra.

Perhaps it was that that triggered his obsession with the notion of bettering not just Emily but her very existence. He put his knowledge at her disposal for a considerable price, which she paid. He spent his savings, put away over the last two years, on a Mercedes like Emily's, and he made a point of humiliating her whenever he could, so of course, she was fascinated by him.

The Artist was introduced to yet another social circle, and yet another round of adulation. I am relaying all this with the Artist as a passive object, but this is because of the way it looks in retrospect. The Artist, as I remembered from the night with Sir Robert and Niamh, was always very mild, even obsequious, in these encounters. I could never tell why. He always seemed to revel in the status, but inside, some engine was turning, and when the moment of crisis came, or more accurately, when he forced the process to a moment of crisis, he would collapse and re-emerge – often completely detached and contemptuous of the life he had deserted. I believe this was a pose, or perhaps merely, conventionally, representative of some deep hurt, such as we all carry. Whatever it was, the price was tremendous. The past did not exist for him; it was all a machine to bring him to the present, he said.

But the past existed for other people. Bouvier and Emily were not fools. They knew, as everybody knew, what had happened with first the university crowd, then with Bain and Babs. They took precautions; Emily travelled alone to the meetings with the people the Artist had helped her contact, drew up documents in her name alone, naming the Artist only as a consultant. When the deals were struck, the Artist was not present.

Bouvier also collaborated with the Artist, but on his own terms. He and the Artist would hole up in his studio for several days, talking and sketching, and discussing ideas. Then as the Artist left, Bouvier would continue to work, making sure none of the work he produced was seen by the Artist, and it was signed by him, Bouvier, alone.

The crisis came when all the work for the opening of Emily's centre had been done. They worked in an office in her father's management complex in the new part of the city. Everyday, O'Malley would come into the office to see his daughter. Often, he would hear them arguing violently over the plans or the manifesto for the new gallery. The Artist would invariably bring up Emily's ignorance about anything artistic. One day, O'Malley came into the office when things were relatively quiet. He looked over the Artist's shoulder at a proposal he was working on.

"I don't think that sentence is in the right tense..." he began.

The Artist turned around. "Is that so?"

"We've had to do a lot of editing before the proposals go out," chimed Emily.

The Artist noted the rehearsed tone. "Editing, yeah? Sorry, Colin, but where's your degree from again? You were trained by whom?"

"That's not the point..." O'Malley began.

"No, that is the point exactly," said the Artist. "I don't need your advice on my tenses, thank you."

The Artist found a letter on his desk the following morning. His contract was terminated forthwith. The grand opening of the project proceeded without him. When he saw the brochures, which were printed weeks before his termination, the Artist was shocked to see his name was not, had never been, included.

I returned to the island a few months before the opening of Emily's centre. My bank was one of the major funders of the enterprise – Emily had used none of her money or O'Malley's contacts with the various international institutions with stations in the island to finance her project – so I was aware of all that was going on. I occasionally saw the Artist's name on correspondence, and tried to get in touch with him.

We'd spoken on the telephone. I didn't tell him who I was working for, since my identity was buried deep inside the bank's inner workings. My position was important because of Oxford and Sir Robert, and because the bank needed to elevate a few locals. I was well-treated, anonymous, and powerful. It suited me.

"Bhagramsingh!" He'd sounded happy to talk to me, and didn't think to ask what I was doing.

"Why don't we meet for a drink?" I said.

"Ah, sorry pal, I can't. I'm working on a huge project now. The funding agencies have given us deadlines..."

The importance in his voice came bursting through the line.

"... But look, leave me your number. You're lucky to get me home. I usually don't answer the phone."

I gave him the number at the apartment the bank had found for me. He never called. I returned to my own life, and was quite happy to begin thinking about the pleasant stasis of living in the hills of the island's northern range, overlooking the sea. I had seen the land and was almost at the end of my probation, when I would qualify for the bank's assistance in constructing a home.

Three months later, at the opening of Emily's centre, contained in some old industrial buildings on the fringes of the city, I looked for the Artist, but he wasn't to be seen. I had found out, bit by bit, about his exploits in the three years since he'd returned to the island, but this was through discreet queries which my secretary made sure would never be traced back to me. It's not that I minded the association, but there was no point in letting my associations and preferences be revealed. Because despite what had happened, despite the Artist's caprices and selfishness, I still felt I owed him nothing less than the life I now lived.

I drove through the country a few times in the first weeks of my return to the island. I thought I would shudder at the sight of the dilapidation, the gnarled roads, the wild greenness skulking around the verges of the settlements, lazily sending tendrils of chaos into the gardens, but I didn't shudder. I knew that if I had to, I could go back there and forget the last few years.

The life was like water. A shape exactly fitting my dimensions would open, accept me, and close itself in the instant of my passing through. Life continued. My departure had affected nothing. So I told myself, until I passed the old house where my girl lived, whose faded photo I still kept inside between the leaves of Malthus.

I had been gone five years. The house had been repaired and painted, had lost the look of frailty behind a smartly varnished porch and pale blue exterior. The gleaming windows were uninterrupted by snaking cracks or moss, and even the fretwork had been restored. The air around the barbered lawns and rose-bushes might have been breathed by someone from a hundred years ago, when bullock carts and indistinct black forms leading them decorated the kind of romantic landscape reproduced in the postcards that tourist-adventurers sent back to their families in the north.

But even more astounding was the lot next to it: the overgrown field with sickly orange trees, which had borne sporadically at best, was no more. Now, there was a recently constructed building, a small supermarket and convenience store, complete with glass and chrome doors and packed aisles.

I saw all this in the few seconds it took me to drive by. I like to think the two buildings were connected; that my money had somehow helped the girl to start all this. I was not interested enough to stop to reassure myself, though later, I reflected that this, too, was the doing of the Artist – inadvertently, to be sure; had I not walked, uninvited, onto the paths he opened, I would be no better off. But it pleased me to think that the Artist's selfishness and myopia had somehow brought all this about.

In none of the speeches at the opening was he mentioned, neither his contribution to the project, nor his importance to the island's artistic community. The opening exhibition was of new and early works from Balthazar Bouvier.

A few months later, about a year after I'd returned to the island, the Artist appeared at my office. I suppose it was inevitable that he would have found out who I was. My secretary was flustered. He looked even wilder than usual. He'd lost weight, his clothes hung off him, his hair was long and pushed-back, framing the dark brown face dramatically; he looked like a dacoit who terrorised the Maharajah's trains through the Khyber pass.

"So, Sundar," he said, a cruel parody of a smile deforming his face, his body splayed out spider-like in the chair, the fingers restless on the armrest, "you've done well for your school-teaching self."

"Yeah," I said, looking around the room, smiling at him gently. "Yeah, I suppose I have. And it's all thanks to you, pal."

As I said it, a new kind of tension entered his body, visibly tautening the skin over the prominent bones of his cheeks and hands. He looked as if he'd been living on coffee and salt biscuits for months. He smiled something close to a real smile.

"You didn't call me," he said. "We should have a drink some-time. Talk about things."

"What about now?" I said, getting up.

"Big man, huh?" he said following. "Take off any time you want."

"Yeah," I said, walking by him.

His Mercedes followed my car to the *Seagull*, an old bar just outside the outskirts of the city where the old close-to-pasture executives came out from three o'clock onwards to spent the rest of the day drinking and arguing about sport. Later in the evening, the younger crowd would come in, and the atmosphere would change. The red brick walls were decorated with sports memo-rabilia, old trophies, and car license plates; in the back was an alcove for darts. This would all disappear at dusk, replaced by a wall of blue and white shirts, pink and black forearms glistening in the fluorescent light, the faces and voices swimming through a haze of smoke and alcoholic spoor.

We sat at a table in the back. The music was low this early in the day, and the old timers were just getting started. A few tables at the back were occupied, collars were being loosed, cuffs undone, hands brushing tired foreheads, and creeping up and back over sparse, rough crowns.

"So tell me about yourself," I said, swigging from the beer bottle, and sighing a little as I leaned back in the chair and reached up to loosen my tie. The furniture was old and solid – tables of thick oak, the chairs old fashioned and round-backed, with grooves carved for the arse.

"Just out there, diggin' my bottom, trying to make it, man," he said, before tipping the beer bottle. "The art shit. You know how it goes."

"Art is shit, huh?" I didn't know if I wanted him to tell me what had happened. There was no closeness between us. But I could sense he was warming up.

"Was it ever anything but?" He grinned, and a little bit of the old Artist returned. "Get us some food, Sambucharan. I'm fucking starving."

He'd gone vegetarian, he told me. The only thing on the *Seagull's* menu he could eat was fries. He ate them one at a time. As he ate, he told me the story of the previous three years, with himself as the star.

I asked him if he didn't think he'd contributed to his own demise. The university lecturers, Babs and Bain, Emily and Balthazar.

"Zarathusthra must enter the world before he can save it, Shivadhar." He grinned. "Do you know all Emily wanted was a gallery? That's all she could see. Balthazar can't see past his past, and Bain, well, what can you say about Bain? You gotta love the guy, you know?"

"I don't have to love anyone," I said.

"Well I do," he said, laughing. "That's the difference between us, Govinda."

"Is it as simple as that?" I asked.

"Oh, for God's sake," he said, not missing a bite. "What do you want? My defence? Got none, Ramchandar. Why? I don't know. I did what I did. The future isn't a straight line from the past. Everything you know, everything you feel, could be forgotten in an instant. Unseen and uncalculated variables affect everything. All I do is point them out at that instant. They could change in the next instant, but that's nothing to do with me."

He spoke matter-of-factly. The words were convincing, but he had excluded himself from responsibility for what he had done, his own hypocrisies.

"So anyway, Saaghbovan," he said, switching smoothly. "Look. I have a proposition."

The bank had just finished constructing its new headquarters. He wanted to be named as consultant for the new building's artwork.

"Contracts have already been signed with Emily," I said. I was going to say I'd thought of him, but he'd never returned my call. The meeting ended soon after that. He became quieter, and as we walked into the darkness, more and more morose.

"What kind of car you got, Ramsingh? A Toyota?"

"It's an Audi," I said. "Your car seems nice too."

"It's not a car, Jugmohan, it's a Mercedes. This is the vehicle of hardened men, the powerful. Not like your Toyota. I get respect when people see me drive up in that."

"I see," I said. "Well, I guess you should have no problem getting work, then. Just send a picture of the car with your cover letter."

He didn't respond, seemed to sink a little lower, and I relented. "Look," I said, "I have a proposition of my own. Do you think you can spare a few minutes? Or are there peasants waiting to be impressed by your car?"

I showed him my land. I told him I wanted him to collaborate with the architect on the design of the house. I suppose it was my way of maintaining contact with him. I paid him more than I paid the architect. I endured his endless calls at all hours of the day and night, to talk of trivialities, under the pretext of being to do with the plans for the house, but always ending up being about himself. He told me about Emily, about Bain, about his experiences with Aixman. He was obsessed with how Emily and Balthazar were faring in their new enterprise. He was always threatening to apply abroad for fellowships and leave the island, never to return, taking only his girlfriend – who he refused to introduce me to – with him. I don't know how true this was. At other times, he would tell me about his feelings of claustrophobia, and his fears that he would be trapped on the island because Emily and Balthazar were maligning him outside the island to the funding agencies and artists he had introduced them to.

When the house was finished, the Artist approached me with another proposition: he wanted to use the foyer of the newly opened office building for a final exhibition before he left the island forever. I said yes. It was his final exhibition.

As before, he sealed the place and refused to allow anyone in. The foyer was one storey up from ground level, and he asked that the elevators not be allowed to stop there. I knew what was going to happen, but I indulged him. The opening night was packed with the bank's directors and one or two people from the head office in the States. I had done my part for him; I'd made a big thing of it.

There were two pieces: one was a series of pillars, seven in all, about four foot square, arranged processionally, each a little taller than the last, and made of a different material: the first was hardened mud, the second wood, the third raw stone, the fourth bronze, and so on. The last was made of fibre optic cables in a transparent container. On top of each was a fist-sized portion of human excrement – it was titled "The Ascent of Man".

In the middle of the floor was a sculpture called "The Muse Inspires the Island Artist". It comprised a detailed mask of a woman's face with a raven black wig set on a body made of steel pipe and iron strips. Around the waist was a strap-on dildo, and one of the hands held onto a leather strap which was attached to the neck of a male figure painted onto a canvas. The figure was on all fours wearing a bondage mask made of the island's flag.

Emily and Bouvier did not attend the show, but there are few secrets on the island. The Artist's luck held. An executive from the bank's head office offered a huge sum for the "Ascent of Man", more than enough to keep the Artist for a year.

It was after the show that the Artist, in a fit of largesse, invited me to his home. I had performed the ultimate homage; I had enriched him. As we drove toward the house, he briefed me about his girlfriend. He had met her when he was teaching at the university.

"A real woman," he said. "Not one a these little town-girls. My girl's from the ghetto. A country girl. But bright. Very bright. She works in the day for the newspaper and goes to the university at night. Studying management. None of this artistic bullshit."

She was young. In her early twenties, I guessed, and I saw immediately why he liked her: the curly hair, the voluptuousness, the dark primality. She seemed defensive in my presence, and I saw why as we talked. The Artist completely dominated her, squelching her attempts to talk about art, his work and the politics of the island. A month later, he was dead.

Her presence in the house woke me. It was early morning. The horizon was just beginning to lighten. The bottle and empty glass still sat on the floor next to the chair.

"Come in," I said. "Sit down."

She slipped past me and sat in the second chair. The redness of her eyes had lightened, but it brought back the night before. The bullet-hole in the Artist's chest. The phone ringing in the middle of the night.

"Did you sleep?"

She nodded and sank back into the chair.

"Are you hungry?" I didn't wait for her to answer, just got up and went to the kitchen. She followed me. I sat her down on one of the high counter stools and rummaged in the fridge. I got out eggs, cocoa, butter, laid it all out and looked at her.

"Let me," she said, a small smile playing on her face for the first time. "Let me do something. I'm tired of doing nothing."

She went into the fridge and took out some chives and onions and looked up enquiringly at me. I pointed to the knife rack. Nothing was hard to find. The kitchen was new and hardly ever used. A woman came in once a week, kept the refrigerator stocked, and at the end of each week, replaced the old things with new.

"He used to talk about you sometimes, you know," she said, as she moved about the kitchen, and I sat watching her. The sun was just starting to creep up the mountains. It was a progression I always enjoyed witnessing.

"He used to say you were a fool. He thought you were gay and

43

just wanted to sleep with him. But after you gave him the job, then got him the show, he used to remember how he met you in London. Did you know he didn't like you?" she said, turning from the stove.

I shook my head from side to side.

"He had bad moods, he liked to fight. He grabbed me by the throat, but I think he just wanted to hold on to me. Then he would say he loved me. And if I ever left him, he'd kill me. I knew he couldn't kill anybody except maybe himself. He used to talk, but outside, when you saw him outside, he was a different man. He said his father put a cutlass by his throat once. Sometimes he used to wake up at night and couldn't breathe."

"Do you know what happened?" I asked. "I mean, how he died?"

"No," she said. "He left one evening, didn't say where he was going. The next thing, a policeman was by the door. Asking me who I was, and then to go with them."

The police did not seem to know anything. The Artist's body had been found on the outskirts of the city. He had been shot through the windshield of his Mercedes. No witnesses. No suspects. Who would want the Artist dead? It seemed that it would all end there. They would release the body in a day or so, she said. It would not be in the newspapers that day, because it had happened so late in the night.

By the time we'd finished eating, I knew what I would do.

"Stay here today," I said. "You have a change of clothes?" She nodded. "Listen to music, read, watch TV, swim. It's alright if you don't have a suit. There's no one to see you up here but God. I'll take care of the arrangements for him. I have a few things to do."

She nodded. I think she was glad to not have to return to the world, at least not today. I gave her my secretary's number if she needed anything, and I left her there early in the morning.

Aixman's gallery did not open before the afternoon, but his apartment was above it. The long avenue he lived on was sunny and deserted. He was waiting for me. I'd never seen him without his hair combed, his trousers seamed and shoes shining. Today, he hadn't shaved, and he wore a bathrobe over yellow-striped pajama bottoms. His red face sagged, and the mean black eyes looked slightly watery peering out the door.

"So eet's you who 'as come," he said opening the door to the side stairs which led to his suite. "I knew someone would come," he said. "You are 'ere about the Artist, of course. I know, he is dead. Colin O'Malley killed him."

I said nothing, following the thick red calves up the stairs. At the top was a landing. The sunlight bounced off several shiny pots which hung on a rack in the kitchen at the left and threw small diamonds of light onto the walls of the airy living room and into the grey corridor separating the two by a passageway leading further into the apartment. The wall's sternness was relieved only by two doors on the right. There were no pictures anywhere I could see. He motioned me down the passageway and through one of the doors.

His study was, uncharacteristically for the island, minimal. His bedroom slippers papped on the grey marble floor. The blinds kept the light from playing off the semi-oval glass and chrome desk. Three leather and chrome chairs sat in front of it and one large, highbacked one behind it. A bottle of scotch and a half-full glass sat next to a black blotter with a platinum pen set, and a computer terminal matching the colours of the room hummed on the far side of the desk. A few glass shelves ran along the side wall with bottles on them, and a small glass and chrome counter with glasses and an ice bucket. The other walls were bare apart from two perspex and steel filing apparatuses.

He saw me looking around the room as he sat behind the desk. "You like this? I copied it out of a French design magazine. Nice, huh? Get yourself a drink."

"No art on the walls," I commented as I dropped ice into one of the thick glasses.

"I tell you a secret. I 'ate fucking art. I graduated from the Ecole Sembable with a degree in Public Administration and was going to be a bureaucrat. I came 'ere on vacation just before I took up my post. I never left. These ignorant bastards will buy anything I say," he said, angrily.

"Is that right?" I asked settling myself into one of the chairs.

"That is right," he said. "Nobody takes thees shit seriously.

Colin didn't 'ave to kill the coolie bastard. Only a few people knew about 'is daughter's situation, and they knew because she told them."

"You're sure Colin killed him?"

"I am sure. Colin told me he was going to 'ave 'im killed the day after the show at your bank. And Colin does not joke about things like this."

Aixman sat back in his chair clutching his glass to his chest and looking up at the ceiling.

"What do you think his work will be worth now?" I asked.

"I don't know," he said. "He could have been an important artist in ten years. It will be worth something."

"Would you handle the transactions?" I asked.

"I will," he said looking at me. "I didn't know 'e 'ad any work left."

"He did," I said. "It belongs to his girlfriend."

As I passed the door into the passageway, I caught a glimpse of a red and gold robe with a gold and green dragon on the back draped about a body whose back was to me, just as a slender black arm with bright red nails stretched out to reach into a cupboard.

"You know something?" he said, padding down the stairs behind me. "Before this, the whole art business here was a joke, a game. Now, no more."

The drive to Emily's estate took you through a few small villages along the main connecting artery, past the opened wooden doors of the rumshops, the knobheaded barstools forlorn in the mid-morning; past the slow, thin trains of people trudging along the roads as they came out of mini-buses; bright shirts and dresses against the jet black and brown skin. My car arrowed past it all. The Artist's death had not made an impact on me the way I expected death would.

Emily was not in her office. The receptionist told me she should be in in a few minutes. Would I care to have a look at the recently installed show? One side of the warehouse had been partitioned into small studios for various visiting artists, but the main gallery was simply a huge expanse of floorspace, about the size of a soccer field with ceilings as high as a cathedral.

The work that had recently been installed was by a woman who painted enormous bleeding vaginas and black and Indian women being sodomised with cane stalks. I found myself horrified and beset with an overpowering urge to laugh out loud as I wondered what the Artist's response to this would be. I stood at the entrance and busied myself reading the artist's biography: she was a foreigner who had come to the island several years ago and had decided to stay, and now divided her time between here and Paris. Her work had been exhibited in several international shows.

"You find this funny?" Balthazar spoke from the entrance.

"Yeah," I said. I suppose I must have been smiling. "Hilarious."

"Ah," he said, coming in, but turning his eyes to the far wall where a woman was being sodomised by the fattest cane-stalk I had ever seen. "So you haven't heard?"

"I heard," I said.

He turned to me. There was nothing in his face I could read; just a dark oval, with darker eyes framed by unkempt curly hair. The two or three days' worth of stubble, and the shorts, T-shirt and sneakers he wore made him look like a passer-by or factory worker who had wandered in.

"The end of a very promising career," he said, looking away again.

"I think it was a little more than promising," I said. "He did get past that, don't you think?"

"It depends on what you consider to be art," said Bouvier. "He always struck me as someone too obsessed with himself, too much personality getting in the way. He lacked concentration; if there'd been internal intensity rather than the outward wasting of energy... He deserted formal technique too soon. It was obvious."

Bouvier spoke impersonally, detachedly, as if he were composing an essay on the Artist.

"This thing I let him into, with Emily," he said. "It was a good thing. He should have made more of it. Been grateful instead of resentful. This situation is not ideal," his eyes flickered around briefly, "but it allows you to keep working. Artists have to eat too, have to put gas in their Mercedes. He was never satisfied. Not with anything. Give him perfect happiness, he'd find a way to fuck it up. We need to stay alive. We need to keep working. That's all that matters in the end."

By the time Bouvier finished speaking his voice was just above a whisper.

"Yeah," I said. "That's one way to look at it." There seemed to be nothing else to say, so I walked past him.

"Do you know who killed him?" I asked at the door.

"Bain," he said without hesitation, his back still to me. "Babs is pregnant."

Emily's jeep pulled up next to mine as I stood at my car door. She came out the passenger side. A large black man in black jeans, dark sunglasses and a blazer over a black tee-shirt came out the driver's side and walked ahead. I could see the straps of his shoulder holster and a flash of nickel from his pistol as the jacket bounced off his chest.

"Hello," she said, throwing my distended face at me from her sunglasses. She looked like an incognito movie star – faded Levis, pointed-toe black cowboy boots and a black leather vest over a white work-shirt, a raven-dark gloss of hair falling smoothly over her cheek, and a peachy scent.

"Did you come to see me?"

"I suppose so," I said, realising that I had no idea what I would actually say to her once I saw her.

"About the contract?"

"Ah," I said. "The contract..."

"Or about your friend?" Her voice was, as always, soft and engaging. She could have been asking me about my sick mother.

"You heard?" I said. There was no change that I could see in the shape of her face, but the dark glasses remained impervious.

"Is there anyone who hasn't heard?" she asked. "But there's nothing I can say. We hadn't spoken in almost a year. It's a loss to the artistic community I suppose."

"You suppose, huh?" The man stood patiently, just out of earshot.

"You sound as if you expect me to be sorry or hurt at the news." The voice still hadn't changed. She smiled sweetly. "Maybe if he'd just known his place, and kept his cock in his pants and out of Babs Jones he'd be alive today."

I smiled back. "I think he and his cock knew their places pretty well, Emily."

Bain's house was at the opposite end of the city; there were no bars, or black people in the streets. He lived in the old French quarter, where large houses nestled indolently in the crests of sleepy hills. The road to his house was steep and winding and led directly into the open iron gates. I had never been to his house before. The driveway wasn't very long, and made a loop, at the crest of which was a covered area where I suppose drivers dropped off their masters and mistresses to be entertained in the great house. A servant came out to meet the car as I drove up.

I fished out a card. "Tell Mr Bain I'd like to see him," I said.

A few minutes later, after being directed to park in a garage at the side of the house, I was led through the hall of the house. It was exactly as the decadent imagination would have fashioned it: a foyer, French doors, a chandelier and marble ornaments, paintings, and there was even a marble fireplace. I vaguely noticed it as we passed through to the back porch, across a lawn to a white stone and marble terrace with several deck chairs laid out on it. Its lower stairs lead to a pool whose far end was off the edge of the hill overlooking the city.

Bain wore khaki shorts and a white shirt. His back was to me, facing the pool, watching a pale body slowly churning through the water.

"How can I help you?" He didn't turn to speak.

When I didn't answer, he turned and I found myself staring at myself from yet another pair of dark glasses, but these seemed strangely at odds with the lined face. "Is it about the boy's death?"

I nodded.

"Then there's nothing to say." He turned back.

"There's always something to say," I said.

"What is your interest in this?"

"He was my friend."

"You're wrong," said Bain, turning to me. "He never had any friends. He was incapable of it. He could only recognise inferiors, whom he loathed; or superiors, whom he despised.

"I would've been an inferior then," I said.

He turned back his attention to the body in the pool. "You know Colin O'Malley killed him, don't you?" he said. "That precious daughter of his. Decadent little bitch."

"I heard you killed him," I said.

"No," he said, turning to me again, but with a strange smile on his lips. "That would have been the reverse of the way it's supposed to go. He is the one who killed me."

Bain removed the sunglasses. His eyes were clear, but his face suddenly looked tired. "Was there anything else you wanted?"

On my way out, before I re-entered the house, I looked back and saw the pale body wrapped in Bain's arms, his hand stroking the damp golden hair. Even from the distance, I could see the passion in the gesture, and the rage.

The visits were absurd. I realised this as I left Bain's house. I was making a fool of myself. The anonymity, the colourlessness I cherished had been splashed with mud, blood, tar, and God knows what else. I drove down Bain's hill and decided to head for the peace and invisibility of my own. My certainty had trickled out of me bit by bit over the course of the morning. I was no longer sure who I was; I was somewhere between myself, the self I knew and owned, and the self the Artist had created, and at some moment, had begun to inhabit. I looked in the mirror at my face. I needed one more thing. The girl would have it.

The Artist's parents lived in the southern town. Their house was in a large suburb away from the agricultural market which collected the produce from the small villages like the one I came from. The houses bore all the marks of the people living in them. Embellishments like dwarf palms and rosebushes could not disguise the claustrophobic smallness. Security wire twined the gates, and a few dobermans trotted lazily up to the fences as I passed tired brown and black bodies in armless vests and worn out work-trousers pushing lawn mowers up and down the few feet of green allotted to each house.

His parents' home was about the same as all the others. I sat with them in their living room staring at effigies of Hindu deities.

"I need to ask you one thing," I said.

They both looked bewildered. Neither had asked why I had

come after I introduced myself to them as his friend. His father was a stern-looking, well-preserved man, younger than Bain, and his mother was the epitome of what she was: a well-kept middle-class wife. They had both been crying for some time before I arrived.

"Do you remember," I asked, "ever having put a cutlass to his neck when he was a boy?"

They looked at each other. Then his father broke into a bitter laugh.

"What do you think of me?" he asked, the Artist's brown bitterness crossing his face for an instant. "Do you think that these walls hide secrets of abuse and torture? Do you think I didn't know his mother was giving him money when he left home? Do you know why he left? We used to have a gardener here when he was about sixteen. I found them in his room together one day. It was the gardener whose neck I put the blade to. After that we never spoke of it. No sign until that day he announced he would be leaving home and giving up on school. I was happy when I heard he'd gotten the scholarship to art school. I went to him and told him I wanted him to come home before he left, that he didn't need a scholarship, that I had been saving all his life for his education. He refused. He never came."

As I drove out, slower than I had driven in, I saw the names on the mail boxes – Choonilal, Sagbhoovan, Sundar, Sagram, Pootoolal, Ramchandar.

So, returning from my journey into the past, looking out again over the sea of faces, I see only the Artist smirking at me. I am not entirely sure when he entered me and began the transformation. I don't really know if it was he who transformed me. I know I, and everyone here, is different from what we would otherwise have been, but for the Artist.

He would have scoffed at anything as naïve as ideas of destiny and ultimate purpose, and I can't conceive him as someone who would be a tool in some other artist's design. His presence among us was a joke, and he was the only one who got it in the end. I don't know if he had ever thought of any of this – or if he believed anything he said. But the words I've written describing his life are foolish and inadequate to say to these people. Still, I have to say something.

"We are all here," I begin, "because the Artist was important to us." The faces are curious, even strangely elated. He moves through them, above them, pausing at his mother and father, sneering a little, floating around the rococo arches and brushing up against the stained-glass windows, floating as if he had done it all his life, as if it was his audience, and not he who was the alien, the outsider bringing us glimpses of things just outside our narrow sight. *It does not matter what you say.* The sneer is gone now for a more benign countenance, another of his masks, his poses.

"These are the words he would have wanted me to say to you: 'This life is nothing but a sport and a pastime; when we wake, we remember nothing'."

THE BLONDE IN THE GARBO DRESS

It used to be that they'd come in, stare at it for a while, then ask some question in their brutish ape way. But lately, in the last few years anyway... time runs differently down here; you can lose track if you not careful... *If you not careful...* . Christ, even starting to think like them. Not like you, my blonde beauty in the Garbo dress. You'll never change. Never escape from that dirty frame hanging on that dirty wall near the cash register. Charmer of animals. They can't take their eyes off you.

In the last few years they've stopped saying anything straight off. Some of them even manage to not ask at all, but they all stare. Shows their growing sophistication. Savage bastards. Before, it used to be a few tourists, a few fishermen, the odd rich entertainer from the mainland – bringing the whores and society women – who didn't want to be recognised. Now the bastards have struck oil. Now the apes have organised themselves into a middle class. An ape middle class. Ape class. Coming in here in shorts and sandals. Talking on cellular phones. About how picturesque the village is. On vacation from the mainland. Vacationing apes.

They'd sit by the bar and gape, but they wouldn't say anything if I was behind the bar. They'd wait until Winston came round. Until they thought I was out of earshot.

Then: "What is dat, boy? Who is dat blonde woman?"

If I was around Winston wouldn't say anything. When I wasn't there, God only knows what he said.

No, not only God. I know what he said: "That was the boss wife, boy, you ain't hear the story...?"

I'll tell a story. When I catch you sneaking cases out when I'm not here, you black bastard. I'll tell the story of how the old nasty white man sent the thieving ape away for ten years for stealing beer. Stupid bastards. They don't even steal money. Steal beer, drink themselves into a stupor, come in with eyes red and lips dried-up white the next day. I turn up their jungle music to full blast. Like calypso? Take it, you savages. Here it is. Thief my rum. Thief my beer. Take the calypso for chaser. On the house.

But in the last few days something strange has been going on. One of them has taken to coming in, sitting directly across from her and just drinking and drinking. Yesterday I heard him mumbling something, looking at my blonde. That's alright. They can do whatever they want, the ignorant pygmies, as long as they don't cause a fuss.

But I don't think this one would cause a fuss. He looks like one of the educated ones. Sent him abroad to school. He forgot how to climb trees and eat bananas. Apes. But I can't say anything. The last time I started cursing the nig... bastards, they told me they'd take my license. Run me out. That big black ape with the fat nose in the sergeant's uniform. Careful. Mustn't even think it. It might slip out one of these days, and I believe they'd do it. Never mind I've been here twenty years. Started this place before ape watching became a tourist attraction. Kept it going. People only started coming to this little speck of a place because a white man was running the hotel. They knew there'd be no entertainers making a racket and harassing their wives. They knew they could leave things in their rooms and come back and find them there. Thieving savages. I had to threaten them, bring the police ape down to talk to them. Now the apes have decided the island is a tourist haven. Hotels going up. Entertainers everywhere. Apes in uniforms. Apes in suits.

I started to wait around in the evenings – to see who Winston was giving my beer to. Then I noticed this fellow would be there all day. In the mornings, when the others were on the beaches. At noon, when they'd go off to eat. At night, for a week now, he's been the last one out of here. Winston had to push him out the door. Never gives any trouble. No arguments. No struggle when Winston takes him by the shoulders and pushes him out. Just goes. And comes back the next morning, wearing different clothes, clean shaven.

"We'll find you a strong island boy." I grinned and put my arm around her, squeezing her to me in that rough cowboy way she liked.

She grinned back and shook her head in her slow, cowgirl way. "I know you think you're joking, but just wait."

"Well, you wouldn't be the first. You know how many poor stockbrokers came to the islands with their wives and went back alone?"

"What is it? Something in the water?"

"They say the island men all have a little something extra."

"That's what they say, huh?"

"Yeah, that's what they say."

"So what happened to yours, cowboy?"

"I had to surrender it to your father before he introduced me to your mother."

Later, as she slept, curled up in the seat, I leaned back and looked with a curious satisfaction and still, after all these years, with disbelief. Her hair had come loose, curved in a delicate wave on her cheek. I could never look at her hair without a small shock at its stark goldenness. And there, forty thousand feet up, where we are closer to our dreams, seeing the golden hair, the pink skin against the white of the shirt, I felt the familiar surge of desire for her. After the sun-starved winter under the heavy coats, the layers of clothing, the hats and scarves and gloves, her skin was even paler, showing the faint green branches of veins beneath the skin around her eyes, like the undersides of her breasts, where the skin was thinner. My body gave no such sign of knowledge of the seasons, and I marvelled that hers did, but I enjoyed the winter – I always had, as much as she hated it.

"You just say that because you had sun for the first twenty-something years of your life. You don't go all pale like a ghost," she'd said. "I look like a stale old hag by the time Spring comes along."

I hadn't thought of the islands in a long time. Then one day, in late January, when all the streets were covered in a whiteness that defeated even my love of the soft silences of winter, I caught sight of a single palm frond through the glazing of frost on a billboard that towered over lower Broadway. I walked into the first travel agency I came to, and had the tickets mailed to her special delivery, with flowers and the truffles she liked.

I hadn't done something like that in a while. But that had been a year of plenty. The bank was having an astonishingly good run, and my team had put away a few large deals, even by our standards, over the past year. Not bad for a third-year associate, I'd heard. Howie Feinstein had hinted at a larger than promised bonus. "You're gonna be able to buy that island you come from, bubbulah," he'd said, giggling, as he waddled out of the sauna after our last lunchtime work out. He wouldn't say any more. I'd find out at the end of the first quarter.

The flowers, tickets and truffles had arrived in the middle of a shoot, and the models had been jealous. I walked through the door that night to red candles, a fine haze of incense hanging lightly through the rooms, and scented oil in the bath water. She was waiting, wearing her boots, belt and hat, and nothing else.

We'd visited home once before, just after the wedding, for her to meet Mama. She lived on the mainland, and we'd stayed only a few days. She was uncomfortable. The old house on the old street, the poorness of everything, the boys next door ogling, but not saying anything because of me. They knew how hard Mama and I had it before I left, and they knew what I'd had to do to get where I was.

"We'll come back for a real vacation," I'd said. But Mama had died the next year. There was no one else for me there. I went back for two days, handled the arrangements, and I left. I was free. The world was mine. That was five years ago.

In the plane, I covered her hand with mine. The contrast startled me, as it had done the first time I undressed her: her skin against mine, so pale, so vulnerable. She scraped my palm gently with her nails and turned away, burrowing herself deeper into the seat, drawing her legs up.

★ ★ ★

I finally caught Winston. His mother came up to beg for him. Brought the whole family. Winston's girlfriend, his children's mother, his brothers. Begging. These people. Only their ape God knows what goes on in their heads.

Standing in my yard, looking up at me on the porch. "Give 'im a chance, sire. He is all these chil'ren have. You go send their father to jail?" Is this how the overseers felt? No. The overseers had power. Could do as they liked. Could order the women to the house from the fields if they wanted.

One of Winston's sisters was a red bitch. That's what these bastards call the fair-skinned blacks. "Red bitches". Men or women. These people. A young girl, not older than about fifteen, she stood aside from the group, there outside my back door, on the cobbled path that led to the road. A wild thing. Long legs, black eyes, little just-sprouting bitch teats with hard nipples under the little white vest. A touch of the Spaniard, a haughty tilt to the chin there amongst the trees in my yard, distracting me from the sea. That irritated me. This was where I came in the evenings, to look out at the sea, away from the eyes of my blonde.

I surveyed the coarse lawn with the few trees, the picket fence along the gravel road. Hands on the railing, I felt the smoothness of the wood, smelled the sea a hundred yards away.

The old woman was endlessly moaning about the virtues of her ape-son. I knew what would happen if he went to jail. I would have to spend months training another ape. I raised my hand.

"Alright. But he's suspended for a month. If I ever catch him stealing again, you won't have to come here begging for me to spare him from jail. I'll just shoot him."

Then they all left. The red bitch at the back of them. As she walked out the gate, she turned and looked at me. Then she spun around, the way children do, and walked behind them, the long brown legs pumping beneath the ragged hem of the pleated grey skirt she wore. It was the school uniform of a Catholic school on the mainland.

So in the month that followed I had to be in the bar every day. That's when I saw him. Around the second week, he spoke to me.

"Where's the other fella?"

He'd been drinking for about three hours. By now I knew his

57

pattern. Arrive in the early afternoon and sit across from my blonde. Buy a nip of white rum. Water chaser. Sit and sip, watching my blonde. Muttering sometimes. If the bar was crowded, he would sit where he could and as soon as the seat at the bar directly across from my blonde became free, he would pick himself up and sit himself down there. He paid for everything straight away. Smart. Less chance of getting robbed that way. No long bills with many entries. No chance to put something in on the sly.

The heavy season was almost over and the crowds were thinning. The bar was hardly full these days. Just the stragglers. I was better placed than the hotels. My bar overlooked the sea, and you could walk down to the water from the bungalows. The rooms were off to the side, along the hill, so each had a sea-view – and no rooms sitting on top of one another. You could come here for privacy, not like in the damned hotels.

"Holidays," I said. "He got caught stealing."

"Ah," he said. "He told me the owner of this dump lets the cabins at better rates in the off season than the hotels."

"That's right," I said.

"Where is he?"

I looked at his face. Nothing special there. Ordinary, black, strong jaw, watery eyes. Only with the liquor did there seem to come some sign of life, and danger.

"Come back in the morning when you're sober. He only interviews drunken bastards before ten o'clock."

The next morning, Samson, the relief bartender was there when he came in. He came and told me the black man who stared at the picture was asking for me, I got out a calypso tape and went out to the front.

He was there, sitting on the stool where he always sat, wearing a clean white shirt, khaki trousers, and fine cordovan shoes. His eyes were red, but he seemed sober. I slipped in the tape and turned the music right up, and was satisfied to see him give a start.

"You wanted to see me?"

"Could you turn the music down?" He put a hand to his temple and grimaced. I noticed the wedding band. It was silver with little gold circles going round it.

"No, I can't. I also don't have time for shitting around with you people. What do you want?"

"I want to hear myself think, for one thing."

"Then go somewhere else. This is a place to drink."

"Christ, alright; I want to talk to somebody about a long term rental."

I told him the cost. He came back later the day with cash for six months. He moved in that evening.

★ ★ ★

I didn't notice it the first few days. Not really. I'd thought it was just what the tourist brochures promised: *Discover a different you in a different world*. We'd arrived late in the night. The island now had its own airstrip, and a modern building through which we were herded by crisp, clear-eyed young black men in white short-sleeved shirts, black ties, and holstered pistols by their sides. Pistols. Dull-black, six-shot revolvers. What could be dangerous here?

Everything hummed quietly, unreally, until we walked out of the building into the warm night and the waiting taxis, driven by sour-faced old men. I'd forgotten this about the place. The progressions, the rapid progress downhill, the weary giving up on life, were much more noticeable here. Here faces were lit with the spark of life for a few years only, long enough to run and survey the hills, to chase the long-legged beauties and hold them down over mossy rocks and grassy beds in the pastures, and revel in their newness for a while. Then they resigned themselves to the place, sinking into the landscape, becoming the faces you saw standing by the side of the road beneath straw hats or disappearing out to sea in a fishing boat.

In the cities the life you lived, the house you slept in, the woman you loved, the streets you walked: nothing really belonged to you. You just used everything, and paid a price for it. When you could no longer afford the price, you moved on. No excuses, no trace of your passing. Here was the other extreme.

Was that how everyone who had been away thought? She was tired and clung to me, draping her legs over mine, putting her arms around my neck. Inside the darkness of the car, I rubbed my cheek in her hair. It was a massive old Chevy, a Caprice Classic, I think, with a soft leather interior, mile-long seats, giving the whole thing a voluptuous feel. I leaned back, looking out of the window. The island darkness was heavier, softer. No blazing neon, no enormous lit-up outlines of buildings in the distance, nothing interrupting the car's beams except the wire fence that separated the endless run of pastoral from the highway. Even the street-lights along the road were resigned to small, mournful circles of light.

I caught the driver's eye on me a few times, reflected in the rear-view mirror. There's something about the eyes down here. They look at you in a knowing kind of way. A few of the young men at the airport had nodded at me furtively, almost conspiratorially, as we walked along, she leaning on my shoulder, coat dragging behind her, hair loose from the pony tail, the paleness of her skin even starker in the fluorescent light of the hall. The dark in the driver's eyes blended with the dark outside. I looked out again. There was a full moon.

She stirred and I whispered in her ear, "We're going to have a great time, baby."

★ ★ ★

I caught the black bastard stealing from me again, not two weeks later. He returned to work the following day as if nothing had happened. Same insolent stare, same apish casualness about everything. I'd said nothing, played along with him. But this time there was nothing to do but call the police. Then there was the delegation from the mother and the wives and the brothers. They brought the red bitch with them again. Again, they stood in a group outside the back porch, begging for their ape son-husband-brother.

Who would think a worthless black bastard like Winston could cause all this misery, could move these people to suffer this humiliation on his behalf? And for what? A few beers, a bottle of rum, a few cigarettes. I will never understand these people. I didn't chase them off. No telling what these apes will do if you

60

insult them like that. I have seen white men come here and interfere with the little girls and leave them with big bellies, and walk off with arms swinging, so long as they left a few dollars behind.

But one time a white man had one of the girls in his room for three days. Wouldn't let her go. The mother came looking. The man slapped her and pulled a gun on the brothers. They all left. Two days later the girl walked out of the room and went home. The cleaner found the man dead in the bed. The apes made a show of an autopsy, but they couldn't find what killed him. They said his heart just stopped. Cause of death indeterminate. The girl couldn't be found, of course, had disappeared into the black sea of them, never to be seen again.

So I listened to the old bitch, with her head tied with white cloth, wearing her best Sunday gingham dress to beg for him. Just listened, just looked. When she saw I wouldn't give in, she pulled forward one of the young apes from behind her.

"Well take this one, sir. Him strong, will work harder than Winston."

"You know," I said, in exasperation, "if you people spent as much effort raising these bastards as you did breeding them, maybe they wouldn't steal and end up in jail."

Another round of begging. It was as if I had said nothing. The red bitch stood apart from the mass of black ape bodies, wearing the same clothes as before. Just standing there, looking on like a hungry cat. Hard little nipples pushing against the white vest. I put my hand up, palm outwards.

"Her," I said, pointing to her. "No more of the bastard men. Send the bitch. I can use her as a maid. Send her up here tonight with her things."

They went quiet. The old woman looked at me, and I couldn't resist looking directly into her eyes. Old, old eyes. Old like the beaches that had felt the weight of the conquistadors, the French, the British, the slaves. Eyes that everyone and everything had walked upon, laid their bodies upon, fucked upon, shat upon. And left there.

The red bitch hadn't changed pose. But now she, too, looked directly at me. Then at the old woman.

"Look here," I said. "I don't have all day. Make up your mind."

"Alright," the old woman said. "By this evening."

Then they left, the red bitch following behind.

★ ★ ★

It was one of the newer hotels; everything bright and sharp. The lounge was an atrium, tables of glass and steel, chairs of beige leather and raw wood. The blazing sun falling on the Hawaiian floral print shirts, the raw pink skin, bouncing off the sunglasses, the white teeth, the floral arrangements on the glistening tables: it all left me dazed. A young woman in a white shirt and khaki skirt greeted us and told us we would have to share a table with another couple.

"Maybe we should go back up, Ki," I said. "Order in."

"Shit no," she said. "I'm starving, Bobo. That'll take at least an hour." She hadn't called me Bobo in a long time. I squeezed her hand.

"Alright, where?"

The woman smiled at Kiki, and pointed to a table with two people at it. A man and a woman. The man was in his early forties, heavy, unshaven, untidy hair, in a white rumpled shirt, folded haphazardly up to the elbows. Dirty-blond, both; she wore a thin white vest against which the nipples of her small breasts pressed.

Ki looked at me and grimaced as the hostess went over to the table. "They look like a porno director and his washed-up star," she said, tapping her camera, which hung off her chest from the leather strap she'd made from Mama's old belt.

"We could wait for a few minutes," I said hopefully. "A table is bound to open up. Those bastards can't feed all day with island boys waiting outside to service them."

"You and your island boys. Stop being so tight-assed and let's have some fun with them, Bobby."

"Asshole..." I muttered as she smiled at the hostess and I pulled out her chair. The couple looked us over, desultorily. They were German. Pieter and Greta. She looked older than she probably was. They looked like people you see in the background of tourist brochures. Disposable, forgettable. I sighed inwardly. They both nodded to Kiki.

"How are you?" the woman asked Kiki. Her accent was harsh and clipped. "First day here?"

Ki nodded.

"That was quick work," the man said, nodding almost imperceptibly in my direction.

"Yeah," Ki said, "I got him at the airport. I figured, why waste the time, you know? I even got some pictures." Ki had put on her cowgirl accent. She put her fingers around the lens and moved the zoom back and forth.

"Good for you," the woman said, "but don't limit yourself, there's plenty more, plenty better."

"Hm'm," said Ki, blowing a kiss at me, "I'll have to keep that in mind. "What'll you have, er, Johnny, is it?"

Maybe if I hadn't played along. Maybe if I'd gotten angry. But it was easier to laugh at it. The people seemed so unreal, inhabitants of a different world, and we were just crossing paths. Allowances were easy to make because nothing was real.

"Y'know wot ah like, m'lady."

She smiled lasciviously. "I sure do."

The Germans laughed and relaxed. I remained silent over the rest of the meal. They spoke about the island, the places they had gone, where Ki could go to take pictures, but, I realised, they said very little about themselves. From Germany, they had been here a few months, or it could have been longer. They didn't seem to be very well off.

After a while I tired of them, and concentrated on my plate. As usual, Ki was taking things much too far. She was a school teacher from Iowa, she said, and had just won money in the lottery, and had taken off for the islands, leaving behind her husband and her obese mother-in-law and retarded brother-in-law in a trailer-town called Pluggit. The Germans seemed remarkably composed at the news, smiling blandly as if they heard such stories every day. We were as unreal to them as they to us. I must have grimaced, because Kiki dropped the pose and said quickly, "What is it baby? You want to go?"

"Yeah," I said.

"Try the beach," said the woman, looking up as Ki rose, "it's alright for the first day. Plenty of time for adventures later." Her eyes flickered briefly as Ki stood up, a flash of strange-coloured light that left me with a stab of emotion, of danger. As we left, the Germanic accents with the muddy local tinge followed us: "We'll meet up later."

We walked along the palm-tree lined path from the hotel to the beach, giggling, holding hands.

"Shit," said Ki, as we settled into two deck chairs. "Shit, I could get used to this, babe."

The beach was a crescent of bone-white sand with yellow and red umbrellas and deckchairs marked with the hotel's logo, set in front of a natural rock wall overgrown with shrubs. It led to a placid, sparkling-green bay. Oily white flesh lapped over the edges of the fabric of many of the deck chairs. From a distance, the prostrate forms looked like the young of a sea creature that had come up on the beach to give birth.

At places amongst the almost formless protoplasmic mass of pink flesh, canvas and sand was the relief of a black outline: young black men with bland faces rubbing lotion onto the freckled backs of middle-aged, thick-ankled women; or long-limbed black girls, in old one-piece bathing suits and cheap sunglasses, lying pristine under the sun, the occasional slim hand reaching over to stroke the old, fat men beside them. Behind it all, between the wall and the beach, a brooding figure sat in a square tower decorated with orange life-preservers, surveying everything.

"You betcha," I said.

"I'm going straight in," she said, and pulled off the T-shirt, smoothly unzipped and dropped the cutoffs onto the sand, and the camera on my lap. Suddenly, startlingly, against the riot of colours, the greens of the water and palm trees, the blue of the sky, the red and yellow of the umbrellas speckling the sand, she became a small, pale thing walking towards the enormous ocean. I felt a surge of tenderness and desire for her. Then I smiled and settled back into my chair. Just like the brochures promised.

Some clouds drifted across the sun. I closed my eyes. When I opened them she was lying on the edge of the sand, where the waves lapped to the shore, talking to Greta. She wore the same vest over a bikini bottom. The vest was plastered to her body, the little breasts with their angry nipples obscene even from the distance. There was no sign of Pieter. A young black man in brief swim trunks walked up to Greta and knelt down in the sand next to her. A wave washed up across the sand, darkening it. As I closed my eyes to it all again, I caught a glimpse of them at the feet of the young man, whose face I could not see, looking up at him with a mixture of awe and blandness, and, I imagined, desire. I shook my head. Sometimes Ki didn't know when to leave things alone.

★ ★ ★

After years of watching the same things happen over and over again in this pisshole of a place, all of a sudden, everything was different. The red bitch came that night. Came in and stood at the door of the bar, not saying a word, wearing the same clothes, carrying a brown paper bag, just staring. I hustled her out the front, and round the side of the house to the back.

She followed like an animal: silent, patient, frightened, along the side path of the house, her flip-flops papping up the stairs. I don't know why, but as she entered behind me, I saw the house as if for the first time; saw with a sense of wonder the empty umbrella stand, the coat-hooks which had not seen a coat in years, the Persian rug with a design of wispy lines running through it, the old sofa covered with the chintz-patterned fabric, acknowledging myself in the cameo mirror on the wall – white-shirted, grey-haired spiky-bearded face with thin lips and snake-cold eyes – as I climbed the stairs.

I took her to the small room down the corridor from my own. I had not thought about her coming, had forgotten the instruction to the old ape woman as soon as I gave it, and had given no thought as to where she would sleep, where the little bitch-body would rest.

I held the door open, and she walked in, looking round the room, at the iron-framed bed, the wicker chair, the windows with the frilly curtains, the white sheets on the bed. It had been like this for as long as I could remember. She looked at me out of those Spanish-dark eyes, the little bitch-teats pointing at me accusingly.

65

Her breathing quickened, and her eyes lit with an instinctive light. Her sex reached out despite her, despite the painfully thin, frightened child-body here in front of me.

"You'll sleep here," I said. She nodded. "I'm right up the hall. We'll discuss your work tomorrow." She nodded again.

I held the knob of the door as I walked out. "I don't want you to come round the front," I said.

She nodded a final time and, as I turned, she spoke for the first time.

"You comin' for me tonight?"

The voice was high, contained nervousness without fear, not a child's but not a woman's. I turned back and faced her. This was no woman.

"Go to sleep, child. I wake at eight. See that you are dressed and waiting for me at that time, downstairs."

The next morning, she was there, wearing the same clothes, her face wearing the same frightened look as the night before.

I had lived alone for years, had come to do things the way I did them, had, in truth, no need of her. The women who cleaned the bungalows and cooked for the guests saw to my needs. I decided to send her back to the old woman and tell her to send her other ape-son. But as I looked at her at the foot of the stairs waiting for me, she raised one foot and used it to scratch the calf of the other. The pose transformed her for an instant into a ballerina, with all the poise little girls are supposed to have. I cursed the house, cursed this godforsaken place, cursed the black savages for what they did to themselves, and what they had done to me.

"Don't you have other clothes?"

She nodded. I remembered the small paper bag she had brought with her. Probably the sum of her possessions.

"Alright." I took her to the kitchen. "Can you cook?" Another nod. I instructed her what to cook, what wares to use, what to clean, where everything went. Then I left her, and went to the bar, where the strange ape, the strangest I had ever seen, would come a few hours later, drink himself into a stupor, and mumble strange things to my blonde, while I watched, waiting. I didn't know for what, but now, after twenty years, it had begun to dawn on me that I was waiting for something – like everybody else who came here.

★ ★ ★

There was a time when to be an illegal alien in New York was an occupation with its own style, its own dress, its own manners. You were expected, budgeted for: immigration hotlines were everywhere; people advertised, nobody questioned a shady-looking piece of identification, an obviously false social security number. The people I knew thrived, lived loud and large, occasionally got in trouble with the police, went to the West Indian day parade, and seemed happy to stay that way.

I envied them. By the time I arrived, the style was becoming passé. People were getting tired of the loudness, and I could never shake off the stigma, could never stop wanting more. I went to every free consultation I could, but each loophole was plugged by the time I asked, and in the end all I learned was the almost infinite possibilities present in the word "say" in dealing with anything official.

So let's say you met a woman in an alley where an immigration seminar was being held, who told you that for a price you could get a stamp in your passport which would get you a work permit. Say, then, once you got that, you did the GED, then started hunting for a college in a state nobody took notice of, like Maine, or Nebraska.

Say you ended up in a town with a forgettable name, say Winslow. Say this town was a university town, with two colleges, one state and one private. Say the folks tended to treat the students pretty well, since they were the town's main source of income. And say it was otherwise a regular town, no different on the face of it to thousands of other towns, with snow piled in the sidewalks in the winter, little gingerbread cottages and large red brick country houses set back from wide roads, giving the whole thing an unreal feeling (which was fine with you since you wanted everything to be as unreal as possible).

Say you were doing well in the place, though getting lonelier as time went on, because you couldn't trust anyone. Say in this town there was something you didn't expect: the *Pen*, a bar run by Stinger, an old Deadhead, just on the edge of town.

Say that in this place the rich students who went to the private

67

school and the rest who had to go to the state college could meet and get high, and whatever happened after, happened and provided nobody got hurt, there were no consequences. Say Stinger, with the long, greying hair, spiky beard and headband with the faded image of a marijuana leaf in the middle, was irascible, generous, and gave you a discount when he heard you were from the islands, since every island to people like that was Jamaica.

Say this was your only relief, because the place was always dark-lit, always filled with the sound of some forgotten band from the 60s, and always friendly. Say posters of Ché and Bob Marley and Huey Newton stared stonily from the walls, making you feel in a small way, closer to home. Say in this place black kids usually came on Tuesday nights because of the Marley and Gregory Isaacs and old Ska records Stinger played on those nights.

Say, there you were one Tuesday night, sitting alone at the bar, listening to Marley's "Is this Love", and you turned around and there she was, the ever-present camera round the neck, in faded Levis and a white working shirt, with cowboy boots, and the hair, always the hair, in your memory.

Say Stinger was saying to her: "Here babe, this'll help you with Mr Joyce," and handing her the largest joint you had ever seen.

Say she said, "Thanks, pardner."

Say you thought *God she's beautiful but what the hell would she want with me* and you continued drinking and humming *We'll share the shel-ter, of my sim-ple bed...*

Say she drew her legs up to put them on one of the bar-stool's crossbars, and bumped into yours.

"Sorry."

Say the booze made you brave, and Marley made you reckless for a few minutes. Say this exchange took place:

"That Mr Joyce must be a real problem."

"Yeah, he is," she said.

"Who is he? A professor hitting on you?"

"Nah," she smiled. "That's easy. When they hit on me I just invite them over to my place and fuck 'em. No more hassle, and my grades are great."

"That's one way to deal with it." You looked at her directly for the first time, and noticed the full lips, the upturned nose, the laugh. The small scar just under the left, dark-green eye.

"So who's the guy?"

"His name's James, and he writes the most irritating goddamn books you ever read."

"Oh, that Joyce," you said. "Look, the trick to Joyce is that you can't read like a reader. Read as if you're writing the book."

Say you had overheard some guy saying that to a freshman he was hot for. After that, your expertise ended abruptly.

"Oh, yeah..." she started to say, looking you in the eye for the first time, but right then, a denim-sleeved hand with long fingers and a slight sprinkling of light brown hair below the knuckles draped itself over her shoulder and slanted through the small valley between her breasts. She reached up and stroked the forearm. The fingers tickled her stomach lightly between the shirt buttons.

"Ready Ki?" Say the head that appeared over her shoulder was blond, handsome, and the voice was level and went with the good looks.

"Yeah, babe," she said. "Just finishing this interview, just a few minutes more."

"Am I being interviewed?" you asked, as the hand and face withdrew.

"Well..." she said.

"When were you going to tell me?"

"Ah... look," the pose dropped, and there almost miraculously before you was a small, delicate thing with eyes as green as the avocados in your Mama's tree (assuming you had a Mama with a tree). "I'm trying to do a story on this place, and I had to get him to come here with me, for, you know..."

"'Cause it ain't safe with us here?" You don't know why you said that. The drink, the disappointment at seeing the handsome hand.

"Oh, shit, come on," she said; "no, no, not that, not at all..." Before you now was a child pleading, and you regretted what you had said.

"...I'm a rich white girl from West Virginia, come on man, gimme a break, will ya? It's about counter-culture and the appeal to people across racial lines..."

She spoke rapidly and excitedly, trying to convince you.

"Well," you said, interrupting her, "if you're going to be a journalist, you're going to have to hold it together better than that, babe." And you turned away, because you remembered handsome.

"Shit," she muttered, and you heard her boots hit the floor.

"Hey," you said, turning back. "You're going to give up that easy? What the hell kind of journalist are you? You should be prepared to sleep with me to get the story."

She turned to you, smiling the first real smile; back on familiar territory. "Only if what you're giving me is good."

"Well, who the hell knows what's good for a rich West Virginia white girl."

You talked a few minutes more, then she left with the handsome man.

Say she came back a month later, and found you sitting alone again.

"Hey, it's James Brown Joyce," she said.

"Lois Lane. Where's Clark Kent?"

"Oh," she said. "Off playing with his cape, somewhere."

Say things moved slowly at first. Say she had never known anything but rich white boys from West Virginia. Say she liked you for no reason you could think of, but she did. Say it was another month before you went out. Another month before you kissed her. Another month before you made love. Then she moved in with you the next week. Say you met her parents – a scotch-drinking red-faced rich father, and her aging blonde mother with an air of desperation at the thought of how she was going to explain this at the club – the next semester break. Say for all that, everybody managed to have a decent time. Say the father was glad you were studying Finance and Economics. Say you got married as soon as you graduated.

Say you moved to New York, because that immigration department was the most overworked in the country, and the least likely to pay close attention to applications. Say her father knew some people, enough to get you an interview at a big bank. Say you, with your state college degree, jumped over the heads of the Harvard and Yale applicants. Say at that moment you came to love America. And you loved her. More each day.

★ ★ ★

I went home tired that night. The apes have a way of doing that to you. Wearing you down, like water through a rock. Just there, the savages, endless waves of them, like the sea. One like another, they were just waiting, waiting for you to slip and fall, to overrun you, absorb you, digest you and hide your bones in their maw. But not me, not me. Never. I'll stay here spitting on them, and when I am ready, I'll go home to die. Won't give them that satisfaction. Never give them the satisfaction of watching my mouth closed up and silent, never give them the satisfaction of giving those insolent, evil grins I know they show my blonde when I'm not there. Black ape bastards. Never.

She was waiting there, on the back porch, standing just as I had left her. There was nothing in the kitchen. No food. Nothing had been touched. Came back out to her. Standing there looking at me with the same glazed-over look that Winston had when I told him to do something.

No food after a day of heat and apes.

"Why is there no food?" I shouted at her.

She just stood there on the porch, back against the night, collar bones stretching the skin tight, eyelids fluttering lightly.

"Why?"

I was up close to her, and met only a stolid silence. Then it occurred to me that she thought that if I saw she wouldn't work, I would send her back. I drew my hand back and slapped her across the face. She fell down on the porch with barely a sound, then rose on her hands and knees, licking the little slit of blood on her lip.

A beast of desire seized me and I dragged her up by the hair. She was light, lighter than I expected. She put her hand on mine and gently moved it from her hair, looking me in the eye, and dragged my hand down to her little bitch teat. I shuddered and reached down and covered her lips with mine. The bitch kissed back as if it were the most natural thing in the world, moving her tongue inside my mouth, driving me further, unbuckling my pants, putting her fingers around me, manipulating me, driving me further and further into the animal world from where I knew if I went, I could never return.

71

The next morning, I woke in my own bed, at first feeling only a lightness I had never felt before. Almost immediately, the memory of what I had done woke and rose in me. I fell back in the bed and cursed myself.

I went looking for her. I'd send her back, let the old bitch send Winston's brother. This was how they worked, these people, this place; they crept up on you. You guarded your flanks for years, so they stopped attacking there, but found where you were weakest, places where you had not thought yourself vulnerable, until they brought you down, down into their own animal world.

She was in the kitchen. Dishes were laid out on the table, food in them: eggs, bacon, bread and butter. She looked up at me as I came in, her face transformed from the previous day; the child was gone, replaced by a creature I had never seen in my life, or even thought of. I hung my head. This was no creature. This was an underage girl, a child I had violated. Now I was no better than the apes. They had done this to me, had made me into one of them.

"Mornin'," she said. Even the voice had changed. Confident of her mastery of me, of where my weakness resided. I sat down mutely and watched her serve me through slitted eyes.

★ ★ ★

The next few days we repeated the routine. Breakfast, then walked to the beach, and lay there, her skin turning first a creamy brown, and successively darker as the days went by, each successive shade registered by the increasing contrast with the pale circles around her breasts and the small pale triangle which marked her crotch. Each night we fell into the bed, exhausted and happy from the heat and salt of the sea and made love. Then I would wake late in the night and sometimes early in the morning to find her over me, her head between my legs, finding myself excited, despite my tiredness, at the glint of her hair as it picked up the full moon's light through the gauzy curtains covering the sliding doors of the room.

A few mornings later, as the sun was just beginning to beat against the gauzy curtains, I fell off her shining body breathing quick, hard breaths and rolled over on the bed and lay spread-eagled.

"Christ I'm dead," I said, "from dehydration."

"You're out of shape baby," she said laughing, her legs still spread, the golden mat still plastered to her mound, heaving stomach still trembling a little.

"Easy for you to say. I do all the work."

"Yeah? Just lie back, I'll do all the work."

"Christ, no. I don't think I have any left. Go to breakfast. I'll meet you on the beach later."

"Look," she spoke to my closed eyes, "I might go off and take some pictures today, OK?"

"Sure," I muttered. "Tire yourself out as much as you want."

When I went down to the beach a few hours later, she wasn't there. The black man with white teeth and cold, calculating eyes from the lifeguard tower remembered us.

"Yeh, she was here," he said, looking at me seriously. "But she leave with two other white people, a man and a woman."

"Old man and a young woman?" I asked. My accent had slipped back into the island drawl.

"Yeh, an' nasty lookin' too. What you worrying about that for? It have plenty others here for you, man. I watching you for the last few days, you know, and you shouldn't get too close to them. Think of it as a business. They won't take you back with them."

I looked at him and smiled. "But she say she would take me back," I said. "And she say she love me."

"Look here, you's a big man or a fool? What's you name?"

"Johnny."

"Call me Joe, man. Look, you new in this business or what?"

"Well, I meet she on the mainland and she say she want to bring me here."

He sucked his teeth. "Look here, man, them people she leave with, you know what they is? They get somebody for the woman, and they want the man to watch."

I felt a wave of revulsion. "Eh heh?"

"I could even tell you where they gone," he said. "It have a place on the other side of the island. Ah old nasty white man own it, and they does all go there. Is like a Mecca for them, a bar this man open

73

when he wife leave him for a calypsonian they meet when they come here twenty years ago. The man have some cabins out in the back, and when they want to do they nasty business they can't do in the hotels, they goes there."

"Oh ho," I said, jovially, and left him to return to his perch. I ignored the chairs and dropped in the sand. I lay there, prone, and watched the sun set, saw the colours change, the sparkle of the ocean turn to a dark, moody green, saw the tourists pick up their shining pale flesh and stroll back to the hotel, concubines and masseurs in tow, kicking up small puffs of sand as they went. Then, I was alone. Perhaps it was the silence of the absence of others, but there, then, I heard something I had never heard before. I heard the waves lapping on the sand, with the regularity of a machine, or magic. Then the sounds of the crickets, cicadas, parrots tearing the silence. Sounds of life. This place was alive. Suddenly the beating of a heart and the flutter of an eyelid became enormous things. I stood up, trying to shake off the feeling, and walked away. As I passed, I looked up at Joe, on his perch. I caught sight of his fingers curled over the edge of the wall. A human hand.

When she came in, later in the evening, I was out on the balcony with a bottle of island rum, looking at the moon.

"Oh, there you are," she said.

"Here I am."

"I was looking for you."

"I was on the beach."

"Ohhh, poor baby, I'm sorry I kept you waiting."

She'd come out on the balcony, and I reached around her waist, hooked my finger in the waistband of her jeans.

"That's alright. I had a good time too."

The sights of the evening silenced my thoughts. Stars always look completely different when you see them over water. The moon had begun to diminish, had by now lost its perfect shape. She stood behind me and ran her hands along my face, then took the bottle and put it up to her lips. Then she knelt on the side of the chair and kissed my ear with small kisses, and then tiny bites.

"Did you miss me, baby?"

I turned and looked her in the eye, ran my hand down the side of her cheek, surprised, as I always was, at its smoothness, but even more surprised at the flushed, hungry look on her face.

"I missed you."

Her lips ran down my jaw to my neck, down to my chest, then she dragged herself around to the front of the chair, and continued down my stomach. I looked at her out of slitted eyes.

★ ★ ★

Outwardly, I maintained that nothing had changed. But the apes knew, somehow, and strangely, they respected me for it. Savages. I despised them more for their respect, for it was not that, not respect. It was a welcoming – welcoming me down to their level of ape existence. I cursed them the more, spat on them more, but the more I did that, the more their admiration, the knowing smiles, seemed to shine, lit by the knowledge beneath. *He is one 'a we now. A man just like we.*

In all this, all that remained constant was the ape who sat there and drank, looking at my blonde.

That morning I went to the bar, not knowing what to do, what to think of myself, not knowing how to negotiate with the pleasure I had felt the night before, or with my satisfaction at her preparing my food, serving me; all that against my own self-revulsion. I passed by my blonde and stopped to look at her. *Are you happy now, you bitch? This is what you have left me with, have brought me to. Now you can come back to me. Now I have become one of them...*

Then he came in, sat there, ordered his nip of rum and bottle of water. I set them in front of him and moved back. He sat there mumbling at her, drinking, ordering more, drinking. The high season was all but over. The numbers of whites had thinned out. It would be a month before the locals started coming in. He had been living here for a few weeks now. Finally, after two hours of looking at him, I said exasperatedly: "Look here, man..." He said nothing, continued looking at the painting.

"Look here man," I said, slapping the bar with my palm. "What the hell is wrong with you? Why the hell do you sit there and stare at the goddamned bitch all day? For God's sake, man."

He looked up at me. "Do I owe you any money?" His voice was slurred and sad.

"No," I answered.

"Then why are you bothering me?"

I was taken aback by the hurt in his tone, and after dealing as I had to deal with the bitch, and my own guilt, I found myself affected by it.

"Look," I said, and softened my voice, "look, you're a young man, you look well off..."

"Yep," he said, smiling, his eyes shining as if he were on the verge of tears, "got a bonus of $1.2 million dollars last week. Can buy this goddamned island if I want. That's what Howie said..."

"What? Look here, man, stop talking foolishness; you're a young man; why are you pissing your life away in this pisshole, staring at that goddamned picture?"

"The same thing you're doing here," he said. "Waiting for her to show up."

I left him alone after that. Damned savage. Let him drink himself to death. Let him miss a payment. He's out on his black ape arse. Him and his $1.2 million.

★ ★ ★

Only a week was left after that night, and in the days following we went to places outside the hotel – a different beach, a different restaurant, walked along marked nature trails. She became browner and more radiant each day. But the changes in the night were more wanton – both exciting and unsettling. She brought native necklaces and wore them. She started putting local phrases here and there in her speech.

I found myself becoming more and more angry, and savage in my desire for her, being rougher with her than I had ever been, and she seemed to revel in it. With just two days left, we had come in after a day trekking up to a waterfall in the hills, and immediately the door shut, as she had in the days after that night, she pushed me down on the bed.

That night she seemed insatiable. As I lay there exhausted, she crawled up the bed and draped herself over my chest. I moved to put my arm around her, to peel her hair away from her face; she turned her face up to me and, for an instant, I barely recognised my wife.

"Fuck me up the ass, baby."

Her hand reached down and stroked my balls, and despite myself, despite the tiredness, something primal in her voice enflamed me. I grabbed her hair and pulled her over.

"Wait," she said, "get some..."

I ignored her, ran my hand between her legs, and ran it up along her anus. Then I pushed myself in. I was surprised at how easily it went in. She grunted and threw her head back, and then she started moaning, softly at first, then louder, then she deserted her humanity, lost the power of articulation, placed her face down in the pillows and reached back and spread her ass-cheeks even further, pushing back into me, pushing, pushing, faster, screaming raggedly, back writhing, the room stretching itself out of shape, until, finally, everything exploded.

When I woke the next morning, she was gone. I found a note. "See you on the beach later. I'm going to walk around and take some more pictures."

The place Joe told me about was at the end of a short, pitched track off the main road that ran right round the island, and whose length you could traverse in a few hours.

The bar was once the living room of an old colonial house. Inside the French doors, the bar-top itself curved around the staircase, blocking-off the upper floor of the house. The inside walls had been knocked out, and wooden tables and chairs sat haphazardly in what had once been the living room. Off to the side were other mismatched lounge-chairs, settees, tables looking out over the estate with palm trees, and the sea behind it all. There was even a chandelier above the bar. More noticeable than any of this, though, was the air of sadness that permeated the place. Everything pointed to desperate preservation. Nothing was new, but the oldness was not graceful, not acknowledging the passage of time as much as trying to forget that time moved at all.

The bungalows were off to the side of the house. There were about ten of them, one or two noticeably older than the rest. They must have been servants' quarters in days not too long past.

All this I noticed afterwards. I went into the bar. It was early in the afternoon, but there were people in there. Once inside the sadness settled into a kind of melancholia. I could see why the tourists would want to come here. In comparison to the slickness of the hotels and the hollow gaiety of the local-run restaurants, this place had its own character. I sat down in the bar, intending to ask the barman about the rooms, and as I sat, I saw her, Kiki, wearing a an old-fashioned dress from the fifties, with shoulder straps which widened downward to her breasts, leaving a white arrow-point of flesh between them. The eyes were glazed and nakedly sexual, as if she had been doped up, with a thick smile. But it couldn't possibly have been Kiki. The picture was at least twenty years old, the frame was cracked, and hung in the middle of the place, where it could be seen by everyone in the bar.

I didn't hear the bartender come up to me as I was staring. When I turned to him he was laughing.

"Don't worry, everybody who come in here does get catch with that."

"Who is she?"

"The boss wife. Leave him for a singer in one of the hotels."

The bartender spoke with a spiteful pleasure that brought me back to my own business. I turned to him. Dark, vicious eyes contrasted with the otherwise bored expression.

"A room," I said. "Some people rented a room here. I need to find out about it."

The edge in my voice must have carried. His face clouded, and he said, "Can't do dat, man. What you want to know for?"

"Ah have to meet them," I said, grinning at him slyly, letting the local drawl creep into my voice, feeling the mud rise in my stomach.

"Oh ho," he said. "You mus' mean the Germans." His face twisted into an expression of revulsion, but I could see excitement at the thought of the Germans. "Number three."

"Ah hah," I said. "Well, no hurry, I could take a drink first." My legs could not support me at that moment. I just sat there and stared at the blonde in the Garbo dress. I heard a cracked voice order a beer and realised it was my own.

A few minutes later I walked out slowly down the path to the third bungalow. The afternoon was deathly still. The sounds I had heard the evening before had gone: no birds, no lapping of waves, no wind. I counted the palm trees as I walked: twenty-three in the whole yard. The bungalow was more of a cabin, all wood, with a rough porch that extended along the front. I paused at the wooden steps.

Footsteps would be amplified by the wood. I walked around to the back. There was a small clearance between the wall of the cabin and the drop of the low, sloping hill. Through the walls came the murmur of voices punctuated by the occasional grunt of rough laughter.

She wouldn't be there. I shook my head and turned to walk away. Then I heard a tick-tick sound followed by a faint whirring: a camera shutter opening and closing, the film being forwarded. I reached the window, and paused. Looked over to the bluer than blue sea, followed the blue up to the white beach, followed the sand to where it disappeared from my field of vision, up the edge of the low hill, then to the window. Another tick tick of the camera, louder now. I looked in. There were six of them. Pieter sat on a chair, facing the sea, one hand masturbating himself. The other hand held the camera loosely pointed at the tangle of black and white bodies on the bed. As I turned away, the last sight I saw was of her, on her hands and knees, the outline of a black body kneeling behind her, black hands seeming to grow out from the white skin where they gripped her waist, her own hands holding onto to a black penis in front of her face, her mouth opening, tongue flicking out, her face contorted in a spasm of pleasure and pain. As I turned, I heard the same primitive grunt I'd heard in the hotel room.

I don't remember doing it, but I went back to the bar and sat there, drinking and staring at the blonde in the Garbo dress.

★ ★ ★

My life continued along this new course. I never touched the red bitch after that night, but she did not seem to mind. Was up at seven every morning, cooking for me. Washed the clothes, cleaned the house. All done in silence, broken only by short, shy responses to my questions. I found myself at times wondering if that night wasn't just a fever-induced dream. But the knowing gleam in her eyes reminded me each time.

Everything seemed to have settled into a rhythm that did not interfere with or contradict my previous life. A week after the red bitch had deposited herself into my house, the old woman appeared at the bar to collect her wages.

I paid her, looking into her eyes for any sign of the laughter or familiarity I had seen in Samson and the tradesmen and the cleaners of the bungalows. There was nothing in those old eyes, nothing – like the emptiness of the island before the footprints of a white man had impressed themselves into the sand.

So I continued, accepting the small pleasures, certain, for the first time, that whatever was coming or to come would happen no matter how I felt about it. And sure enough, a few weeks later I saw it, as she turned after serving me, on her way back to the sink. The slight tumescence, and then the hook and clasp above the zipper of the skirt undone, the white vest riding up ever so slightly on the new roundness of the belly, the slight curving of the flesh that had been flat a month before.

The next week, when the old bitch came for the wages, I took her round the back, and sat her down on one of the chairs in the porch.

"Was she bred-up before she came here?" My rage bore into the empty eyes, and the old bitch saw it.

"No sir."

"You know there are ways of finding out. The doctors can tell me."

The eyes continued staring without a flicker.

"If I find out you have done this thing to me, I will burn your houses to the ground. Do you understand me? And I will see that Winston stays in jail for the rest of his life."

She nodded.

★ ★ ★

The moon was at its lowest point; a small, curved blade scything the blue-blackness of the sky. Without the moon, I foresaw a blackness not even the stars could allay would settle would over the island, a darkness I could not find my way through.

Inside the darkness, I knew, was a world with houses, with people in them, with mothers and sons, with fathers and daughters, and in the houses was a familiarity, a knowing of each other and each thing around them. In those houses, the personalities put on in the day to earn their livings, to sell their bodies, were banished. In those houses they could be as they truly were; they could laugh real laughter, not the plastic grins and hollow smiles they showed outsiders.

It's just a business. I tried to think of the men who had participated in it, but I could attach no faces, no substantial persons to the thought. These were not men, just bodies – unfeeling, uncaring; just performing. They were mere props, though perhaps part of the payment they exacted was the pain they caused me; perhaps they took pleasure in that. Or perhaps they were just savage bastards who would fuck anything and tell all their friends what the white woman did for them, and what they did to her. Perhaps, perhaps...

I heard the door shut, heard the soft padding of her feet across the carpet, then she was out on the balcony.

"Hi, baby." The voice was warm, nothing different, nothing I could see in the darkness.

"Hi."

She put her arms around me and kissed the top of my head, then ran her hands along my chest. I held onto her wrists.

"No, Ki, not tonight. I'm exhausted. You wore me out." I smiled quickly at her. "We have a long day tomorrow."

"Oh, you're no fun," she said. "I'll just have to get me a strong island boy." She grinned and kissed me on the head again. "Alright, I'm kinda tired too. I'm going to bed. Don't stay out here too long."

The next day, we sat in the terminal building with our bags, waiting for the flight to be called. I wasn't sure what I was going to do, and when she saw I wasn't responding to her attempts at conversation, she sat there, looking out at the palm trees of the pastoral that surrounded the airport.

When the call for the flight came, I walked with her onto the open tarmac, to the foot of the stairs to the plane. I held one of her wrists and pulled her aside.

"Look," I said as she faced me. "Look, this is it."

"This is what?" she asked, casually, her other hand on the railing.

"This is it for us," I said. "It's over. You're going back alone."

"What? What the fuck are you talking about, Bobby?" Her eyes were on me now, fear in them. "Whadd'you mean it's over? What's over? I'm not going anywhere without you."

I gripped her shoulder, my thumb falling just below her neck, and for a moment, allowed the anger I had not acknowledged till that instant to rise.

"It's over, Ki." And just as she was about to open her mouth again, I said, "I followed you."

She searched my eyes. Tears welled up in her beautiful, green eyes, the pose dropped and the little girl I'd seen those years ago stood there.

"I want to stay. I want to stay with you. I'm sorry, Bobby, so sorry..."

"It's too late, Ki. If you'd stayed, the man I'd become is not a man you'd want to know. Go."

I turned and walked away, did not look back until I reached the terminal building. I waited there till the plane was nosing up into the clouds. Then I went back to the bungalow bar and sat across from her picture, and prayed she would come back.

★ ★ ★

— Months passed, and I sat there staring at the picture.

— God, the red bitch's belly is enormous now. I wouldn't have thought such a little child could get that big, but she still wakes up every morning and serves me.

— And I wish and I wish and I wish she would come back to me, wish she would walk through the door and say, *Hey it's James Brown Joyce.*

— I don't know why, exactly, but the child growing in that belly has brought a change in the house. Now, I even find myself smiling at the apes sometimes, and they smile back

— but I know what the smiles mean when they see me here, just drinking, and staring at the blonde in the Garbo dress. They all knew, they all saw, when I thought no one was looking, they all know all about me

— and I don't care that the apes smile at me, sometimes. But I can't let them feel I'm getting soft. I still curse their black bastard asses when they don't do what I say, still call them apes and scream in their faces, but we all know something is different here now. Something I have never felt before is happening to me, and I fear I am losing myself to it, I fear that this, the bitch's child, is just an omen of something else that's coming. Even the ape who sits drinking all day has started to look like a sad man to me now, not just another one of these animals. I even talk to him, and sometimes, he even answers. "The millionaire," I say to him, and he responds, "The dirty old white man".

— Howard Feinstein's letter came with the cheque: *I've told the old man you caught some voodoo illness down there, bubbulah, but that's only going to hold them off so long. There's plenty more to be made, and if you wait too long, they'll forget you...* My life in the city, if I didn't want it, someone else would take it.

— "You know the story behind that?" I asked him one night when we were the only two left there.

"I think I do," he said.

"I know what the apes have told you," I said. "But there's more, much more."

— Isn't there always more, old man? To everything under the sun, there's more, like there's more to you now since I've started to come here. I see the life returning in you; perhaps it is the life I have lost.

— Then, one day, my blonde walked in, not in the Garbo dress, but in a pair of old Levis with a white shirt, wearing cowboy boots, with a camera slung round her neck by an old leather belt.

— I heard the taps behind me. *Hi, can I interview you? I'm doing a story about this place.* My heart almost burst at the sight of her

— Where from after all these years? And so young, so beautiful. My heart almost burst at the sound of her voice, at the golden hair, the green eyes, but no, she couldn't be my blonde.

— So I answered her: "Sorry, there's nothing to say."

— And the ape said, "Nothing to say." I held my breath, waiting. This is what he had sat here waiting for all these months.

— Out of the corner of my eye, I caught sight of the dirty old man staring in a kind of wonder at her, and at the same time she caught sight of the picture, and we all looked at the picture and I said, "Goodbye, goodbye, my blonde in the Greta Garbo dress."

— And I said goodbye to the old picture of her that had been put there for me to meditate on, to pray to. *I waited and waited for you to come, Bobby, and I went home, and I told my mom what I'd done...*

— And she just stared and looked out of the frame of the picture, my blonde, looked at my spirit walking away into the world where the little girl waited, her belly big with a child.

— And I looked at her face, my cowgirl in the blue jeans. Why should I take you back? Apart from the fact that I want you so desperately, that if I let you walk out now I'd crumble into dust.

— Maybe the life I haven't lived the last twenty years, maybe...

—*... and I didn't know how to explain what I'd done, Bobby, she just asked me if I'd like to take pictures of her, and the first time it was ok...* But what about the next time, what about when it happens again? What happens when a wolf that's been domesticated tastes blood for the first time? And I don't care now where you went, because the world, even this little part of it, this little part... *but the second time, I just sat there watching them and it was like I was someone else, Bobby, another woman was taking off my clothes, and I just lost myself, but even inside it, I was thinking with the small part of me that could still think, of...*

You were just being human, Ki. We're fragile, dissatisfied creatures, and sometimes our desire drives us into unknown places where we lose sight of what we desire and we desire illusions that cannot exist anywhere but in our minds. Do you understand that? The path is high and low, as my own desire for the world led me to you, Ki, my little girl from West Virginia, whom I love more than the sun and the air I breathe, but I began seeing only a white girl who made my place and status in the world complete, but now, now we leave here together...

— Let me move you from here, from that dirty frame, away from their leering eyes, and place you where you belong, in the fire of my memory. A child is coming,

— *A child is coming, Bobby.*

NEW YORK STORY

He'd decided to use the *Pierre* on 54th Street, for no other reason than he'd read in a book – a Ludlum novel or something like that – that it was discreet. He wasn't altogether sure why or if discretion was required; he'd never done this before. Laughed to himself: *I've never done this before, she said, as she feverishly ripped his clothes off and showed him exactly how it was done.* Uh huh. Laughed again: *You've come a long way, baby.* That ad. Yeah. He thought of them back at 122 Grant Avenue and wondered idly what it would cost to order a hit – not necessarily to kill them all, just a little drive-by at night, aiming at the ground floor when they'd all be asleep on the top floor or in the basement. *And what if a couple of them were wandering around the ground floor and got shot?* Well I tried, didn't I? Fuck 'em if they can't take a joke. Besides, it's not a crime, is it? Not like they're human or anything. He thought he'd managed to stop thinking about them in the last few months, although Anya had told him that sometimes he would mutter foul curses in his sleep. One morning, a few days after they'd moved in, she asked him over breakfast: "Vat iz a coooleee?"

"What?" He'd been startled, but only for a moment. *Of course, talking in my sleep.* "Uhm an animal that likes to play in shit and eat it," he said.

"Really? Zheet eeting? Zhour pets?" The Russian Bond-chick accent made anything she said sound sexy, especially when she knew he was putting her on and then overdid it.

"No, my father's," he'd said grinning. "What's for breakfast, porridge?"

The room: a blue suite, mahogany writing desk off to the side, a couple of chintzy highbacked Victorian chairs with low, curved legs and matching footstools; a big bed, nice wool sheets, reminding him of the winter outside – he loved the winter – big TV; soft rich robes and towels in the bathroom; glistening taps reflecting the pale light; a clock on the blue wall above the writing desk; a window looking out over the city and its lights – fiery soulpoints embedded in growths of evil.

Eight-thirty. She should be there any time now, but the snow was coming down even harder. If she'd taken the subway she'd be OK. She'd mentioned cab fare, but you never knew; sometimes they pocketed the cab fare and took the subway. He hoped she'd taken a train; this wasn't going to happen again. He absent-mindedly started replaying the INS scenario again. There were about five agents with blue windbreakers with "I-N-S" in big yellow letters on the back, and blue official-looking caps with "INS" in smaller yellow letters above the brims; a truck to put them in; guns – automatic rifles and Glocks. He would wait in the car until they were herded out, then he'd come out for them to see him. The agents would surround the house, then bang on the door. Komay would open it and poke her crooked nose outside.

The INS man would say a few words. She'd close the door. They'd bang on it, and perhaps bring out the battering ram. Break in the door. Yeah, the battering ram. Herd them up: Colo, bare-chested and confused with his big black gut protruding out of his plaid bathrobe; Az, his short black self cowardly before the INS officers; Bucky with his teeth; the wives with the babies, bawling and crying like cattle, thinking of the island they were going back to. Not Sarah and her baby. A call could be made. Something...

The phone rang. "Your guest has arrived, Sir." The desk clerk sounded uninterested. The discreet *Pierre*. No doubt trained to be that way. He'd been sitting in one of the chintzy chairs, with his feet up, looking out the window at the snow. The lights in the room were low, making the view of the city outside more unreal: the terrorized neon stream running along Broadway, the dimming window-lights; everything slowing, letting the soft blackness into the blood; feelings of languor, slowness; the momentary pleasures of evil. *Unreal city in an unreal time.* He fingered his tie; suddenly felt silly. Why had he bothered to wear a suit? Oh, yeah;

I've never done this before. What would she expect? Apart from the cash. Not much else. The knock on the door.

She was beautiful. *Blonde bombshell, liquid blue eyes, lovely D cups, long luscious legs. Let me rub you with warm oil...* It was all true. He started to relax; beautiful women have a way of making that happen to moral dilemmas, he thought.

"Hell-loo," he said, smiling. "Come in." She smiled sweetly and walked in.

He hadn't been sure what to expect; he'd half-expected a fur coat, silver high heels, tight satin pants. A *Starsky & Hutch* hooker. She was about his height, in a long camelhair coat over a dark, wool suit and a body-hugging turtleneck. She'd loosened the scarf on her way up, and the dirty blonde hair drooped carelessly over it. She could have been somebody's wife; a college professor; even, with a tight skirt and mules, one of those Madison Avenue publicist Barbies.

She turned, sliding off the scarf, shaking out her hair. "We aim to please." Her voice was throaty, surprisingly deep. When they'd talked on the phone, he thought the connection, something in the machine, had made her voice seem heavier than it was, than he'd expected. But here she was with the throaty voice. "Can we take care of the financial part of the evening before we get started?"

"Uh, sure." He reached into his pocket uncertainly. "Is this, uh, how it's... I mean..."

"You've never done this before, right?" She sat in one of the chintzy chairs. "Not sure how it works?" She grinned and leaned back and put her feet up on the footstool. Black pumps. Her face lit up; the cheeks, pinked from the cold, played off against the eyes; the lips not pulpy but firm, not red but dark, still glistening from the balm she put on; a hint of the white teeth. Strong jaw. She brushed her hair back, strong fingers short nails, not feminine; all business. The laugh put him off. *Fuck, working her way through college. Probably reads Cixous or Kristeva or whoever the hell is bitching these days.* Stop it. No reason to think about it; this isn't real. Unreal night in an unreal city.

"Yeah. You've got it. And you must be what, a college student? Working on your degree in psychology? Call-outs beat waitressing in Hooters, getting groped by stockbrokers. Right?"

He drew the bills out of his pocket and held them up between his index and middle finger.

"Right first time," she said, smiling, not moving toward him. He liked that. He walked toward her and handed her the cash. She slipped it into the inner pocket of the coat without counting. He liked that too.

"So what now?" He stood over her, not sure what to do with his hands.

"Well, whaddya think, sport? What're you up for?"

"Surprise me," he said.

She laughed again; got up and left the coat on the chair, walked over to him. Ran her hands over his lapels.

"Nice suit."

"Thanks." She was tall for a woman, but maybe the pumps added a couple of inches. He liked looking her straight in the eye.

She slid the jacket off, holding his gaze, ran her hand down the front of his shirt, wrapped her hand around the belt buckle, pulled him over to the bed. She was stronger than she looked. Leaned into him, rubbing her breasts on his chest, biting him lightly on the neck, pushed him down, back first on the bed. *Strong 'un; probably kick yer ass.* Slid off the tie, the shirt, biting him again on the nipples. Raised herself, undid her belt, drew the turtleneck over her head; they were spectacular; he reached up, she bit his fingers.

"Wait." She stopped and looked down at him. "What's your name?"

"Amanda." She grinned conspiratorially.

"Amanda?"

"Amanda What's yours?"

Her head was near his bellybutton now, hands squeezing him. The contrast of her skin on his skin was not so stark as to be arousing: brown and pink, *who the fuck gets turned on by that,* he was thinking when he felt it: the warm, unmistakable protuberance on his thigh where she straddled him.

"Call me Mr Aaaaaahhhhhh," he started to say as the realisation hit; his legs on their own accord began scrambling and he sprang back, rolling off the bed. He managed to get out, "What the *fuck* is that?" before he fell head first onto the carpet.

"What the fuck is what?" She was startled, flustered for the first time since she'd come in.

"Tell me you've got a banana in your pocket," he said, feeling ridiculous for saying it; shirt undone, pants undone, kneeling on the floor looking over the side of the bed, panting foolishly, looking at her breasts heaving slightly. *The Crying Game*.

"What? You mean you... Aw, shit." She sighed and slid her pants down, along with the panties, and there it was – a good sized, not quite semi-erect penis.

He was mesmerised. His mouth opened twice to speak but nothing came out. He retreated a few inches, and bumped into the chair.

Fucking coolie bastards. Fucking coolie bastards. Though he wondered briefly: *How is this their fault?*

She dropped on her back and laughed. "You fucking asshole. Didn't you read the code in the ad?"

"What code?" Fucking *Village Voice*. Fucking space-saving assholes.

"T-S-S-H-M."

"That means something? I thought it was an advertising code or something. Can't they just say 'chick with dick' or something? How the fuck am I supposed to know that?"

"'Transsexual seeks heterosexual male.' Everybody knows that." *You asshole.*

"Not everybody."

"Obviously not." Her self-possession was back. They remained like that for about a minute: him kneeling at the side of the bed, she on her back looking up. He got up and dropped himself down in the same chair he'd sat in before she arrived.

"Well this is just fucking great."

"No refunds."

He thought about it. What was he going to do? Call the cops? Fight her? Call the desk clerk? He sighed. She had him. No refund. Fucking *Village Voice* assholes.

"Alright," he said. "Forget it. Let's call it quits." *Well, there goes that goddamned idea. Happy now, you Armenian trollop?*

She got off the bed and walked to the window. His eyes moved from the bouncing breasts to the bouncing cock, and he was paralysed as the waves of lust and revulsion clashed, and started to mix along the edges. He felt slightly nauseous.

"It's really coming down out there," she said. She turned to face him, and again the straight-jawed pretty/handsome face, the breasts, the flat stomach, the cock, stopped him dead. She saw the confusion in his face and sighed; walked back to the trousers, pulled them on.

"Psheeeew." She pulled the turtleneck over her head then reached for the phone. He closed his eyes and lay back on the thick carpet. Fuck fuck. *Ah, well*. He thought of his money; his apartment; Anya. Started to laugh. You were the one who said to go do the stag thing. Pulled himself up off the floor. She was nodding into the phone.

"No taxis?" Shook her head. "All of it, huh?"

By the time she put down the phone, he knew what was going to happen. He was going to be here all night. So was she. He went to the phone, buttoning his pants.

"...You got what you wanted all right. I'm stuck here with the snow."

"Stuck vhere? Vat do you mean?" Suddenly there was a note of concern in her voice. The accent thickened when she got agitated.

"I'm at...the P...place..."

"Vat focking place? I'm vaiting for zhou here..."

He understood. The *Eets a tradition in Armenia, the man goes out the night before the vedding, giving zuh vorld a chance to reclaim him while zuh bride offers a mass* was all Armenian goat shit. A small bell went off. It was probably best if she got the simple version.

"Uh... the subway's closed; the streets are blocked... I'm in a hotel."

She sat in the same position he'd sat in waiting for her; legs up, looking out at the city. He gathered his things; belt, shoes, shirt, and dropped in the chair next to her, feeling a slight involuntary rise at the sight of her breasts against the turtleneck which was doused almost immediately by a vision of her bouncing cock. He buttoned his shirt, slipped into his loafers, sat back and sighed.

"Trouble with the little woman?" She didn't look at him; was still in character, but he ignored the light sarcastic edge; it would've been too easy.

"You don't know the half of it, babe," he said. "Sure you want to be one?"

She laughed. "Sure you don't want to try one? Of me, I mean. You never know, sweetie. You might discover a whole other side of the street."

"No thanks. I like this side."

"Suit yourself; it's all paid for."

He stared out the window for a while; the snow was coming harder and harder; the lights of the city were weakening; the night was devouring the whiteness of the snow. In the morning, it would all be beautiful, but tonight, he was nowhere; the hotel room, the satyr next to him; it was a dream. He thought of 122 Grant Avenue – *the scum*; thought of what they'd do if they were trapped here with Amanda. *A Man Da. Cute.* He laughed.

"The name part of the act?" he said.

"Sure, any blonde you meet named Amanda has a penis." She was starting to enjoy scoring points off him.

"I'll keep that in mind," he said. "So you want to be a psychologist, huh?"

"Sure," she said looking at him. "A psychologist."

"Put on your jacket, cover those tits, they're too distracting," he said buttoning his shirt and pulling on his jacket. "You've got your first patient."

She put on the jacket. He pushed the chairs so they faced each other but obliquely, then settled himself in one. She sat in the other and crossed her legs, looking at him with amusement.

"I came to America from a small island..." he started, then stopped. "Wait, aren't you going to take notes?"

"I'll let you in on a little secret," she said. "We just doodle on the pads, write grocery lists, that kind of thing. Go ahead."

He leaned back into the chair and closed his eyes.

II

I grew up in a small piece of shit island in the Caribbean. My old man was well off, but stupid. You know the story: drank it, pissed it away, died, left wife and children kind of dazed, not as rich as they thought. He was a dumb, generous bastard, always taking in strays, and fucking them whenever he could.

I wasn't what you'd call a hard-working dude. I went to the university down there, fell in with a bad crowd; intellectuals, writers, artists, that kind of thing. Did the radical thing; you know – drinking, fucking, drugs. Then I really went downhill; I got into journalism. They thought all the drinking and leftist shit made me interesting; columnist material. It was fun for a while, but, well, you know how things go in these fucking Third World shit-holes; you're interesting as long as you don't do anything that resembles the right thing. Some politician was fucking some bimbo who'd worked on a cruise ship and got thrown off for giving the Captain crabs, and he organised a national literary competition and let her win. I blew the whistle and, well, they threatened to kill me if I didn't leave the country. Can you fucking believe it? I did it as a gag. But white pussy is no joke down there. They gave me three days; I couldn't even sell anything off, get any money together. So there I was in Crapola County, Long Island, broke except for a couple of grand my Mama had spotted me, living with some of my father's strays.

The Colos weren't people the way you know people. Think of the mountain people in *Deliverance*. Back home, they would've been whores, labourers, petty thieves, drug pushers, that kind of thing; kinda sad if you think about it. My dad had grown up in the same village with Colo, the father of the family. I don't think he went to school or anything like that, but my grandfather made sure my father went. So a few years later, my dad was working as a salesman, had married my mom, was living in a pretty nice house in a nice suburb. Colo was living in a sugar company shack, had married a goat woman and they were breeding like rabbits. My dad helped them out over the years; got them a house, helped the kids to get into school, that kind of thing.

They'd come over to our house sometimes when we were younger; holidays, things like that. If they'd been black they'd be po'ass niggers. As it is, they were po'ass coolies. I kind of felt sorry for them in those days. They weren't *bad* people, y'know? Salt of the earth types, who'd looked after us as kids. But we grew up; my sister and I went to college; I don't know where they went.

Somebody had to shovel the shit, and it was them. That's the way it went. Ma told me a few years ago that one of them had gone away, found a backdoor into the States, dragged up the rest of them. They used to come back home every year or so, and visit my mother. They always said anytime any one of us wanted to come, we could stay as long as we wanted.

Everytime they said it, Ma would smile weakly, and my sister and I would elbow each other in the ribs, and we'd all promise to visit soon. Funny how the shit you say comes back and kicks you in the ass. I arrived one cold February day. Colo and one of the boys, Az, were waiting for me. I'd been to America before; an old girlfriend had gone to school there and I'd spent a few summers into the Fall, so I knew the place pretty well. But that had been years ago; we had money in those days. I didn't know anyone there that cold February.

Something had changed since I'd been there those years ago. The place knew I wasn't a young man anymore, wasn't coming to see a young woman, or skip about the Village like an asshole. A lot of shit had happened in the last few years. Immigrants were flooding out the place; the white folks were getting pissed, and it showed.

I got the first stab when I walked out of the customs area where Colo was waiting for me, a little troll of a man, wearing an oversized K-Mart coat, oil-stained work-boots and a cheap baseball cap under which his gray spiky hair and jowly black face stuck out. The pink faces around me were rich and happy, peering out of expensive coats, suits, scarves; completely oblivious of my very existence. Their world moved at a different speed; different dimensions of the mind operated. Colo was barely visible in this expanse of the moving world with its carpeted floors, high steel pillars, glass, bright sterile newsstands with red-sweatered, turbaned Sikhs behind them, electronic flight boards. I didn't see it at first, but what stabbed was our invisibility, smallness; an utter and absolute powerlessness.

"How you goin' boy?" said Colo. The voice hadn't changed; he still sounded as if he had stumbled out of a rice field from the Stone Age, as if his native language was broken Hindustani rather than broken English. Az, the middle boy, stood in the back, smirking at me. "Ah'll git the car, Pap," he said. The accent was a confection of island dialect and New Yorkese. We got the bags in the battered old Subaru and took off. Colo had never owned a car before, but things were different now; for me as well. All those things I'd taken for granted were suddenly on the other side of the tracks.

The roads were long and wide and mesmerizing, leading to places pregnant with promise; only now I was aware that I wasn't going anywhere near them. Where I was going was past a blur of lawyers' offices, video stores, realty brokers, doctors, housing agencies, employment agencies, Dunkin Donuts, McDonalds, Home Depot, Caldor, Interstate signs, exit ramps, orthodontists, chiropractors, plumbing contractors, licensed bailiffs, government tax offices, police stations, fire stations, dog-grooming salons, nail salons, hairdressing salons, Chinese fast food joints, Thai, Korean, Vietnamese fast-food joints, immigration lawyers, property consultants, real estate agencies, landscape contractors, gyms, variety stores, speciality stores, Nation of Islam recruiting offices, Army Navy recruiting offices, temporary employment agencies, permanent employment agencies, temp-to-perm employment agencies, butchers shops, electronics repair shops, lawyers offices, video stores, realty brokers...

I was dizzy and depressed by the time we swung down Long Island, down desperate Grant Avenue, a long line of misery with a few reminders of the white owners who had fled from the encroaching immigrant line – a tattered American flag; the emaciated remains of what was once a carefully tended hedge; a few polished oak front doors with brass knockers. One twenty-two Grant Ave was a big old house with a forbidding peaked roof, showing a soiled, double-hung attic window.

Colo and his sons were handy around the house; they'd done that at home, so they'd done a lot of the repairs themselves. The living room walls were done in pink; the furniture was covered with some sort of shiny orange plastic material that looked like it'd give you a rash if you rubbed on it too hard; there were doilies, pink heart-shaped cushions on the sofa; a little fake wicker basket of pot pourri on the picture window seat; white lacey curtains; a closed-up fireplace with a few ceramic ornaments on it; some pictures of the Colo girls in cowgirl get-up – broad-brimmed hats, dancehall dresses, six-shooters – grinning whorishly at the camera.

As I stepped in the house, the strong scent of curry spread like a thick coating of muslin over everything; it seeped out of the walls, out of the furniture, out of the sweat-suit wrapped around Komay, Colo's wife, who was waiting for me at the door. Crooked yellow teeth grinned welcomingly from a burnt-black head, topped with short curly hair, that poked out of the oversized neck of a grey sweat shirt.

"Oh Gaaard boy, how you goin'?"

She led me to the kitchen and sat me down with her as she cooked, sharing the wisdom she had acquired in her years in America.

"Boy, dis country is 'bout wuk and wuk. You mus' wuk in dis country. Everything is wuk. You will have to wuk in dis country." The cheap wallpaper that plastered the kitchen was almost liquid in the heat, releasing the nauseous smell of spices; the floor, covered in linoleum, was uneven and lumpy.

"Uh huh," I said.

The rest of the Colos filtered in over the next hour. Colo and Az had left me to pick up one of the daughters from the train station; they returned minutes later with Sooz, who worked for American Express in the city. She had to be picked up at the train station everyday, even though it was only a few minutes' walk away. She was a small, dark, delicate thing with a pageboy haircut and a Valley Girl accent.

"Ohmigaad haw yew dewin'?" she asked, as she dropped her shopping bags; Macy's, Parade of Shoes, Filene's. "We haven't seen yew in *yeers*." She wore Reeboks and a dark green skirt suit, an American Express pin on the lapel. She carried her pumps in one of the bags.

Bucky, the parents' favourite, came in later. He was the good-looking one; light-skinned, with buck teeth and a strange head of hair. At the front and back, its texture, consistency and direction of growth were different. He worked in the shipping department of a computer firm and had worked his way up to a supervisory position. The family depended on him; Colo was out of work because all he could do was manual labour, and things were slow. Az, who looked like Colo only thinner, was also the shithead of the family; he was involved in a lawsuit with a construction company, which getting a job would have put an end to. He passed his days watching the OJ Simpson trial.

The youngest, Pinky, who worked in a store in Queens, came in last. She was slim and tall with long straight hair and baby-doll features. Whenever she went into Manhattan, people ("weirdos"), she confided to me later, came up to her offering modelling contracts, which she refused. She showed me some of the cards: they were from a vice president of Donna Karan, an agent from Ford, and an associate designer at Prada. She kept them for souvenirs; she'd never heard of these companies. There were the other boys' wives, Toggy and Sarah, and their children. Another brother and sister lived away from Colo central, but they visited often with their own families; various friends, relations, and refugees also visited from time to time.

The house was divided into three levels. Colo and Komay, least in importance, occupied the basement; the children and the grandchildren occupied the upper floor. Each of the boys had a room which was dominated by a large television and personal paraphernalia, which they shared with their wives and children. In the scheme of things I contributed nothing to the progress of the family, so I was put in the converted garage which also served as a storeroom, and which, I found out the hard way, was unheated.

But at the dinner table later that evening, they seemed happy to see me. They asked me what I was going to do. I put it out that I was hoping to make a go of America.

"Aw," Sooz said, "well, Pop knows people, doncha Pop?"

It seemed the Colos had somehow managed to find a way out of the immigration net that was tightening in the US at that time. I was anxious to find out how. Then came my first inclination that all was not as it seemed.

"Well boy," Colo said, "that thing we do…"

"It over now Pap," piped in Bucky. "Cain't do it no maw."

"But what was it?" I persisted.

"Well, it had a fella with a farm down in Miami," said Colo, "an' we pay him and go down there for a couple of days. Then he carry we to the office. The officer ask a few question. Ask if you could talk English and thing. Say we could only talk Spanish. Then they take the picture and thing."

That was as much as I could get out of them. Later, I pieced together that they had posed as Cubans; those were the final days of the Cuban amnesty and they had just managed to slip in under the wire before the loophole was closed. I marvelled that they had, by pure dumb luck, managed to find one crook who kept his word and not taken their money and shot them through the backs of their empty heads.

Later that first night, the conversation turned away from me and onto their lives: their credit cards, their vacations, their jobs – it all loomed large and impressive inside the house. I crawled into my small bed with their warbling voices echoing in my ears. I slept dreamlessly, but woke several times in the night with a sense of foreboding. Or maybe it was just the cold.

The next morning I took a couple hundred dollars and fled to the city for relief from the scents of curry, coolie body odours and the general muddiness of the Colos' world. But the change, whose tendrils I'd encountered at the airport, felt even more palpable. I came out at the 34th Street station with the dregs of the rush-hour crowd – the cell-phone carrying, cashmere coat and Brooks Brothers suit-wearing, pale pink petty-bourgeoisie. February, cold as hell. The sidewalk was dry and grey, and city was covered with soupy grey clouds. My boots were too thin, and so were my sweaters; the jeans got colder and colder against my skin. I couldn't walk far, but at least I was out in the open. I was confused, nauseous, though I didn't realise the nausea was a result of the confusion. I caught a look at myself in a shop window as I walked by – the old coat, the hair pushed back, the eyes desperate and dull at the same time. I'd always been a good-looking fella, well-browned, square jaw, straight nose, good firm lips, dark hair and eyes. Maybe that's why I got away with the things I got away with on the island – handsome radicals are always more successful than ugly ones. I was like a minor piece of art, good to look at, ok for conversation, something interesting you wouldn't miss if it were to disappear. Here, what I saw looking at back from the plate glass was just some Asian-Paki fuck, some immigrant come to take jobs away from hard-working Americans. No one would ever know how interesting I was because I would never be heard.

There was a porno store just outside the 8th Avenue entrance to the station. I went in and roamed around the stacks of Ass Masters, White Bitches Sucking Black Cocks, Asian Sluts, Bizarre Sluts, Chicks with Dicks Taking it Both Ways, Barely 18, Oral Cum Shot Extravaganzas, Euro Bestiality. The balding fat white men with glasses who'd minded the stores in the 80s had sold out to Indians, who stood behind the counters ashen-faced, mean-looking and pathetic; if selling jizz in America was the last stop on your opportunity train, it had to take something out of you. The place was small; walls were lined with video boxes and sex toys: butt plugs, whips, handcuffs, dildos, inflate-a-dates. The books were stacked in trays on a large table in the middle of the room. The men poring over them wore suits, carried briefcases; some were hayseed tourists in jeans, sneakers and cheap athletic jackets. The sign over the video boxes announced: *All Movies Available in Booths.*

I went in and started flicking around. The desperation, the tension of hopelessness was glad to spend itself in sexual desire. The booth was small, covered in orange arborite and smelling of bleach and stale ejaculate. I had undone my pants and slipped my cock out and, balancing on the small chair, hiked up the tail of the coat so it wouldn't trail on the floor. The whole operation took less than three minutes, but afterwards, with my ears roaring, I realised I had nothing to wipe up with. I whipped my hand to flick it on the floor, and dried the remainder on my undershorts. I made a mental note for return trips.

I stumbled out of the porn shop onto 34th Street and walked dazedly up to Sixth Avenue, then turned down Broadway. It was cold, but the numbness spreading below my skin frightened me even more. I walked down to the Village. There were people there, but they didn't see me: not the cars crawling past, not the people skittering along, not the hooded messengers, limbs and torsos thickened by several layers of sweat clothes, on their fragile bikes wheeling around the cars, not the immigrants buried in enormous cheap parkas, not the hucksters: no one who was unlucky enough to be out in the streets saw me. A strange thing: the buildings, canyons of stone and glass, towered above; vertigo, another kind of fear, but I never looked up.

I drifted into the *Angelika* and bought a ticket for the movie that was about to start right then – some lesbian flick I gratefully surrendered to; crying as the heroine ditched her stockbroker boyfriend for a jeans-and-construction boot-wearing woman performance artist. As the lights came up, I saw I was the only man in the auditorium; everyone else was short-haired, spectacled, determined looking; women who wouldn't take any shit about their lovers from any one. A few of them scowled at me. I would have scowled at me, too.

On the way back to Grant Avenue I read the *Village Voice* and the *New York Press*. By the time I stepped past the green front door of 122 Grant Avenue, I was in a New York fucked-me-up-the-ass frame of mind.

"Oh Gard, boy," said Komay as she let me in, "we was worryin' 'bout you."

"Yeah," said Colo, from behind her, "dis city dangerous, boy, you mus' lewwe know way you is. You mus' call. Use the phone an' call."

I was overwhelmed by their concern for me, and said so. The New York shaft eased out of my ass. At least someone cared for me. They led me into dinner; I sat and dutifully ate the curry that was put in front of me. Then I went downstairs to the basement and finished the evening lying on an old sofa in front of the television with Colo. He was a Western man; liked Caroll O'Connor in *In the Heat of the Night*, Chuck Norris in *Walker, Texas Ranger* – moronic action stuff. Once or twice I tried to swing him to the Sci Fi Channel – *Mystery Science Theatre 3000*, *Star Trek* reruns, *Saturday Night Live* reruns on the Comedy Channel; but he wouldn't budge from the Westerns.

During the commercials we discussed the idea of finding me a menial job till I could find some loophole that hadn't been closed yet to get a green card; all the Colos had promised to activate their contacts to help me find a store-watching or ditch-digging position. A few weeks passed, but nothing happened. Colo seemed happy to have me around to run errands; Komay seemed happy to have me do the dishes, to be there to listen to her imbecilic babbling about America. The young ones were too taken up with America to think about my problems. The dinnertimes I had looked forward to for talking to them, to find out if anything had come up, were filled by discussions of their vacation plans, the places they'd been to, the purchases they planned, their outings, their friends. My distance from everything seemed immeasurable as I sat there listening. I was nowhere, had no friends, knew no one. Outside was a nameless blur. I was trapped in the house most of the time; I'd calculated I would be able to go into the city about once a week until I started earning. I bought the *Village Voice* and the *Times* as often as I could. Sometimes I brought myself a bagel, a milkshake, tried three Baskin-Robbins flavours, or sushi, just to taste a difference; to banish the taste of oil- and sugar-laden stews and curries; becoming, with each small outlay, painfully aware that however bad it was at that point, it would be infinitely worse without money.

More frightening were the other types of atrophy. The Colos bought no newspapers, so I took to stacking them in my room. During the day, Az would be in his room watching the Simpson trial while his baby slept; his wife, Sarah, and Bucky's wife, Toggy, went out to work as a baby-sitters. The wives were illegals who had married the Colo boys and were awaiting their green cards. I filled the days rereading the papers in my room or going downstairs with Colo to watch television. I couldn't talk to them about what I read in the papers; beside the OJ Simpson trial, the vicissitudes of American life passed above their heads. I felt my mind beginning to liquefy into mulch, accompanied by the theme music from Colo's Westerns. The Fridays I spent in the city began, more and more, to seem like an interrupted dream: my movements through the cheap art galleries, the cheap movie houses, the free poetry readings I saw in the *Voice* – it all became more and more insubstantial. I left no footprints; no one noticed me. I was fading away. And even at moments when there were small rips in the emptiness – when I saw a man holding a little child's hand; two people kissing on a train; a young woman blowing into her cupped palms for warmth – the hopelessness of my situation began to solidify, as did my realisation that the Colos would do nothing to help. I couldn't understand why at first; it wasn't that they lacked the contacts.

At least two weekends each month there was a gathering at the Colo house. The first was after I'd been there two weeks. All the Colos and their friends – mostly people who'd lived in the same village with them, and several of whom knew me – began arriving early in the morning, each bringing some freshly killed animal – a goat or pig – or as much liquor as their minimum wages could buy. Loud, irritating Coolie music, imported from home, started up around 8 am. By noon there were fifty people in the house. I was mesmerized by the plaid, the cheap boots, the knock-off Levis, the polystyrene coats which would melt or burst into flame near a lit stove, the sallow brown faces which became more and more droopy and blank as the day progressed; the noise, the smoke, the music in the background. I'd never experienced anything like it, except for a few times when my father's coolie family got married and we were forced to go to the wedding. At first I sat in a corner stupefied, not sure where to go or what to do amidst the tramping boots, the talk of white women, work and the fabulous $15 an hour jobs like Bucky's. The women had disappeared into the upper floor of the house with a hoard of liquor and chocolates, from where they'd emerge later to engage in drunken embraces and wet, ursine copulations with the men. I wandered around the house nervously; you never knew when one of these retards would recover some lost memory and turn into a homicidal lunatic. Az stood with a group of men, and I drifted in with them.

"All you know dis man?" Az had been drunk all morning. He put his arm around my shoulders. "Dis man is de man who fadder carry me in de horsepital..."

I nodded around through the thick haze and the smells of tobacco and rum and beer. A few rayon mesh caps bobbed in return through the smoky atmosphere.

"So ah tell 'im," Az continued from where he'd left off to introduce me, "if you ain't wanna geemee $200 ah day, fuhgid it. An' he cuff me dong."

The entire collection of bearded snouts peering out from under Dodge and GMC plastic mesh and Yankee baseball caps, gurgled and snorted indecipherable encouragements. I stood for about an hour listening to each talk about how the white, Puerto Rican and nigger supervisors at their jobs knew nothing, and how each man there had saved his company from certain bankruptcy at least once a week; although how this was effected from the fucking loading docks, mailrooms, or the toilets they cleaned, I couldn't work out.

I considered getting hammered, but decided against it. Who knew what I'd say to them drunk? Who knew what fifteen of them might decide to do to me if I got drunk and told them they were morons? To the Colos and their ilk, drink wasn't a lubricant for the mind and libido as it was among civilized people; here it was just fuel for ignorance. I wandered around for an hour, then out of desperation grabbed a six-pack of beer and retreated into my garage-storage room.

It was February, still cold as hell, so I sat on the floor with my back against the wall connected to the house for the feel of the heat. I finally fell into a light sleep, punctured every few minutes by someone tramping down the steps to grab an extra bottle of rum, a roll of toilet paper, or stumbling into the room with a pudgy little cock in hand looking for a place to pee.

Sometime late in the night I woke. The house was quiet; the music had stopped, the lights were off, the storeroom door was open. I was half-awake, still dreaming of falling and having the Empire State Building rammed up my ass, when I heard soft sobbing and sniffling. I woke up completely, but didn't move. The sniffling, and some faint grunts like a child or a small animal crying, continued for a few minutes. A light padding of footsteps, then Komay's voice.

"Wha happin wid you, gyal?"

"Ma..." More sniffles.

"You sick, gyal? You want me to go an' call you Pa?"

"Nooooo... doh call Pa." This started a fresh muffled staccato of sobs.

"Wha happen, gyal? Ah have to shit," said Komay.

"Is Pa, Ma," replied the voice.

"Wha happen to Pa, gyal?"

"He... he bull me, Ma," the sobbing continued.

"Oh Gard, dat is arl, gyal? Look lemme shit an' we go talk."

The toilet belched and gurgled a few minutes later. Then Komay's voice.

"Oh Lard, gyal, that ain't nutten. When I did jes marrid Pa, he pappy and he bredda bull me."

"Buh he bull mih in me bam bam, Ma."

"Dat is because he ain't want to breed you up, gyal. Wha' happin? You bam bam burnin you? Ah few good shit go ease dat up, gyal. You mus' leave de shit and doh wipe it. It go pass fas fas."

The sniffling became fainter as the two pairs of footsteps padded away. I reckoned it must be Sarah, Az's wife; she was not well-liked among the Colos. I had once seen a strange exchange between her and Toggy, Bucky's wife. Sarah was a country girl from the island whom Az had met and promised to marry during one of his trips back, and had completely forgotten about it once he sobered up. Sarah had acquired a stolen passport and presented herself at 122 Grant Avenue one summer evening a year and a half before I arrived. There was nothing Az could do but marry her; coolies took that kind of thing seriously. Still, it was a fair deal. Az was one of those men who fucked obese, shut-in women, or those with mental problems; if a group of eight men fucked a hooker, he would be last; if the hooker could be persuaded to have another go, she'd say "everybody but that one". Sarah was plain, flat-chested, had thin legs and was illiterate, but there was a glint in her eyes none of the Colos had; I suspected this was why they disliked her: she was spunky. Soon after the wedding, she was pregnant, and the baby sealed the issue: she was locked into the family. The family idiot got a wife, she got off the island: a fair exchange.

The incident I had witnessed involved the babies. Toggy's son was playing with Sarah's child's toy. Sarah took her child to Toggy's child and said to her baby: "Say, 'Gimme back mih toy'."

Toggy was nearby. She guided her son's hand toward Sarah's child and said: "Say, 'Take it, you likkul piece a shit'." She laughed as she said it; making a joke of it.

Sarah said to her baby: "Say, 'Doh call mih dat'."

Toggy kept laughing and saying: "You likkul piece ah shit."

Toggy had gotten pregnant after a drunken Saturday party, and entrapped Bucky into marriage. She was short, had thick, hairy legs, and her face was round and flat with a wart below her nose, which was made more apparent by the light sprouting of hair which she attempted to cover with a cake of foundation. But she was the wife of the favoured son; that meant something. Sarah was plain, but she was a kind soul. Sometimes I saw her hold her child and draw her knees up and put her forehead on them, forming a circle around the baby. I knew that one day, as soon as she had the green card in her hand, she and the baby would simply disappear from the house. That made me glad; it allowed me to fall asleep.

Life with the Colos continued like this for about seven weeks, but it seemed much longer. The only change was that I adjusted my schedule to be away from the house during the gatherings. By the seventh week, of the original $1400, I now had about $700 left, and the desperation was beginning to intensify. I'd put on weight, a lot of it. On that Saturday in late March, the winter had turned wet and cold; everything was dark grey as I went into Manhattan, to a pisshole movie house on 42nd Street I'd seen advertised in the *Voice*, where new movies cost $4 and they let you stay as long as you liked if you could stand the sticky seats, the smells, and the sounds of security guards, Wall Street brokers, and orthodontists from Long Island sodomising hustlers and transvestites in the back rows.

Walking from the train station to the movie house, it dawned on me just how completely forlorn I was. My money would run out in a few weeks, then I'd be at their mercy. Not escaping into the city at least once a week was not an option. I had to come out otherwise my brain would dissolve. I spent more and more money – as much as fifty dollars an outing – going to the paying museums, buying sushi and Japanese plums from Dean & DeLuca as a way of pinching myself into consciousness, to fight my fading into the sidewalks. It felt like my previous life had been a dream I'd just woken from to find myself in a prison. I was passing another porn store and I went in, found a booth, flipped to a channel with two black men with huge cocks being sucked off by a blonde with huge tits, and jerked myself off in less than a minute.

I sat there with my shrivelled cock hanging out of my pants, dribbling semen onto the floor. I'd not cut my nails in all the time I'd been at the Colos, and I'd handled myself so roughly the skin on the underside had been rubbed raw; I could feel it starting to burn. I could see little blobs of semen other desperate assholes had left on the floor, glistening in the light of the screen. I leaned back, closed my eyes, and wondered how much lower than this there was to go. I'd never been a praying man, but I looked up at the dark roof of the booth. One of the black men held on to the blonde's head with one hand and started jerking his cock, coming on her tongue, on her cheeks, on her tits, while she opened her mouth as wide as it could go and stuck her tongue out further to catch the thick gobs of semen while she pumped the other man's cock frantically. I said: "God, what the fuck did I ever do to you?" Then I wiped myself off with the Colos' kitchen towel and stumbled out.

I bumped into him just outside the porn store. God, in the incarnation of Steve Bamford, one of my island strays. While I'd worked as a columnist for the papers, every now and then one or other of my leftist pals would dump a charity case on me. Steve was a poor black kid who'd gotten arrested on a marijuana charge: the charge was not paying off the policeman he was supposed to. His mother came to my office and told me the story – you can guess it. She told me she had a sister in Brooklyn, and she'd send him there if I could talk to someone. I managed, through bribing the chief crime reporter who knew some people, to make it go away. Then I talked to somebody at the American Embassy who owed me a favour and got the kid a visa. Every once in a while, I tried to do something I felt good about; it was like a protest that I wasn't *that* much of an asshole.

He'd come to the office with his mother to thank me; a vicious-looking little rat-faced miscreant, wearing oversized clothes that had obviously been borrowed, who'd stood off to the side sullenly while his mother embraced me. Now here he was, walking down 42nd St on a dark, wet evening in Spring, basking in the carnivalesque twinkling lights announcing human degra-dation for as low as a quarter, wearing enough gold to buy off the island's entire police force; a leather jacket, jeans and boots, all of which seemed at least three sizes too big for him – but now on purpose, not the result of charity – and a Kangol hat of the approved fashion and cut. Beside him walked a sullen, heavily made-up brown gangsta bitch with fake hair, long orange finger-nails, large droopy tits and a big, tired-looking gash of a cunt imprinted on tight Gaultier stretch pants peeking out from the fur-trimmed leather coat.

"Oh fug yo'," he said, embracing me effusively, displaying an impressive set of gold teeth. "Yawyawyaw, homie. Whadda fug you doin uppyere and ain't call me fo?"

He'd graduated, was a connected guy now – not a Donnie Brasco type, just one of those loudmouth deat-wish niggers who walked around looking mean, talking tough and packing a Glock, waiting for someone to shoot them and put them out of their misery. We repaired in his Lexus to a saloon on Greenwich St. He walked into the place, along the steel and chrome bar, with the electric pink and blue neon lighting and industrial cables snaking round everything, baring his gold teeth at the bartenders and the yuppies wearing the $1000-a-pop loafers and their Nine West-wearing, too-expensive-for-your-poor-ass bimbos; daring them to tell him he couldn't afford the joint. I followed docilely to the table feeling poor, fat and pathetic. As we sat, a waiter appeared, though the place was crowded, and was dispatched by Steve for a bottle of Moet or something in that price range. I explained my problem as we waited, resisting the urge to grab his Glock and pop myself.

He knew some people. I said I didn't want to do anything with drugs, except use them from time to time.

"Thadda be hard, Gee, but call dis fella here; nigga owes me money." As we parted, he put his hand in his pocket and pulled out a roll of bills and a business card. His other hand produced a heavy gold pen and scrawled a name and a number on the back of the card.

"Nah, man, I can't take your money," I said, eyeing it lustfully. The brown bitch's tits heaved spitefully. She'd followed us to the Lexus, sat in the back while he drove us downtown and sat at the table sneering at the pale pink mass of tit-jobs and chin- and neck-tucks that surrounded us, while we talked for more than an hour without saying a word herself. Occasionally, Steve ran his hand over her, squeezing one of the droopy breasts. When he noticed me watching, he said: "You wanna ride this ho, Gee? Be mah guest. Take da bitch into da alley an let 'er git you off."

I considered it briefly, then said: "You got here a little late, man, I got off already for the day."

"Suit yo'sef, Gee."

The bitch's eyes never wavered.

"Whachyou mean 'my money', nigga?" he said, pressing it into my coat pocket. "Thas yo money, homie; cause my ass would be rottin in some fuckin' hole now if it wasn't fer you. Take it. You want mo', I git you mo'. You want somebody fucked, I fuck 'em up for yeh. Ah owes you, baby."

His accent was flawless. I briefly contemplated setting him on the Colos, decided against it, then took the money; it was about $2,000. I called the number he gave me the next day. That's how I ended up at the Olympus Messenger Service.

The dispatcher, Lou, was a miserable-looking Italian man who liked getting high more than he liked a life of familial happiness. He'd been an accountant in the life before cocaine, had lost his job, his wife and little girl, and was now working as a dispatcher for Olympus, paying half his week's salary to Steve and his associates, doing the occasional favour to clear up the vig. The office was a little hole in the wall on 58th Street, not big enough to be anything else but a hole in the wall; but it was like walking through a magic portal into some shithole or jail cell of my island. All the messengers were from there, but not from the part of it I was from; so far as I could tell, they had all absconded from the police at home and made their way here thanks to some gay American tourist lured into an alleyway on the pretext of some hard black cock up their ass, and instead got some hard boots up there and, as an added bonus, were relieved of money, passports, several pints of blood, and frequently of consciousness, or the ability to walk without a limp for the rest of their lives.

I introduced myself to Lou, whose emaciated body and face still carried the shifty desperation and cruelty of his previous life. He told me where to buy a bike and the gear I'd need; in a week, I was settled into the job.

Messengers are like alligators in the New York City sewers:

everybody knows they're there, and one day one might show up at your apartment. Until that day, though, nobody really sees them. You learn a lot about the city riding around; you get to know yourself, because you're the only one there is to talk to; you remember every advertising jingle you ever knew; you plot elaborate scenarios around your plans for world domination, lottery wins and wreaking untold violence on your enemies – like setting the INS on their coolie asses. You also learn where everything is: where the cheap food is, where the free bathrooms are. And you learn just how much the rich and poor really hate each other. This is something you really don't know until you've delivered a package to an upscale restaurant and seen the chef pissing into a pot of soup; or gone to a Madison Avenue office where the Waspy pink publicists have a dirty, broken phone for the messengers, which they spray with ammonia after they're done.

Each side is correct about the other: messengers are fucking animals – the same species as bellboys, waiters and servicemen in the uptown buildings; they'd fuck a dying comatose 86-year old woman for money or fun. The rich white people are cheap, lying, thieving shit-bags who pretend you don't exist in elevators in the World Financial Centre, while they casually drop insider information about IPOs, or boast about raping their Haitian maids and throwing them out when they got pregnant.

The messengers in the Olympus office were scary even by those standards; those Madison Avenue white girls' cunts must have frozen in horror at the sight of those dreadlocked niggers talking island pidgin. A lot of them had done time, usually for drug pushing; the rest of them were illegals, fresh off the plane and out of their Brooklyn basements, waiting to graduate to drug pushing. In that nether space I existed for a few weeks.

By the second week, I was making more money than the others because I was able to write the names and addresses faster than they were; I was able to read the maps, talk to the receptionists, and read the addresses on the packages. I guess it might have palled after a while, but in the beginning, just being outside, away from the Colos, was like moving from a box at the Port Authority into the Plaza. I'd bought a bike for the price of a used car thanks to Steve's money; and I think Lou had told the Shaka Zulu wannabes I was a friend of Steve's, so they left me alone.

My weekend jaunts to the city also became less macabre: I still made the occasional trip to the jerk-off emporia, but now I was able to buy the odd book, and found to my amazement that the Barnes & Noble slacker book-packers didn't care if you just lounged around the store all day and read the books – and even encouraged you to put your feet up on the chairs. I was able to go to a comedy club now and then, even some cheap theatre in the Village. The invisibility was beginning to lift. My face and stomach had begun to flatten, thanks to the eight-hour days biking through the city. Now I had to put up with the Colos only one day a week, on Sunday mornings; in the afternoons I went to the movies at a multiplex I'd discovered not far from their home; but from the outset of my starting to work, I began to notice changes in their attitude toward me.

Before, it seemed that they were happy to tolerate my loafing around the house, watching television, doing errands, and getting fatter and more depressed as the days dragged on. Now, with my new-found independence, acquired without their help, little resentments began to emerge. There were mutterings, always just outside the door, and just loud enough for me to hear, about how hard life in America was, and how expensive it was to live there, especially as Colo wasn't working. The messenger's pay was modest; I gave them half of it, but it wasn't enough.

When I came home one evening, and left my clothes off in the bathroom hamper, Komay told me later: "It did smellin' kinna fonnee". I started doing laundry every day; until I heard a murmur that the washing machine was old, and could not take the pressure. Once Komay saw me using the phone to call Moviefone. A few days later she told me – because the $100 I gave her couldn't "covah mih eggspenzes" – I was to stop using the phone.

The Colos' talk of their purchases, their credit cards, and their vacations I now regarded with bemusement at the dinner table on the odd occasions I was there; a bemusement reinforced by their cheap shoes, the 14th Street and Pitkin Avenue knockoffs they wore, the tacky fake jewellery, the caked-on, too light for their faces make-up. I never said anything, never showed any visible sign, but the bastards who couldn't spell their own names most of them, or recognise my alienation and move their black asses to help me, could intuit my harmless amusement at their gaucheries enough to resent it. The end began, though, when I offered to help Sarah and Toggy with their GED studies.

One Sunday afternoon as I was leaving on my movie outing, I saw them at the table with some books. I looked over Sarah's shoulder; she was struggling with Pythagoras's theorem, biting the pencil.

"What's the problem?" I asked.

"Cyah unnerstan' what dey sayin'," she muttered. I read the instructions. Then I took the pencil and drew the diagram on the paper. I explained what a square and square root were and showed her how it was done.

"If you want to understand what they saying," I said, "you have to start learning how they does talk. Try to figger out what they sayin' when you watchin TV. Or I have newspapers in the store room; you could come and take them out and read them."

"Arright," she said, shyly.

"You too, Toggy," I said.

Toggy had sat there looking at the whole exchange stolidly; she turned her head down to her books without a word.

Komay was waiting for me as I came home: "Dem papers in de room does cause cockroach. I take dem out and trow dem 'way," she said, eyeing the *Times* in my hand. "You muss'n bring dem in de house."

"OK," I said. I had adopted a policy of absolute non-resistance. I was still an illegal immigrant; if they threw me out I knew I was fucked. I began to wonder how long I could hold out. The way the house had turned against me, I knew it was only a matter of time. I still had some of Steve's money, but acquiring a place to live was a complicated process requiring documents. The money alone wasn't enough. I needed something momentous to happen. As it turned out, two momentous things happened.

The first thing had already been happening for some time. My Saturdays always began with a few hours at the B&N on Union Square. I'd read the *Times*, have coffee in the bar, and then move over to the poetry section, sometimes the politics section, sometimes the philosophy section, make a few selections, find a comfy chair, and read for the next two or three hours. It was springtime by then, so most people were outdoors; I had the place to myself early in the day. On the third week, I'd read an essay on a Russian poet in the *Times* and decided to poke around for the book. I couldn't find it in the poetry section. I wandered around, looking for an attendant. I was directed to the floor supervisor, Anya.

Anya had a Gothic thing happening; she was dark-haired, with a pierced septum and tongue. Under the B&N polo shirt, she wore a black, ultra-thin undershirt, through which her pale white arms glistened; she wore black velvet underwear, but I wouldn't discover that until a few weeks later. Her lipstick was black – like her hair and her dramatically arched eyebrows – but beneath the lipstick and the nose ring, I could see her lips were round and soft. The poorly-fitting khaki trousers she wore couldn't hide the curves of her ass and the lines of her long legs.

"Akhmatowa?" she said. "Zey haf all zold out seence zuh *Times* article."

"Oh," I said, "that's too bad." Her eyes were were like liquid onyx. Suddenly I realised I hadn't had sex with a real woman since I'd been in America. "But," she said, "I haf a personal copy I bot tozay, I vill lend it to you iv you zit over zere and look at eet."

I sat looking at the book for about a half-an-hour. When I was done I returned it and said: "Can I buy you some coffee or something?" Apparently coffee was a sexual aid in the New York dating world, and invoking it was like a mantra.

She smiled, beautiful strong white teeth, and said: "Ve're not allowed to date wit zuh customers."

"I haven't bought anything," I said. "So I'm not really a customer."

"I hate zuh coffee," she said, making a face.

"Me too," I said. "We could have tumblers of tea. You know, like in Dr Zhivago."

"I'm Armenian," she said. "I hate zuh focking Russians."

"Me too," I said. "Commie bastards."

She laughed. "I get off at zeeex," she said. "Be on time."

The second momentous thing came from Lou. At about the time the Colos were beginning to turn on me, he called me outside one morning. "Moe," he said (the name attached to the Social Security number I was using was Morris), "let's getta cup a' cawffee."

"You asking me on a date, Lou?" I asked.

His face twisted into a pained look, than a hate-filled look, then back to its normal miserable cast.

"Ha ha," he said, sourly.

As we walked to the deli down the street from the Olympus store front, he said: "I got a special job for yez. Itta mean extra money, but ya gotta keep yer fuckin' ma't shut."

The Colo business was just starting to heat up, so I asked no questions. Lou, it seemed, was a slave to many masters. Not only did he owe Steve's friends, he was also indebted to the Mob. He couldn't trust the niggers, he said; they were too fucking dumb to be scared; they might try to rip off the Mob and get everybody killed.

The job was picking up a tightly wrapped, hefty package from 95th on the West Side and taking it down to Mott in the Village. I took it though an iron slot in the door uptown and passed it through a similar slot downtown. A $50 bill accompanied it each time.

After two weeks of making the same run, I was given more specific instructions. I was not to deliver to Mott; I was sent to another street in Little Italy. I had to locate a pizza parlour, pass through a basement entrance, and take a short walk underground. I was let into a scene from *Goodfellas*: a darklit room with several menacing, enormous men around a pool table and others sitting playing cards. I was to go in, hand the package to Vito, and wait for another package or until I was told I could go.

At the back of the room there was a door through which Vito, looking like he'd just stepped off the set of a Scorsese film – slicked-back hair, jowls, enormous gut, shiny suit – took my package. I was terrified, but Lou implied that if I tried to get out of it, they'd take it badly. I was stuck. I sat in small wooden chair in the corner Vito pointed out, read a book or newspaper, and tried not to look anyone in the eye. Mostly they ignored me. After two weeks, one of the card players looked over at me and said: "You Italian?"

"Nah," I said. "From the Caribbean."

"Yeah?" The speaker was a youngish hood; he wore loafers and chinos with an expensive looking Paul Smith shirt under a Zegna jacket – an exact replica of an outfit that had been in *New York* magazine a few weeks earlier. Who was copying who? I'd begun to distinguish regulars around the room.

"I thot they wuz only fuckin' niggers down dere. You know, fuckin' rum an' fuckin' coco cola, straw hats, limbo, calypso, shit like that."

"Not all niggers," I said. "But the fuckers talk so fuckin' loud, no one else can get a word in."

A few of them laughed. The young hood laughed. Then they went to their own business. But after that, the bartender would bring over a beer for me while I waited.

Once or twice I saw a middle-aged man with them, playing cards or watching the ball games on the television. He was obviously a boss. If he was out in the open when I arrived Vito would give him the package and he would disappear into the back room. Once I made the drop late in the evening and saw him having his dinner: some kind of – what else? – pasta with a bottle of wine on a small table set for one. He had the day's *Times* quarter-folded on the crossword page as I came in. He looked up as I was let in the door. He waved to Vito to sit and motioned me to hand him the package. I handed it to him and turned to go.

"Hey kid." His voice was not as coarse as the other hoods; like Al Pacino's in *The Godfather*, softer but not cultured. I turned and looked at him, and then Vito.

"Yes, uh, Sir?" I didn't like to say "sir" but I figured I should; a little ass-kissing never hurt the tipping hand.

"You wouldn't know a 12-letter word meaning the way knowledge and information are organised and their validity evaluated, would you?"

"Epistemology," I said. I waited as he wrote it down. He nodded satisfactorily at me, then looked back down into the paper. From the next day, my tips went up to $100.

My new arrangement meant that my reporting in to Lou was now a formality. I merely stored my bike there, and did no work apart from the sometimes one, sometimes two or three special deliveries a day for Vito's boss. This meant a lot of extra money and a lot of spare time. I bought myself some expensive walking shoes and shorts, so I'd look like a tourist rather than a messenger, and spent most of the days in the B&N on Union Square. I took Anya to lunch every day and fell in love with her. It wasn't hard or unexpected. She lived with her parents in Greenpoint; they were an Eastern Orthodox family, and she had five brothers and sisters. She confided in me she wanted to leave, but she wasn't paid enough. They'd only been in America a year or two, and her Armenian degree in Architecture wasn't recognised: she had to start from the bottom. We were the same age and in the same boat. Almost.

I sketched a slightly retouched version of my situation: my life with the Colos, my job – but not the complicated bits about not having a green card and running contraband for the Mafia. I told her I had just moved to America and was waiting on job interviews, messengering for a while. It was plausible. She didn't know me; it would be too easy for her to cut out the complications and proceed with her life as it had gone before I arrived. Love in New York was just another negotiation: sometimes it wasn't worth it; sometimes it was just too complicated.

I knew it was all more dangerous than it looked; none of it could last; the Mob pick-ups would last only until the police found out about it, which from television shows I knew could not be very far off; or somebody could come to the goombah game room in a bad mood and shoot me. Visions of the scene in *Goodfellas* where Joe Pesci whacked Spider, the kid in the wiseguy clubhouse, started flickering into my dreams. After two months of making the special deliveries I had about $3500 saved, but I still had not found a way to get a bank account, or legitimate identification. I carried my money with me in a money belt. One evening it suddenly occurred to wonder what had happened to whoever had made the deliveries before me.

The Colos had faded into the background. I arrived late and left early; the trouble was that they hadn't given me a key, so I couldn't arrive too late. One night, I arrived when they were around the dinner table. It was a scene I'd been dreading, because I knew the only card they had left to play was my expulsion; and I had no place to go. The tension in the room went up as I came in, but to pass the table straight would have been the greater evil, so I sat, and attempted to be jovial.

"So how the OJ business goin', Az?" I asked.

"Awright."

We lapsed into silence. The food tasted like shit, and I watched them shovel it in with old spoons in their gnarled hands. I suppressed a little fart-laugh I felt their hatred of me intensify. I understood it by then. The Colos had been shitkickers on the island; I had been privileged. Here they had, after years of hard work and eating shit, bathing in it and making casseroles with it, made something of themselves. Having me in the house had been like having an ornament; something that reminded them of the place they'd come from and how far they'd progressed in the world. Seeing me degraded made them feel better: I'd only been ahead on the island because of luck; here in America, on the level playing field, where each man was equal, their quality had shone through. So my managing to land on my feet in a mere three months was a kick in their yellowed, rotting teeth. The fact that they were morons who, without my father wouldn't have been able to live in their own house, much less get a travel visa to get to America, seemed to have been forgotten. Then, without meaning to, I gave them just the excuse they needed.

Sooz was talking about her job; something about a Christmas bonus that the company had managed to negotiate away from the union – apparently Sooz was a member of her department's negotiating team – in lieu of which there'd be incentives linked to the company's stock market performance.

"It's rully gre-ate," said Sooz in her coolie Valley girl accent. "Naw all the bonuhsiz ull be hiyur."

I knew I shouldn't have said anything, but I'd read an article in the *Times* about it; a lot of the bigger companies were offering similar deals to their employees. I said: "Are you crazy? It means if there's even a slight recession, and the stock drops, you not only get nothing, but you might have to take a pay cut."

The table went quiet. I don't think anyone heard anything after "Are you crazy". To talk to Sooz like that was unthinkable. To question her intelligence was heresy. I saw Sarah's eyes glint briefly as she leaned over to pat her baby. Sooz's lower lip trembled. In that moment, in the smelly house, on the table that looked as it had once been a butcher's block (covered with a bright pink table cloth beneath a plastic slip cover); seeing my reflection in the glass of the cabinet which contained the mismatched china, fake crystal and Elvis plates the Colo girls had brought back from Atlantic City – in that moment, the dumb-looking shitholes in their tacky shirts and walking shorts showing sallow, black, pig-like flesh, who sat there as if posing for a bizarre Norman Rockwell painting – the kind you'd find in a KKK headquarters with concentric target circles drawn round it and the bullseye on Colo's dumb-fuck face – in that moment, if they could have given their resentment physical form, it would have shaped itself into a grinder to crush me. Then it could have gone two ways: they could have killed me at that point and buried me in the back yard, or they could just pretend I hadn't said anything.

Sooz decided I hadn't said anything, and continued talking, as if there hadn't been an interruption. The next day Komay was waiting for me. "You know boy, you wit' we 'bout tree monts now. You uncle Colo family have somebody else to sen' up fo we to help. You go have to get you own place. De boy comin' in two weeks time. You go have to be gone by den."

"OK," I said, wondering whether I should phone in an anony-mous tip to the INS to raid the place when they had their fucking coolie party. I tried calling Steve, but the number he'd given me just rang and rang. I contemplated telling all to Anya, but it was too risky; if she knew I'd been lying to her, she might just dispose of me.

I started trawling the *Daily News* room-for-rent ads. Some island nigger in Brooklyn might be sympathetic; if I never saw another coolie again it would suit me just fine. I suppose my rage at the Colos is what did it; they were prepared to cut me loose, despite the enormous debt they owed my family, into a world in which I had almost no chance, as far as they knew. But then, if everything had been okay, I probably wouldn't've been mad enough to charge when the time came.

Two days later, as I left out the back way as usual in Little Italy and was taking the long way round to my bike, I saw something unusual: a Puerto Rican man – the beard and leather jacket, like in the movies, was a dead giveaway – walking by the alleyway. I'd come to know every step of the two hundred yards of Little Italy between the alleyway and the pizza parlour where I left my bike. The alley was short – a red brick rectangle of walls running up into the sky, open at one end only. It was just ten yards from the back door to the street, punctuated midway by a dumpster with a few garbage cans around it, so it was hard to look nonchalant peering down the passage. My eyes met the Puerto Rican's. I looked away. I had my package; it was none of my business.

I'd come to recognise the different kinds of people who came to the Pizza parlour: Italian wiseguys, Italian grandmas and grandpas, tourists. The two men with sadistic moustaches, lupine eyes and mean-assed looks sitting there, as I collected my bike, were not part of the usual traffic. By themselves they looked suspicious; combined with the other one lounging in the back alley, it was like a fire engine with bells clanging. My knees began to shake as I wheeled out the bike. They sat at the counter; when I left, it would just be them and the young paisano who minded the store. I walked out with a tingle running from ass to neck.

I got on the bike and rode down to Canal St, to meet Sixth Avenue and head back uptown. As I got to Houston St, I turned right, crossed Broadway and headed back to Little Italy down the Bowery. I still had the package. I got off the bike and peered around the corner, down the alley. It was quite late in the evening. Little Italy was slowing down. The Puerto Rican I'd seen earlier and another one were walking slowly down the alley with their arms clasped in front of them, holding guns. A few faint pops sounded – gunshots from the club. The back door opened and two hoods came out, guns first. The two men walking down the alley fired at them. Both men from the club fell, but one got off a few rounds, one of which slapped one of the Puerto Ricans back, pitching him to the ground. The remaining Puerto Rican advanced on the doorway, then stopped.

"Come out, muthafuckah," he screamed, "and hold the brief-case in front of you." The boss came forward with the briefcase in both hands. "Open it," demanded the Puerto Rican. The boss obeyed. I was behind the dumpster; they were about eight yards from me. I looked around for a weapon. The only thing I could find was a garbage-can cover. The whole thing had taken about twenty seconds so far; those from the front would be coming round the back soon, but it'd take about a minute for them to get there.

The Puerto Rican was peering into the opened briefcase. Then his gun arm rose.

"Aaahhhh," I screamed, and rushed forward with the garbage-can cover. The Puerto Rican whirled, and I tripped and fell face first onto the cover. By the time the Puerto Rican looked back the boss had a gun pointed at him; they both fired simultaneously. The Puerto Rican fell, and a red slash appeared just below the boss's right ear. As the Puerto Rican was falling he fired again, shooting the boss's leg out from under him. I got up and ran to him.

"Get the case," he said, as I grabbed his arm and helped him up. The door he'd just come out of was metal and dead-bolted. A muffled staccato of bullets thunked into the door from the inside as we hobbled to the head of the alley and into the street. Little Italy still strummed to its dolorous nighttime rhythms. The darkness of the evening and his dark suit made the blood invisible. The red gash on his face was beginning to thicken, but he was strong and lucid.

"A cab," he said, as we walked three-legged away from the pizza parlour onto one of the busy streets. A cab stopped. I helped him in and got in beside him. He put the gun to the head of the driver, an old black man.

"Beat it," he said to me; but his face seemed ashen, his voice weaker. The exertion had taken a lot from him; he was losing blood.

"Don't worry," I said. "I'll get you home. What's the address?"

We stopped at a Long Island mansion at the end of a private drive about forty-five minutes later. I had undone his tie and torniqueted his leg. He held his pocket square across his cheek. As the cab pulled up to the gates, two men in suits came out. I got out and helped him out. As soon as they saw him they went from lazy and tough to quick and mean. One spoke into a walkie-talkie and went to the driver, the other rushed over to me and took hold of the boss. Three men rushed out of the house and took hold of him. I stood by the gate. One of the first two said to me: "The driver'll take you home." He turned to the driver and said: "Remember what we discussed."

The next morning two of them were waiting for me at the office. My bike, left on the sidewalk, had disappeared; but that was the least of my worries. I had about $4000 in my money belt and the package in my bag. I hadn't delivered it. As I walked in the door, they both stood up. I nodded to Lou. The niggers in the back were quiet as I walked out with the men to the waiting Town Car.

By day, the mansion was a white, marble-pillared affair surrounded by immaculate green lawns, a high wall and black iron gates which opened silently as we drove through. I was ushered into a large room with enormous bay windows, white curtains and a bed in the middle. An antique writing desk with a matching high-backed chair stood off to the side; a few hoods stood at the back; up front at the bed were spectacled men in business suits holding files and clipboards, murmuring and scribbling as the boss spoke.

As he saw me, he broke off. "Mr Epistemology," he said.

"Hi there," I said.

I left the house with the package I'd carried home in my bag. Within a week I had a green card, and a deed to a Brooklyn Heights Brownstone with a lifetime lease at a rent of $1 per year, a bunch of new friends, and, of course, a stockbroker.

III

He'd been talking for three hours. She was leaning back in the chair, peering at him sideways with eyebrows knitted, lips pursed. He looked over at her. She handed him a glass of water.

"You need this," she said, still unwilling to relinquish the pose, but unable to keep the fascination out of her voice.

"Great story, huh?" he asked, sipping the water gratefully.

"It's not that great," she said. "I heard a story like that just last week."

"So much for the movie deal then."

She laughed, baring those strong white teeth again, and he felt the desire surge again between his legs; he was too tired to suppress it immediately; it circulated for a few seconds; the memory of the bouncing breasts and the bouncing cock at opposite ends of the same smooth, lightly-muscled torso was more distant now.

"So you wanted a blowjob from a blonde, huh?"

"Well, that would be one way of looking at it. I'm getting married tomorrow. Anya told me about this Armenian custom that the groom goes out the night before the wedding, and the bride offers a mass while she waits for him; praying he won't find someone else. So I figured that blonde blowjob thing was the only thing I hadn't really figured out in all this. I still get the *Voice*. Looking through, I saw the ad. It kind of, uh, gelled. You know how it goes."

"Yeah, I know how it goes," she said. She sat up in the chair and pulled the turtleneck off in one clean motion over her head. They looked even more real than they'd looked a few hours earlier. She smiled at him and ran her hands over them lightly. He felt himself beginning to stir.

"Stop that," he said, surprised to hear the huskiness in his own voice. He'd said it, but even he didn't believe he meant it. "No kidding around," he said again. He was sprawled out on the chair with his feet splayed out, eyes half-closed, lulled by the softness of the room's heat, lulled by the thought of being shielded from the cold outside the window; stimulated by his invulnerability.

She dropped to her knees and slid herself over to his chair; took his hand and kissed it softly, biting the thumb, then running her tongue around it, then biting the soft vee between his thumb and forefinger. Nothing he could do now could stop it. Her hands were busy, undoing his shirt, the belt-buckle. She made her way between his legs, drew the trousers down, then the boxers. He half expected her to say something about his boxers. Then he was a spectator, outside the pleasure of it all, looking through her eyes up into his own, out of his own into hers, looking up at him glazed with artificial lust; looking down on them both through the walls. The corners of the room curved strangely, deserted their real-ness. *Nothing here is real.* He was between lives now, on the threshold. He could still see the fear of death from the old existence, the longing to taste the flesh of life, to feel the blood running down the sides of his mouth; the pleasure he felt at the lightness of flight. Breathing in the strange atmosphere between these worlds far surpassed the pleasure at the sight of her lips, her goldenness, wrapped around him; the feel of the soft, doughy breasts and their hard tips against his thighs, the fingers raking, raking his legs, the variety of the sensations along the length. When he finally ejaculated, she allowed it to splash off the roof of her mouth, so he would have the pleasure, if he wished, of seeing it against her lips, dripping out of the sides of her mouth.

In slow motion, she helped him off the chair and onto the bed, stripped him, then reached into her bag for a small vial of oil. He was naked, face down on the bed. She sat astride his buttocks. She'd taken off her pants, and he felt the soft bundle of her phallus and testicles fall into the cleavage of his bottom. She leaned over him and began to rub his neck and his back with long, slow strokes. She moved down both legs, careful to straddle each all the way down; always careful he was aware of her maleness. He felt her begin to become firmer; he did nothing. He himself began to stiffen; he did nothing. Her hands began to work down the cleft of his buttocks; probing, oiling. He was powerless in between the definitions of either world, like the snow swirling outside the window, floating in inconceivable patterns, describing unthought orbits around unseen, inviolable forces. The sky was one reality, the earth was another; between them was a short space where the laws of neither applied.

He slept, dreaming of falling; then he dreamt of nothing. When he woke in early in the morning, she was gone. He lay in the bed: the light had not yet begun to sear the new whiteness of the city. He showered, slowly, washing the previous night, and the previous life off him. He ordered breakfast and ate it slowly, carefully. It was as if his body had been reformed; the taste of the food felt new and strange and pleasurable. He moved with a new sureness; a new ownership of everything he saw and touched. He thought of Anya waiting in their castle across the river.

He walked out of the *Pierre* to a new world draped in a white chrysalis. The sun was out, glistening on the white mats spread out on the sidewalk, the white striations clinging to the faces of the buildings, the death mask of the old world. He wondered briefly what the Colos would make of the new city which would emerge from under the whiteness. Then he laughed. The world made itself into many things, shaped itself to fit the dimensions of the mind that opened itself to it. Anya loved him. His mother would adore her. He smiled to himself as his shoes scrunched the soft white snow. Soon it would be a brown sludge, soon it would disappear and the other life of the city would resume. Soon, even the memory of it would be gone, like the memory of his father, whose life had never seen anything like this, and whose like would never again kiss the face of the passionate, welcoming earth.

THE ABDUCTION OF SITA

"Master, what's this I hear? Who can they be,
These people so distraught with grief?" I said.

And he replied: "The dismal company
Of wretched spirits thus find their guerdon due
Whose lives knew neither praise nor infamy."
(Dante, *Inferno*)

"Hey, Dara Singh…"

I recognized the words as his lips formed them rather than heard them. The rain was thundering onto the awning I was trapped under, its jarring staccato adding a martial dimension to my imprisonment. My back was pressed up against a store window, a backdrop of cut-rate faux-silks and curtain taffetas, and my feet were turned inward, toes curled inside the shoes, away from the relentless rain. I don't know how long he'd been there. It was getting late, and darker than usual, and I'd broken off from staring at the discoloured sky to look down. My shoes were drenched and, if it continued like this, they and my trousers would be ruined. And that was when I saw him through the rolled-up window of his car. He met my eyes, nodded, and leaned across from the driver's side to the passenger's door. It cracked open and I ran to it. My mincing rush over the slippery concrete, the awkward hop over the shallow gutter and slide into the car had exposed me to the rain's full force for only a few seconds, but I was soaked.

"Shit," I muttered loudly as I slid into the seat. "Shit, shit. Fuckin' rain."

"Here." A white towel with *Port of Spain General Hospital*

stencilled on the bottom in thick blue letters dropped into my lap.

"Hospital." I fingered it tentatively.

"What?"

"Hospital?"

"That's what it says." He spoke as if to a precocious child. His eyes were already on the road, steering the car into the traffic. I took in his profile as I unfolded the towel, saw, along the curve of his forehead and through the dark, straight hair that dropped across his brow, the fine-boned, almost elfin boy I'd sat next to all those years ago. He was still handsome in a weak sort of way, but heavier; the brown skin around his cheek was bloated, and faint striations of excess flesh were visible along the line of his jaw.

"Well," I said, in between patting my face dry and carefully pressing the towel into my hair, "this is a coincidence. Twice in a week, after not seeing you for years. You're literally the last person in the world I would've expected to pick me up."

He half-smiled, still staring intently through the rain.

I'd met him the week before at a Hindu thing in Chaguanas. Thinking back on it, that was it – the *going back*, I suppose, that was the one random act that had set in motion the series of events that took my life off the road I'd chosen, to the place I'd spent years trying to convince myself did not exist. But perhaps the circumstances were inconsequential, and it would've happened anyway in another form, but the essence would have been the same. For months before, I'd been caught in the grip of an unmistakable weariness. I would lie in bed in the morning, looking around at the room with a vague dissatisfaction, and go through my days robotically, coming to life only in the afternoons to go to the bar, knowing I'd provoke an argument with Val and not really caring.

I was jaundiced, bored and tired. Nothing about love and stability had remained the way I'd thought it would remain. There was no easy movement through the happiness; that had to be worked for, harder and harder, and I began to romanticize what I'd left behind. I had been allowed to roam, and now a cord I did not know I was bound by was being pulled tight, inexorably bringing me back. I felt like a man who has accidentally averted a terrible misfortune and returns to the spot to mourn his salvation.

I saw the god from way off, surveying the landscape, looking for me, towering a hundred feet over his vassals. The sight awakened the stirrings of a faint dread, but it was all so long ago I deceived myself by considering the artistry of the creation. A hundred feet tall, of papier-mache and depicting Rama, the hero of the *Ramayana*, who had killed Ravana, usurper of heavenly harmony. The god's face was fleshy and powerful, and even in the obvious plainness of his construction, the cruelty in the curve of the moustache and in the painted eyes was evident. The display was out in the open, on a plot of land cleared amidst a sea of canefields.

Walking down the hillside from St Ann's, I'd looked out towards the central plain of the island and been struck by the verdure, like a sea, with the little patches of brown in relief. Closer to the god, I felt the peculiar familiarity pervading it all; the engine of a battered carnival ride – the kind that lifted the rider aloft and spun him in a circle for several minutes – bleated loud and continuously; tents and booths huddled together displaying religious effigies, books and food; and people in Indian costumes walked around self-consciously, handing out leaflets and gazing reverently at everything.

The ground had been hastily pitched so it was lumpy and uneven, and the display booths were of gnarled wood, quickly put together, and decorated with perfunctory strips of crepe paper. The textures of the wood and paper, the meanness of the construction, the scent of the food, the colours of the clothes, the hum of voices and the washes of high-intensity light from pillars sprouting out of the pitch, tingeing it all to a hyperreal pallor, took me back to my childhood: to a relative's house where I'd be trapped for a day, or a weekend; stultifying heat, blaring Indian music, raucous voices, odious children, crushes of people I feared, oily food that made me sick. It was terrifying.

I held on to one of the light-posts, savouring the feel of the cold metal and brought myself back to the present. Nothing had changed: old, bovine grandmothers were being led by children in cheap, colourful clothes; there were giggling teenage girls in

Hindu costumes, and boys with their dark-eyed beauty, even in early adolescence, already infused with the germ of the dissolution I knew and abhorred. As I drew back from them, they formed set-piece images from my memory, images that accompanied the silent rages, the suffocation, the longings for escape.

I'd forgotten the power of those images. My other life had become more real to me in the years I'd been away, but now the soft curve of Val's jaw I saw in the mornings over the sheets, the black and white faces of the painting that Oudwen had given us for our housewarming which hung over our bed, the spare white walls, Coltrane in the evenings – all of it seemed far away and ludicrous.

The feeling of distance, as of watching a plane lift off, stayed with me as I walked. People thronged on all sides, but I was unaware of them. I felt only the strange silence of childhood. I walked to stand at the flower-festooned feet of the god and looked up at his face, and the lines of cruelty were unmistakable. Unmistakable, familiar.

I backed away from him into a tent, and found myself looking at photographs of the oldest man and woman I had ever seen. They were the only living survivors of the journey across the black water by the last batch of indentured workers in the early part of the last century. The legend "Revere The Past, It Will Guide You To The Future" was written in flourishing script below the heavy, gilt-edged frames, and facsimiles of the original indentureship agreements which bound them here were spread out below.

The objects of reverence looked to me just painfully old. The man was wrapped in a striped blanket and stood in front of a door constructed of splintered boards. Behind his brittle shoulder, with its collarbone protruding from beneath the tight skin, the door, its hinge rusted and held by a single nail, hung at an angle. They had probably only been able to get him as far as the door. The photograph of the woman was indoors. She sat in an old chair. Her image occupied most of the photograph; no details of the room were visible, but I could guess them. Her face was the saddest thing I have ever seen – no sign of femininity remained, nothing that had ever made her beautiful beneath the gray fabric that shielded her from the world.

I looked away, suddenly angry that I had come here. I fumbled in my pocket for my keys, the keys to our house. This was not real, and I wanted to return to my reality. As my fingers closed around the keys, I caught sight of another photo, of their family, a wretched group of souls, young-old, ground-down men, blighted children, worn-out, emaciated daughters, huddled in the same verandah as the survivors.

I walked toward the exit. I had neither spoken to nor looked directly at anyone since I'd arrived.

"Hey, Dara Singh."

And the images stopped. My name hadn't been used like that, both in rapid succession, as if they were one word, in years.

I turned. He was much bigger than he used to be, but there was no mistaking.

"Sunil." I smiled broadly and took his hand. "Sunil, how the hell are you?"

I had not seen him for years and had not, during that time, thought of him once. But at that moment, another flood of memories rushed in: carefully tended lawns, cool white shirts and the white robes of the priests in the College of the Sacred Virgin, an extraordinary oasis of Catholicism in the flatlands in the centre of the island whose inhabitants practised a religion that was older than the Church, and who held it in as much contempt as those men of God held their heathenism.

Sunil and I had been the first in our families to go to the college. Even then, he'd wanted to be a doctor, but I don't think he ever shared my longing for escape. Looking at him smile that shy smile of his, I wondered briefly if I had done the right thing, but only briefly.

He was heavier, too, than his years. His shoulders were broad and he extended beyond me in all directions now. But the old weakness hovered in his face.

"I'm alright."

"Or is it Dr Varana?"

"Last year of internship," he said, diffidently. "I read you all the time in the paper."

"Oh?" I was relieved to fall into a comfortable script. "So you're the one."

"What?"

"Nothing. Bad joke."

"You remember my sister, Veela?"

I noticed for the first time a fair, fine-featured young woman standing next to him in an expensive looking shalwar kameez, worn with a colourful scarf (as paraded by the giggling girls who flitted about the uneven ground). I'd seen that outfit many times, worn by the heroines in the Indian films my father used to cart us off to see in the drive-inn on Thursday nights.

"Hello."

I smiled vaguely, remembering the small pigtails in yellow ribbons with red polka dots that bounced around inside the car that came to pick him up from school. "How are you?"

"Well, right now I'm looking for my husband."

"Mm..."

"...He's one of those who don't like what you write."

"...Hmm," I said. "Do convey my apologies."

"Look, Sunil," she tossed a sheet of black hair impatiently, "I'm going to look for him, you stay here."

He nodded docilely as she walked off purposefully.

"So," I said, "what about you? Married yet? Found God?"

"About to, in a few months, we're not sure about the date."

"Where is she?"

"She...?"

"The wife to be?"

"Oh, not here."

"Ah. So..." I gestured at the stalls behind him, "you're involved in all this..."

"Well, I suppose..." he said, uncertainly.

"...the devout Hindu, pillar of the community..."

"Oh," he smiled faintly. "You don't think much about this kind of thing."

"Well, you've got to admit..." I vacillated a moment, looking at him and chose the placatory route. "I might not know enough about it to know better."

The withdrawal pacified him. "My father became quite involved in it, you know," he continued, "the religious thing, before he died. He got quite close to Baba Ji..."

"The Baba Ji that writes a column in the *Standard*?"

"Yes," he said, brightening. "You know him?"

"Do you know him?" I asked, cautiously. What I knew of Baba Ji did not accord with the image Sunil seemed to have of him.

"Yes, he helped me through the time after my father died. We were never close you know..." He drifted off uncomfortably.

"Hey." There'd been a disturbing tremor in his voice. "Hey, were any of us? I was glad when the bastard died... but now... I suppose it wasn't all their fault. That's what this kind of life," I nodded around, "this obsession with dead things does to you. That's why I never come back."

I'd spoken in a rush, said things I'd wanted to say for years and which were not what he wanted or needed to hear, and I instantly regretted it. I waited anxiously for him to answer, to laugh it off.

"Sunil." The voice came from behind me and jolted us.

"I couldn't find him. Baba Ji is looking for you." Veela placed herself directly between us.

"Ah. We," he said, turning to me, "are going over there."

I understood, but out of perversity I said: "Well, look at that, so was I." And I followed them. The place they were going to was a small stage where a portion of the *Ramayana* was being enacted. It was being done with music and dance, but no words that I could hear. The scene was of a man, wearing in a crown, but dressed in a peasant's dhoti, apparently chastising a woman, who was looking down to the ground, as if in distress.

"So what's happening here?" I asked. "Do you know the story?"

"Rama has just rescued Sita from Ravana," he said. "He's telling her how unworthy she is."

"But why?" I asked, intrigued despite myself. "It's not her fault. And why bother to rescue her if he's going to cuss her out?"

"It was his duty to recover his wife. But she's become unclean because she was around Ravana, and Ram can't have anything to do with her any more."

"You mean he can't... uhm, make any little Hindus?"

"That's one way to put it," he said, unsmilingly.

"If you have no respect for our religion..." his sister said, looking sharply at me.

"Well, did it occur to you that Ram might be gay? And he's not sleeping with her because he had a thing with, you know, one of the generals or something? Or maybe Ravana isn't such a bad guy, and just did what he did to get to Ram?" I knew I shouldn't have said this. They both looked ahead and adjusted their faces so I was out of their range of vision. I shook my head and walked away, and in another minute he had evaporated from my mind. I suppose if I'd thought about it, it might have seemed strange that he was getting married in a few weeks and the woman he was getting married to was nowhere in sight, but I did not give it a second thought. I walked out to the street and got into the first taxi that came by and went home.

"So, where are you going?" His voice barely registered above the rain beating down on the car.

"Good question. Where are you going?"

"Nowhere. Home."

"Home?"

He shrugged.

"Well," I considered. Val wouldn't be home yet. "Why not come to my place, let me get changed and we'll go where I was going."

"Where's that?

"*Wendy's*." I wanted to impress him, for some reason, so I let it drop with more casualness than I felt.

"Wendy's? Who's Wendy? Friend of yours?"

I turned across to him in amazement. "Are you serious?"

"Not a friend?"

I laughed. "Yes. No. You'll see."

Two hours later, the black looks that shot at us as we slipped past the hundred or so people in the line bothered him initially.

"Are you sure this is alright?" he shouted in my ear over the music that blasted out of the dark tinted doors, pushing against us with physical force. I thrust my press badge into the face of the huge, bald black man who stood with his arms folded, surveying the throng of men and women pressed into a tight circle around the velvet rope that secured the club's entrance.

He studied the pass for a moment then leaned down and raised the rope.

"Power to the press," I shouted as we walked in, separating ourselves from the throbbing mass of pouting lips and taut arms perched on hips.

Inside, past the music and the strobe lights and smoke and crush of people in the dance club, were stairs which led to a lounge. I nodded to the second guard, almost identical to the one outside, as I led Sunil up behind a ragged stream of men in jackets and open-necked silk shirts and women in short black dresses with deadly serious faces. The lounge was darkly lit, with a long, polished bar and crowded tables. There were booths off to the side. The mood here was less frenetic. The music was jazzy and cool, and a few prints by artists of the moment hung on the walls.

I led him to the back past the bar and waved to the bartender. A few minutes later, as the waiter left, I sank back into the seat, resting my back comfortably against the wall. I felt my shoulders sag and I took a long drink.

"So tell me..." I started to say.

"Dara, darling," a body dropped into my lap and kissed me on the lips. I pushed it away.

"Jesus, Sey, I told you if you're going to do that, shave, dammit."

"You never minded before." Sey batted his lashes at me, breaking off to admire himself in the mirror that ran along the wall above my head. He was a hairdresser in his early twenties, with long, curly hair, sensuous lips and an intensity many young women found irresistible – an attraction which, they discovered after five minutes, was quite misplaced – but his appointment books were always full.

"Stop that fag stuff, you damned invert, you're scaring my friend."

But Sunil seemed remarkably composed.

"Hello." Sey offered his best business voice and a limp hand, which Sunil, seemingly dazzled by the thumb ring and the rubies and silver bands that adorned the fingers, cautiously inched his hand toward.

"You don't have to shake his hand, Sunil, you don't know

where it's been. Or actually you might know better than he does where it's been."

Sunil smiled weakly and shook Sey's hand.

"Nice to meet you."

"Now, it is nice to meet a gentleman with breeding." Sey deposited himself next to Sunil. "You could learn something from him, Dara."

"So could you," I said. "He's a doctor. Free testing. Just how much a rectum can stretch. The scientific view." My words came fluidly now, and a sharp joy flowed beneath them.

Sey tossed his mane and cut back at me out of slitted eyes. "Now that is being too bitchy, you bitch."

"What's the matter, Sey? That time of the month? His wife giving him a hard time? I warned you about married men."

Sey got up, produced a pink card and said to Sunil, "With my compliments, sir." Then he turned to me; "Fuck you, Dara. And you'd better look at your own marriage."

"Fuck you too, Sey."

The waiter knew me well enough that I didn't have to signal, and by that time I'd finished off the first drink, I was nursing a second.

I shook my head sympathetically at Sunil as Sey left. He was contemplating his drink, fastidiously ignoring my eyes.

In the instant before I opened my mouth to speak, I caught a glimpse of myself in the mirror, the slight tremble of the hair as if fell over my cheek. I brushed it over my ear and said, "Hey, sailor..." but my voice was slurred, so I let it trail off.

I felt the warmth brought by the liquor spread to my face, and the familiar routine of entering the larger life began. Everything around me suddenly revealed itself to me: I was aware of the textures of the seat, the table, the coolness of the water that had condensed and was rolling off the glass, the red light that fell onto the table. Each note of the music expanded, everything began to envelope me in a comforting, safe embrace.

"...Uh huh, you," I laughed as he looked slowly up at me. Our eyes met, and I saw nothing there I could penetrate. I was reminded of the god in the middle of that little world I'd returned to. "Oh, for god's sake, you're safe, I won't have my toes up your pants' leg anytime tonight, I promise. We're harmless. Didn't they teach you that in medical school? Or do they still tell you it's a disease you can cure?"

He remained silent.

"Yep, everyone in school was right. Hey, Maryse..."

She'd already seen me and was on her way over. She slid into the seat and sat carefully next to me, smiling. Maryse did everything with a delightful languor. Even the way her body passed through the air was careful and elegant.

"Hello Dara. Only two?" She pointed a red-painted nail at the glasses on the table. "Rain slow you up?"

"Now now, my dear, let us not be catty, let us, rather, be otherwise." I reached over and gently took a handful of her brown, lustrous hair and pulled her over to me, and as her face came close to mine and her lips parted, I looked just below her eyes to her ebony skin, thinking that the red of her lips looked like the pulp of an exotic fruit, and slowly bit the lower one and pulled back. Her eyes were faintly amused.

"Display for your fri...?"

I kissed her suddenly, harshly, and I held the kiss until she started to kiss back. Then I broke off.

"It's magic. He can convince everyone." I caressed her hair and brushed a strand over a perfect ear.

He looked over at me, and then her, and I recognized in his eyes a calmness I was too far gone to be afraid of. She removed my hand from her hair and said, "I'm not in the mood tonight, Dara."

"Wait." He reached over the table and put a hand on hers. "Please, don't leave, stay a while."

"Yes, stay, Maryse," I said. A strange cruelty welled. "Let me introduce you. This is my friend, Sunil. He is a doctor. Sunil, this is Maryse, who... well, what can I say that is not evident to any man worth the name within three miles?"

"Cut it out, Dara."

She smiled at Sunil. It reminded me of Sita, watching her beauty fade as the years passed, waiting for Rama to rescue her, only to find out he would never touch her again. "And I really have to go. I'm with... a friend."

"Hmmm," I said. "Progress."

"What I came over to tell you, Dara," she said as she slid out of the seat, "is that I saw Val here earlier. He was with someone."

And she was gone.

"Was she...?" Sunil let the words trail off.

"Was she what?"

I looked him straight in the eye.

He looked away.

"Did your father ever know?"

"My father," I took the glass from the waiter and signalled him to bring another, "is fucking dead."

That was the last thing I remembered saying that night.

In the three months between the time I last saw Sunil and first day of June, the only things I remember are Val's moving out a month later and the invitation arriving. I had a moment of sobriety and I begged him to stay. But things had been happening for too long. I knew someone was waiting, but Val wouldn't let him come round to help get his things out of the house. He was always sweet like that.

The rest of the time coagulated into a formless mass. I saw no one, but I did try without success to call Maryse to apologize. To occupy myself I stayed at work far longer than I needed to. My taste for liquor evaporated. The unhappiness I had felt, I realized, was purely my own, and our life had just been a mirror, showing me what I feared most about myself. Now, with the mirror gone, there was nothing; no reflection, no sound, no sensation. How long I might have continued like that I don't know, but on the first day of June something flicked on inside me. I got up, got the blue suit out, shaved, and made my way to the Hilton. The invitation was a gold embossed affair, with a picture of a slender Hindu goddess showering flowers which fell over the text of the announcement of Sunil's marriage to Vidia. The reception would be in the Water Room of the Hilton.

It's my fault, I suppose. I could have said no at any time. I could have told him to go away, to not come back, to fuck off. But I didn't. I didn't say anything. I kept answering the phone, and I waited for him, and I went where he said, and I did what he asked. Damn Dara. Damn him. Damn him for being weak. Damn him for everything.

He'd come to me as I was leaving. Dara was sick, he said, he didn't know where to take him, would I come with him. Dara was as bad as I'd ever seen him, so drunk he didn't even struggle when we each took a hand and limped with him to the car. His head drooped onto his chest and the fingers of the arm round my shoulder were loose and limp, almost caressing me as we struggled through the night. As he fell into the back seat his head lolled to the side, and for an instant I saw his face in the moment of confusion and pain as the mask lifted, and I felt a shudder. I sat in the back seat with Dara's head on my breast till we got him home. Val wasn't there, and we put him to bed, and he took me home. He said nothing to me, and I had nothing to say to him.

He called me the next day.

"I want to see you."

"Look," I said, "if this is about Dara, I'm not..."

"No. Not about Dara."

And I agreed. I don't know why. I think I'd meant to say no, but the surprise, the unexpectedness of it – and there was his tone. He hadn't asked me. He'd told me he wanted to see me. And I found myself waiting with a little expectation. I didn't even remember what he looked like. But he was, well, boyish; the voice, the shyness and although I didn't know what he wanted, I couldn't stop thinking about Dara, his weakness, his sickness, and his absence, most of all.

After all that time. I remember the last time Dara and I walked up Chancellor Hill, right up at the very top where you can look out to the sea over the city. It was late evening and he'd just told me and the tears were swelling in my eyes and my nails were beginning to dig through his T-shirt into his shoulders as he stopped me.

"Wait."

He took my hand off his shoulder and kissed it and said: "Look at the sea."

The bay was dull grey, and there were no ships, not a cloud, not a bird, just the sun, reaching for the water, to rest, to hide.

"Just look at it for a while. Look at the sun. It's warping itself to reach the water. It's not a perfect circle when it touches; the end is stretched out, yearning so strong it doesn't care about being perfect. But the deformity lasts only a short time, and then even the sun has to go back to being what it was made to be. For a short, precious moment, a second in endless time, it seems to defy its own nature, but it's just an illusion. What we see and feel are meaningless to the world, to the god that made us the way we are. What we feel is like the sun reaching for the sea. But the moment of illusion is still beautiful. Still precious. The sun in its dreams probably remembers the sea it can never touch."

That was the one moment in my life that I've ever felt more than the sum of my flesh. That someone could feel that way for me, could spread himself so wide for me, to encompass the sun and the sea and time, changed the dimensions of my world, destroyed them, and me along with them.

Outside of that, I've done nothing out of the ordinary, accomplished nothing. This beauty I wear came with its own rules, it steers my life without me, makes it... easier. Sometimes even the way I move surprises me. The way I talk, laugh, how I stretch my arms along the contour of my stomach and spread the fingers slightly as they curve along my thigh, how my hips curve in an arch, like a bow stretched to its limit, when I'm fucking. I don't control it, this body; most times I think I only observe it. Dara recognized me inside the body and, in that instant, showed me something outside it. But even before, there was something else. There was a lightness about him, surrounded by a semidarkness; a wonder about life inside a vague revulsion for living with the sweat of the world. Everything we did, even the mundane things, had a careful privacy about it.

We did what people do, we walked together, we held hands, we spoke of inconsequential things: the blueness of the sky on that particular day, the pleasantness of the wind at a particular moment. And he couldn't satisfy a woman if his life depended on it.

But even then, there was always the sense of the separate existence of the world apart from us. We belonged together, the way
two pieces of a branch broken by a violent storm can be fitted
together, but can never be joined as before. I suppose if it had been
different, we would have married and lived as close to happiness
as anyone gets, but it didn't happen that way.

That's why I agreed to see him. Despite everything, I still
needed to know Dara was safe.

I wasn't ready when he came to my house. I don't remember
what he wore, except that his trousers were black and he wore a
belt, and I don't even remember what I said, what I planned to say.
He seemed tired. Not a tiredness of exhaustion, more of frustra-
tion, constraint.

"I'll be just a minute," I said, and pointed him to a chair and
turned to go inside.

"No."

That was the first word he said.

"What? No?"

He hadn't raised his voice, but alongside the tiredness, there
was an arresting force.

He took my hand, and that is what I remember most clearly:
his hand closing around mine, the bigness of his hand around my
wrist, and the feeling of weakness, of inevitability. He took me on
the bed, face down. He didn't take his pants off. He unbuckled
them, that's how I remember the belt.

When he was finished, he said "I'll call you when I want you."
And he left.

I could say that somehow I saw him as if he was Dara, but that
would be untrue. I knew all the time who and what he was, and
the deep, cancerous hatred behind it all. And I shared in it. Hatred
for the body that bound me to the world and all the pain I could
not control. Here was pain of my own choosing, and I revelled in
it.

He never wanted me to come to him, meet him anywhere,
show me off. He came to me, in the night, always. He never called
my name. He would look me in the eye and I'd know what he
wanted. Some nights he just told me to take my clothes off and sit
on the floor. He would sit on a chair and talk to me. He'd tell me

what an ugly nigger bitch I was and that someone like me deserved to have a faggot fuck them. Sometimes he grabbed me between the legs as he came in and once or twice he hit me. The bruises never showed. I think the reason he didn't hit me more often was that hitting was an effort for him. The exertion was too much for his small darkness. (Yes, and I suppose that made my life and Dara's all the more pitiable. His darkness was a small, insignificant one, thriving only on our weakness and desolation. Even the slightest resistance would have been enough to defeat it. Yet it overpowered me, the both of us, so completely. Strange.)

This went on for three months. During that time, Dara would also try to call me, but I never took his calls. Each time I heard the voice on the answering machine, I became more repulsed with Dara and with myself.

And then, one night he told me he was getting married and I was to come to the wedding. I was to be beautiful and then I was to disappear. I was never to be seen again. And on that final day, as I prepared for invisibility, I saw Dara at the wedding.

III

"Maryse... oh Maryse." I was overjoyed to see her. I'd walked in to the Water Room, not quite sure of myself, or sure of anything. The geography of the place seemed immense and unnavigable. The light was soft and a low roar of voices came ominously from all directions, and then I saw her, like an island in a raging sea and the heaviness fell off me.

She stood in profile, her eyes fixed intently on something I couldn't see. She was breathtaking, a soft white dress that bent along the curves of her magical body, and in profile her face seemed as perfect as an image on a Grecian vase, or a cameo set in onyx: the straight nose, the lips, the air of regality that surrounded her. She did not see me approach, and I followed her eyes to Sunil. He stood in the middle of a group of older men who looked like versions of himself, heavy-set, jowly and for the first time, I realised, evil.

"Maryse."

She turned to me, and I found myself staring into the face of someone I did not know.

"Hello, Dara."

Her voice was listless and sad.

"What's wrong, Maryse? Why are you here? What happened?"

She laughed quietly and for an instant, I saw a flash of the easy, satin elegance she kept about her like a shawl.

"I'm preparing for invisibility."

"What are you talking about, Maryse?" I reached over to touch her face, and stopped short as she pulled back.

"Invisibility?"

"Invisibility." Sunil had come up to us. "She is going to disappear."

He smiled as he spoke. He could have been discussing the decor of the room.

"What the fuck is going on, Sunil?" I tried to drop my voice, to muster some menace, and was astonished at the emptiness I found inside me.

He looked at me and laughed. That was the first time I'd heard him laugh. It was a full, booming laugh; the laugh of a man who was sure of everything.

"You don't know, do you?" He shook his head in amazement. "That day I picked you up in the rain, did you think it was an accident? I'd looked for you for three days. You know why? But when I saw what a sorry bastard you were I changed my mind. And decided to fuck her instead."

He leaned over and kissed me on the cheek and whispered in my ear: "You think you're the only bastard whose father ever fucked him up the ass, Dara? You're such a weak shit." Then he was gone.

I stumbled out a door on to a terrace and sat staring out at the sea. She came out after me, as I knew she would. I took her hand, and put my arm around her, suddenly enraged that I could not protect her, that I could not save her from him, and now that it was over, I could never protect her from it. She put her head on my shoulder, and there, just as the sun began its painful descent to the sea, just for that little interval, it was perfect, or so it looked.

FROUDE'S ARROW

Languidly charming as it all was, I could not help asking myself of what use such a possession could be either to England or the English nation. We could not colonize it, could not cultivate it, could not draw a revenue from it [...] If it were not for the honour of the thing, as the Irishman said after being carried in a sedan chair which had no bottom, we might have spared ourselves so unnecessary a conquest.

I

The name – J.A. Froude – had been appearing in the *Standard* for more than twenty years, sometimes beneath long, esoteric articles on history or foreign trade, sometimes acidic opinion pieces on politics or rural underdevelopment; sometimes accounts of events as mundane as the flawed spectacle of the independence day parade or the theological lacunae in the Archbishop's Easter homily. And in all the time the name had appeared, I realized, long after I'd fitted it to a body and mind, so had the letters responding to the articles it accompanied, signed J.J. Thomas. I'd wondered, once I realized it, whether anyone else had noticed it. Someone else must have, but there was never any debate about it, no letters, articles or conversations commenting on the exchanges or showing knowledge of what they echoed. Much later, after I'd known him for several years, and he'd left the newspaper and disappeared, and I landed up at the university, and became friends with Corinne Rajah, I spoke to her about it.

"So tell me," I said one muggy day in June, after a departmental meeting had ended in uncharacteristic heat, "you must have noticed the articles by J.A. Froude and the responses by J.J. Thomas in the *Standard*. It went on for years."

Corinne was a slightly overweight Scotswoman who had migrated to the island about 35 years before. She had fallen in love with Narayan Rajah, a young Asiatic island scholar who had been awarded a scholarship to the University of Edinburgh to study engineering in the 1960s, so he could return home to help build the island. Over three decades, she had borne two daughters who had become doctors and migrated back to Scotland, had studied history at the university, and was now, at 60, a professor with dyed blonde hair (cut short in a style which distressed her daughters), her once aquiline features now rounded by age, giving her the appearance of a slightly raucous hawk, particularly when she exercised the trait that made us friends: her machete-like sense of humour.

"Oh, caught on, have you?" she said, with a laugh that sounded like a cackle, showing small, sharp pearl-coloured incisors. "Decades later. And they say our graduates are getting dumber by the year."

"We're only as good as our illustrious teachers," I said. She knew, she said, little about the contemporary J.J. Thomas. But Froude had passed through the university about twenty years before and, upon graduating with a doctorate in history, had elected to work in the newspapers.

"But do you know why the newspapers?" I asked. "When I knew I him it seemed natural enough; he fitted in as well as any one else and it never occurred to me to ask him. But surely he could have…"

"Oh, he was *difficult*. I might even say idealistic. Not at all like you, just beavering away, quietly ambitious and sly, the way you Asiatics are. Those were the Black Power days, you know. He refused to apologize for being white, which at that time was almost *de rigeur* – he wouldn't, he was always looking for a fight, and always finding one. Life wasn't as easy for us Europeans…"

"You're a European now? The Glaswegian slums are in Europe? They moved them?"

"Oh, we all look and sound alike to the rabble, you know. Glasgow, Geneva, you should read some of the undergraduate geography essays… but Froude. Stay on topic, will you? Froude. Those were the days when your lot was acting up, calling us devils and vampires. He'd been abroad as an undergraduate and read Economics – the University of London, I believe – intending to take up a career in commerce. He came back here and enrolled in the postgraduate programme in marketing, and one day read some reference to Froude, and followed it up. Then he switched to history, and that's where his troubles started. His thesis was titled 'The Arrow Of Ulysses: A Botched Experiment in Civilisation'."

"Really, did you…?"

"Good heavens no, we'd have both been lynched. He started working with Miller, then, when they fell out, Balramsingh. He was lucky he graduated; there was a strong movement to fail him, but the thesis was brilliant. He was able to prove all the unpleasant things he was saying, about how the transference of power from the British to locals actually caused the economy and society to deteriorate, using econometrics or ecological statistics or some such thing – a new field the academics here weren't familiar with, but the British external markers were, and if it wasn't for them he wouldn't have passed. It left him angry, and that's why he went to the newspapers, I think. To, uhm, be on the front line."

It made sense, I suppose. You had to know a bit about the history of this place to understand Froude's position in it. To appreciate his ideas, mainly his ideas about himself, you really had to understand the brutal comedy of our lot. When his namesake, the Regius Professor of History at Oxford, visited here two decades before the 19th century closed, what he saw, compared to what he had seen before, was absurdly comic – the new black politicians bent on stirring their less fortunate devotees into a frenzy at the injustice of their betters being denied power; the corruption of the colonial bureaucracy and the decadence of the emigrant merchants who were intent upon enriching themselves without a care for the place; and most of all he realized, and famously said: Civilization had failed to take root here. The road to self-annihilation might be interrupted by the influence of the British, but its path was as certain as the seas that surrounded us. Naturally, the locals were enflamed, and a local schoolmaster, J.J. Thomas, had written a tract dismantling the great historian's imprecations. Thomas, about the same time as Froude was released from his ordination into the Church of England in 1870, had been the first black man to be elected to the Royal Philological Society for developing a theory of linguistics based on his own investigation of the island's patois, and the battle had gone on ever since on the island, between the descendants of those two.

The descendants of the Europeans, Englishmen, Scotsmen and Irishmen, who had come to the island more than a hundred years before to manage the plantations, or to occupy the colonial civil service posts which, because of their treacherous ambition, could not be entrusted to the former African slaves, or the indentured Asiatics who had replaced them on the plantations, had developed an unshakeable conviction in their superiority over the coloured natives. This idea survived their relative impoverishment, the crumbling of the firms directly descended from those flourishing a hundred years ago, and the newly discovered beauty of blackness.

Froude's people usually belonged to the only country club in the island, never used public transport, or the public hospital, or the public schools, or the public jail, and always managed to secure a residence in West Moorings, Victoria Park, Glencoe, or Cascade. Those unfortunate enough to have to avail themselves of the island's university usually kept to themselves, made few friends, and glided through by contemptuously but faithfully reproducing the ethnocentric nonsense their lecturers spouted – if they were in the humanities, or they took refuge in the abstractions of engineering, the physical sciences, or linguistics, the latter favoured because it allowed them to acquire UN jobs as translators.

The unluckier members of the group were forced into an unwilling, arm's-length intimacy with the upwardly mobile coloured population who inhabited the large new communities bordering the old privileged areas. The poorer whites were able to acquire large house-lots in these areas because they were usually owned by white landowners who, before developing them, made generous portions available to their less fortunate brethren, at prices a fraction of what the ambitious coloured classes would have to pay. Once proximity was established, miscegenation was eagerly pursued by the not- and not-quite-white, and staunchly resisted by the wholly white, resulting in an inexorable mingling of desire and repulsion – a destructive tension which they transferred into a resentment of the ambitious Asiatics, and exorcised in punishing the African poor.

But while Froude's pursuit of so inconsequential a vocation as mere journalism was anomalous, it was not unique; there were, as always, anomalies. There was Sunny Cheval, who had been to Cambridge and been converted by the doctrine of free love, who, on her sojourn to Paris in 1968, had also become infected with the ideas that enraged the rioting students. She had brought these ideas back to the island and was tolerated for a time in the Black Power movement. But the incongruous facts of her beauty, her generosity with her body, and her father's ownership of an enormous amount of land and businesses (and his publicly issued threat to shoot the first Black Power activist that touched any of it), proved too much of a strain on the movement's leaders' wives and consorts, and she was soon expelled.

She had then moved to the *Guardian*, and had remained there for several years, as its fount of liberal virtues. She had written art, theatre and book reviews, managing to ensure that both liberalism and art were derided by her peers, despised by the lower orders and ignored by those who might be otherwise been enriched by them, and a joke to all. This was how the rare exceptions were treated: with ridicule or hostility. They were sheep that strayed from the herd, like the thick-necked, red-faced, illiterate middle-managers who wore short-sleeved shirts and ties and sweated like slaves, some of whom would inexplicably leave their pale wives for a black or Asiatic woman. Conversely, on rare occasions, it was a local white woman who picked up with a steel pan player who became the cautionary tale. Sometimes, Europeans or Britons would stray to the island in search of the moon and sixpence, taking up residence with the coloured races before disappearing, some after many years, leaving any number of light-skinned children in the care of their bereft, sloe-eyed mothers. Sometimes, like Corinne, they would accompany scholarship winners home as wives. But for the most part, Froude and his people remained hovering above the rest of us.

By the time I got to the *Standard*, just after I'd finished my first degree, he was there, entrenched, as approachable as a sheer rock face. Black Power had come, gone, and been quite forgotten. The black middle classes had shed their momentary flirtation with their origins and returned to their love affair with the evil but irresistible coloniser. These were the days of the IMF, globalizing commerce and multiculturalism. It wasn't just alright to be white; it was, as it had been in the past, nearly equal to divine favour, and Froude bathed in it the way Raleigh might have bathed in the streams of El Dorado. Even the mention of his name was a little pantomime whose performance always managed to evoke some extraordinary emotion from him. Sometimes he took offence if it were pronounced to rhyme with *proud*; at others, if it sounded like *crude*. All this evoked equally stark emotions from his colleagues – which would not be fully apparent until some years later.

Quite unlike Froude, I had drifted into the *Standard* because it seemed a perfect place to remain uncommitted until something undemanding and profitable presented itself. The rigours of commerce, banking, or the public service – which I had briefly sampled – did not attract me as they had most of my graduating class, and the *Standard's* management seemed to hold shallowness as its editorial touchstone. All anyone seemed to care about was that nothing really changed, but that the appearance of polemic or dissatisfaction be maintained on behalf of the suffering eighty percent of the population about whom no one, who was not one of them, really cared. I was put in the features department to review books and plays, and to do the odd article on local characters or visiting personages, or the aging queen who tripped along on the stage, and in and out of Senators' back doors, who was about to expire and required a requiem. It was pleasantly languid, though sometimes you got the distinct scent of formaldehyde coming off the *Standard's* chaotic columns, but you could persuade yourself it was important because the publisher, Kingsley Gardener – mainly because his wife despised her – was determined to save art and literature from the rdiculousness of Sunny Cheval.

So I saw Froude. I couldn't avoid it, the place was so small; but I had little to do with him for a couple of years and it did not occur to me to ask, then, how he'd got there and why he'd stayed. This was mainly because my boss, Rebah (whose descriptions of her family history involved anecdotes invariably beginning, ending with, or involving the phrase "first black person to ever…") hated him passionately. Her uncle, St George Garvey King, was an eminent journalist; the first black man to edit a local newspaper, whose longevity – he simply refused to die – had made him an institution. He had been granted awards, honorary titles, national medals, simply because he was able to walk out to collect them, and he duly trotted out to receive them every few months, brimming over with platitudes about the press, and press freedom, and his nimbleness in evading death. At other times, he trolled the corridors of the *Standard*, where he was paid a retainer as a consultant, and occasionally held forth on the op-ed page.

St George was incapable of hating Froude, because he was white, and much of his long life had been devoted to disproving the white man's idea that he, St George, was inferior to him, and that he secretly desired the white woman. So although Rebah hated Froude on her own account, because she worshipped her uncle, she treated him with deference and as much show of friendliness as her hatred would allow. Rebah's mother, I would discover later, was a distant relative of St George's, who lived in one of the country districts, had been seduced by a rich colonial merchant, and deserted when she became pregnant. St George had taken her in, and cared for her and her child without ever asking a question, treating Rebah like his own child.

Rebah had repaid his kindness with devotion, and followed him into the profession, and embraced his beliefs with a fervour driven by the absence of her own father. And that inner animus became inverted outside her skin: she wore her curly hair pulled austerely back from her delicate, oval, brown face; wore starched white blouses, with lace-string ties at the neck, prim, knee-length pleated skirts, and the kind of low-heeled pumps that nurses wore; and she peered at the world from behind thick spectacles which might have seemed more at home in a mortician's shop. Inside this carefully assembled camouflage of frumpiness, there were perfect olive calves, artistic fingers, and fine white teeth. Sometimes a soft, teasing nature broke through the armour of severity – though she could smile and cut down any person almost simultaneously.

I had been discouraged from associating with Froude when we had gotten drunk at my first office Christmas party, and she pulled me aside and groped my chest, as if she were a man feeling up a woman's breasts, and said, "I'm drunk, and if you don't fuck me, and I ever see you talking to Froude, I'll fucking kill you and eat your balls with spaghetti." I never had the chance to ask her to elaborate because she passed out on making this utterance. But after that, it was inevitable I would meet him, and become as close to a friend as he was capable of having.

One of the perks of writing in what was referred to by the Sports Department as "The Homo Section" – and displaying the ability to write complete sentences in English – was that there were people whose job it was to meet you. These were the cultural attachés of the foreign missions resident in the island, who were always interested in penetrating, or being penetrated by, local culture, and would go to extraordinary lengths to achieve it. This involved inviting steel pan players and calypsonians to stage mini-concerts on the spacious lawns of the embassy residences, and afterwards, to fuck their hosts' wives while their hosts watched impassively; and sometimes, after copious amounts of hashish smuggled in through diplomatic pouches, and crumpled US hundred-dollar notes had been pressed into those dexterous, dark fingers, fuck the middle aged, pale-pink men with thinning hair and yellow teeth.

So I'd begun, after a year or two, to be invited to functions at the various embassies: to celebrate Bastille Day among the French; Independence Day among the Americans; and the birthday of Queen Beatrix with the Dutch. Once they got to know you, there were many more, less important evenings, when you were invited to help welcome a trade delegation, a visiting artist, a new embassy official, or celebrate the signing of a new trade treaty – all invariably followed by drinking, passionate, husky-voiced conversations and brief, sordid liaisons, which were forgotten by the next morning. It was a pleasant, slippery decadence all too easy to fall into. And here is where my connection with Froude was cemented; here, in this suspended space, neither in the island nor outside it, was where my crucial knowledge of Froude would emerge.

At every function I went to, he was there, standing in the wide, pale blue ballrooms, smirking at the chandeliers and the potted palms beside the buffet tables; shaking his head at the steel pan players as they stood forlornly, being spoken to by their vapid, pale hosts; sneering at the calypsonians who were attempting to seduce the hosts' wives; all the while sipping at a glass of scotch or expensive wine, or speaking sardonically to the embassy attachés who never spoke to journalists, or staring morosely at Sunny Cheval, who flitted about the room in a deluge of tie-dye wraps and whorish eye make-up, giving watery, approving nods to everyone whose eye she caught. I was usually accompanied by Rebah, and I had no idea that he ever saw me, till one of the nights Rebah was not there.

The Dutch mission was unique in that its cultural attaché was a youngish woman, Mary Gansvroot, whose ankles had not yet begun to thicken, and who wore tailored pants suits and severe, unfashionably slim-framed glasses, and nurtured a passion for South-South trade and liberal socialism. One evening I saw her at the South Korean ambassador's house. She was eating a particularly spicy dish whose heat she had not expected. She squirmed, her surprisingly thick lips pressed together, her grey eyes beginning to water, a frantic look on her pale, heart-shaped face. It all looked strangely, surprisingly erotic, and I began to wonder what her face would look like red, sweating, and contorted in ecstasy.

"Milk," I said. "Cold milk helps."

She looked at me, her expression unchanged, seemingly paralysed. I remembered that on the dessert table sat some small, green, leaf-shaped cups of ice cream, and I got her one. Her slender fingers trembled as she spooned it into her mouth, and I noticed that the cuticles around the narrow, unpainted nails were slightly yellow, and her teeth, as her lips parted, were surprisingly white, a refreshing change from the yellow, crooked teeth that seemed to be a requirement for the European diplomatic corps.

"Thank you," she said. It was the first time I had spoken to her, the first time I'd really looked at her, and when she'd recovered herself, I realized why. Her expression was usually severe and unsmiling, and her dark suits were boxily cut, perhaps even a half-size too large; you'd have to look closely to notice the long, gentle curves of her thigh and calf as the fabric played on them as she walked. I didn't have too long to think about it, though, because Froude appeared.

"Good thinking, old man," he said to me. "You're quick on your feet. Impressive."

"Oh, James, you know each other?" she asked, as if noticing me for the first time, placing her hand familiarly on Froude's elbow. And from then on, he began speaking to me as if he'd known me for years.

So I actually got to know them both at the same time. Thereafter, she would exchange a few polite words with me whenever she saw me, and each encounter was a little warmer than the last, though still I marvelled at her ability to remain unemotional. It was a kind of alertness, I suppose, and each meeting intensified my desire to see those features splayed in unanticipated, unfamiliar emotion, and I knew that moment drew closer with every facile word we exchanged. I formulated little questions on trade and export opportunities for when I saw her, to which she always responded patiently and elaborately. Once, after a longish answer about the requirements for labelling goods entering the European Union, I said: "Would you like to go to a concert with me on Sunday?"

She looked at me seriously, without a hint of warmth in those grey eyes, and said: "Yes, here is my address and telephone number." She handed me a card and moved on to speak to someone else.

Froude was another matter. Once the ice was broken, a veritable geyser of communication erupted. The first spume bubbled the next day in the corridor of the *Standard*. I was walking by and Froude and St George were talking. As I passed within earshot, Froude said: "What do you think of that, old boy?" I could not avoid stopping, because there was no one else in the corridor, and he continued talking before I had a chance to evade them.

"I am of the view that political reporting should be essayed in an ironic mode rather than the present pretence at literal objectivity. We just should not take it seriously, you know. If we've learned one thing after a generation of *independence*," he stressed the word contemptuously, "it's that power has actually caused a form of ontological decay. They become drunk on it, you see. Like the

American aborigines on whisky. Like you Asiatics on rum, you know, when you first came here – an unfamiliar compound introduced into bodies simply incapable of ingesting it without building up their constitution. By reporting their obliquity as fact, when we all know it's rot, we are actually communicating that malaise to the populace. Mr King is of the opposite opinion, but what does a literary man make of this, hmm?"

I looked at Froude as if for the first time, and surmised his illustrious namesake would have been the Victorian equivalent of a human jackdaw, dark-eyed and voracious, and invisible in a crowd of his fellows, but who would stand out surreally against the backdrop of the island's riotous, multicoloured luminosity. The Froude of a hundred years later was a little above average height, slim, but not fit, with a narrow, unremarkable face a brown moustache did little to distinguish. Only his pale blue eyes hinted at some remarkable inner life. On any London street – and I would remember this moment years later, walking with him on a street in London – he would fade into the greyness, but here, in the grey corridor of the *Standard* building, he towered over St George, who, to his credit, did not look the least intimidated. He laughed, baring strong white teeth, and shook his snowy head.

"How is it that a man can be amused by the same desiccated joke for so many years?" he asked, in a tone of mocking wonderment. "Perhaps we need a medical man to tell us whether some change in the biology occurred when these grey nocturnal creatures found more than five minutes of sunlight for the year."

That finished it for him, and he turned to go, shaking his head, the smile sliding off his lips. But as his dark, watery eyes met mine, something other than laughter floated there.

"Well, what do you think?" Froude persisted.

"Asiatics and rum – you know what comes with rum, don't you? The cutlass, then it's a hankering for the white woman, and then even the white man's saggy arse begins to look inviting," I said.

"Oh, you're one of the civilized ones, old boy, I've seen you drinking scotch." He smiled playfully as he said it, and I realized that I could be offended and walk away and never speak to him again, but I didn't. Instead I said, "And don't forget eating white pussy," but smiled as I walked away.

150

I was not at all surprised that Froude's comments were re-peated almost verbatim in an opinion column the following week, and that two days later, a response from J.J. Thomas was published.

> It is gratifying to see that the *Standard* retains a sense of humour in its opinion pages, far too often overburdened by sedulous prescriptions or hieratic harangues about morality in public affairs or development economics. And I must compliment your resident humorist, Dr J.A. Froude, who, like his illustrious namesake, reaches for convenient con-clusions without the dreadful inconvenience of actually seeking the facts.

The article then proceeded to an explication of the history of imperial doctrine on self-rule for the colonies, from Pitt's through Churchill's administrations. Such letters had appeared in the *Standard* from time to time, genteel but combative: Froude cited Milton Friedman or J.M. Keynes, Thomas countered with Arthur Lewis or Lloyd Best; Froude cited Eliot on a fractured, dispirited world, Thomas countered with Césaire's multiplicitous vision; Froude cited Nietzsche on the will to power, Thomas countered with Fanon on the rage of the oppressed, and so it went: poetry-calypso; austere Calvinism-conservative Catholicism; theatre-the island's yearly Carnival.

I would have forgotten about the exchange, were it not for the American ambassador. Occasionally, St George would be present at some of the more elaborate evenings I attended, and a week later, at the American ambassador's on the fourth of July, I stood in a small circle with Froude, the ambassador and her husband, discussing the paintings they had acquired from the local artist, Mokombo Cojo, when St George made his entrance.

"Mr King, so glad you could come," said Callie Sowell, the ambassador, a slim, small woman with spiky, corn-coloured hair and a surprisingly aggressive posture for a diplomat, who wore short white linen dresses and broad-brimmed hats be-cause, as she would sometimes complain: "It's just too damn hot. How do you people stand it?" to any local who happened to be in earshot.

"How could I refuse such a gracious invitation?" said St George effusively. "And particularly on such an occasion, to celebrate the birth of the most powerful engine of democracy of our time?"

"Well, it's so nice of you to say so, when your own democracy is taking a beating," said the ambassador. "I've been looking at your Parliamentary reports."

This was Callie's style. At any time, she might let loose with a dose of truth that was too blunt to do anything but club the respondent. She might tell the UN representative about the obscenity of sybaritic foreign experts here to initiate poverty-relief programmes. She might tell the Archbishop about the idiocy of trying to hamstring birth control programmes when "they're breeding like fruit flies". Naturally, Froude was a great favourite of hers.

"Did you read Froude's column, Mr King?" She nodded at Froude, who, along with me, St George had not acknowledged.

"I have not had that pleasure, Madam Ambassador," he replied, smiling charmingly. "But a small nation must be given the privilege of finding its own way, to develop its own ideas and carve the great idea of democracy to fit itself."

"Yeah, privilege is the one thing the government seems to understand," said Callie. "I was at the foreign minister's the other night. Damn, he has a wine cellar."

"Surely the Ambassador would not begrudge the minister his little indulgences." St George's smile and his anodyne appearance never wavered. "These fellows might not always get it right, but they work like beasts in the field, you know."

I was surprised, too, that Froude remained silent, looking on somberly.

"And on the note of indulgences, let me compliment you on your taste in art." St George turned his attention to the painting we were looking at. It was a slightly surreal rendition of a spectral woman with angular features, painted with a metallic geometry, in a white habit surrounded by layers of dark emerald shapes encasing what looked like a forest. "Ah, a Cojo. My dear Ambassador," he turned to her with a smug smile, "he's a genius, you know, and completely self-taught. It is so gratifying to see your appreciation of our local culture."

"God, he practically extorted us into taking it. You should have heard the guy – slavery, colonialism, the black man and his struggle. We bought it to shut him up," said Callie as her husband nodded wearily.

"Oh, he's passionate, to be sure," said St George, "but what great artist wasn't? I have several of his pieces myself. I know the Prime Minister is reputed to be a great patron of his."

I looked on silently. I had heard many conversations like this. It was widely known that St George was a foundation member of the national party which had occupied power for more than twenty-five years since independence, and had run the country into the ground. Ministers and various other party oligarchs, who were given positions on state boards and in public companies, were usually at evenings such as this, and it was commonplace to see the reporters and editors getting on in chummy, barely professional terms with them. On this occasion, a few of the ministers had turned out, and St George slid easily among them, all smiles, wit, and deference. He was so overwhelmed that he even invited me over, later in the evening, when the empty scotch and champagne bottles were stacked on the side of the bar like war trophies, to meet a minor minister. I went over, and St George turned with a flourish to the minister, who seemed half-drunk, and more interested in a waitress passing with glasses of expensive scotch.

"My dear minister, meet one of our young talents…"

The minister looked at me without interest. He wore an expensive blazer, garishly patterned red and blue shirt, and grey trousers. Earlier in the evening he'd looked quite forbidding, but now, the alcohol and ketchup stains on his shirt, and his slurriness made him slightly pathetic. However, the square, black face, the powerful jaws and broad nose told another, more intimidating story.

"Don't know this one, Georgie," he said, in a heavy, grating voice, taking my hand in his large, flaccid one, his eyes moving between St George and the buxom black waitress as she moved carefully through the crowd, which was now smaller, but considerably drunker than a few hours ago. Froude was deeply engrossed in conversation with a soldier in uniform, the commander of the detachment stationed at the embassy.

153

"Ah, the young man writes about the arts for the *Standard*. You would not see him at your conferences…"

The limp slab of a hand was withdrawn and a brief look of contempt flashed across the rock-like face, and he leered at St George and turned away without a word. I stood rubbing my forefinger with my thumb, and muttered: "Ignorant motherfucker."

"Now, now, my dear fellow," said an unabashed St George. "Not to worry. I recall when I was a youngster like you, I was presented to the Colonial Secretary, number two man in the government, Englishman you know. A long, long time ago. The fellow just stared bemusedly at me and turned away. Not to worry about the minister. He has an excellent memory. He knows who you are now. It'll be better next time, and remember, he is a member of our highest institution of government. We must be aware of the enormous pressures they work under and allow them these little indelicacies."

And this was how St George and the people like him saw the world. They seemed as resigned to the brutes in power as they were to the decay and degradation they perpetrated. If the masses of the poor and wretched saw this as an inevitable consequence of their rulers' collective ascent to long-denied, long-desired power, St George and his like saw no such connection. There was now no doubt in my mind as to the identity of the polemical Mr Thomas, and the next day, I went to see Blake Jones, the editor of the *Standard*.

Blake was named for the poet by his father, Byron Jones, who had studied classics, had missed a scholarship to Oxford by one point, and had spent the rest of his life salving his disappointment with food, drink, and sexual profligacy. Blake was his first child, and the closest in his love for poetry and life; the other twelve had each incrementally moved away from that ideal, and the last had ended up as a morgue attendant.

Blake was, in his sixtieth year, a compendium of the best and worst of his father: he was a reformed cocaine addict, a closet homosexual who was inching to the closet door at a glacial rate, probably because he was weighted down by an extra one hundred pounds, in addition to his constitutional two hundred – bequeathed by chocolate and sweets, oily stews, and a giddying range of alcohol. His epicurean nature produced a stream of tenderness in his articles – about the plight of rural labourers, the urban poor, the sufferers whom St George's government had created, or the Hindu Festival of Lights. Such articles ordinarily had no place in the humourless, unimaginative local press, but they were indulged by Kingsley Gardener because Blake possessed that most desirable of traits: he did not appear to possess a backbone, and would do anything to please. He had met Gardener early in his career as a journalist and had fixated on him as a substitute father. It was a relationship that would end only when one of them died, and Blake would probably have fainted if any dissolution of that relationship were suggested.

Religiously the janitors cleaned his office, but by noon each day it was littered with bottles, coffee cups and empty food and sweet boxes. By then, Blake would display the temperament of a hungry bear as the sugar began to dissipate from his system. I took the precaution of taking him three donuts. As he consumed them, I asked:

"So tell me, Blake, is there some centuries-old ethical precept which prevents you from showing me the raw letters to the editor?"

"What do you want?" His eyes were fixed on the pages in front of him, and the black bald pate glinted dully as the folds at the back of the neck wobbled gently.

"The J.J. Thomas letter."

His eyes lifted off the page proofs in front of him, and met mine, levelly. They were black, round, and not entirely comforting.

"The Thomas letter."

"Yes."

"Why?" He had deserted the donut entirely now, and was looking directly at me with a clarity you might forget was there when you watched him galumph through the *Standard's* corridors, cadging food off desks, and drooling messily over the young male reporters at editorial meetings.

"Curiosity."

"Curiosity. A good trait in a journalist. But…" he paused archly as he rifled through his desk and withdrew a white envelope. "…you just write about homo stuff in the back of the paper. Lucky for you, I like homo stuff," and he threw the envelope at me. "Next time, bring me some pastries from those soirees you go out to. Donuts are too cheap."

The letter was written in an old-fashioned, ornate script, the kind one finds in wills, Victorian diaries, and old schoolteachers' letters. Its contents were published word for word. There was neither an address nor a postmark. The paper was textured and carried a faint scent I could not quite place. I wondered why St George would go through the trouble of a pseudonym. I finally asked Froude about Thomas's identity.

"How the fuck would I know? I believe he's a queer," Froude replied.

And I forgot all about it.

A little time passed and things settled into a pleasant stasis; I drew closer and closer to Mary, and eventually saw her face as I had imagined it, red and flushed and for the barest instant, pushing at the barriers of the last century of European complacency. I saw the saturnine gloss around Froude lose much of its lustre and reveal the mundane reality beneath. Far from the Olympian engagements with J.J. Thomas, his battles were as quotidian as they were many and mystifying.

During evenings at the larger diplomatic functions, as we stood to the side, watching trade missions and cultural ambassadors surrounded by fluttering expats and local commercial pirates, Froude would grow increasingly incensed. And they all seemed to seek out his contempt. Circles would form around him as we stood there. Kurtz, freelance correspondent for various foreign papers would appear, tall, gangly, but with the dangerous dark eyes of a man who had met his demons and sodomised them – and always with some foreign substance caught between his teeth. There'd be Edgar Wegg, an expatriate who had come to the island as a cabin boy on a cruise ship several decades before, who had married a local to stay and was now publisher of national promotional magazines, which featured only white writers. Sunny Cheval would turn up, along with some associate of her father's who sought, if only for a night, to bring her back into the presence of the favoured.

"So how goes the fiction business, old boy?" Froude was staring with undisguised contempt at Kurtz, who reproduced government press releases as fact in his dispatches, published in *Economy* magazine.

"Why I'm sure I don't know what you mean, old man," said Kurtz with a sneering smile of his own. It was interesting observing the snarls and the gnashing of the teeth of these two beasts. The Froude beast enjoyed wealth and status that went back a century, and drew its strength from that; the Kurtz beast enjoyed the conquistador's élan. Because of his accent, his statements had automatic power, and did not need substance.

"Oh, you know that interesting genre I see your little magazine experimenting with – channelling the voices of semiliterate kleptocrats as journalism. Does it pay well? Or is it comedy to amuse your betters in England at our expense?"

"Oh, dear, has the slave market fallen off, old man? Are you trying to branch out? Let me check around for you. I'm sure the *News of the World* could free up a few bob."

"Yes, I'm sure you know all about prising loose change off punters, *old man*. But that's the trouble with the lower orders: they don't know the difference between money and finance…"

"'Lower orders'? Now, Jimmy, are you playing not nice again?" Sunny Cheval appeared in a whirl of long, dark, bouncy curls.

"Ah, my dear, even if I were, I should have to defer to your expertise in playing with the lower organs…"

"Now, Jimmy," said Sunny, half-smiling, half-grimacing, "meet Edward Farraday, the new credit analyst at Barclays." She nodded to a sharp-faced young man with watery-blue eyes who seemed to be drowning in his light blue lounge suit. "This is Mr James Froude, our resident expert on everything."

"Alright, mate," the hatchet-faced young man said, nodding at Froude.

"Ah, an imported scholar," said Froude, smiling sardonically. "So your talents will be directed at lightening up the dreadful record Barclays has on denying credit to small, local businesses?"

"Well, we'll certainly give it a look," said Farraday, unsure whether Froude was joking.

"Now that's what I like to hear. That old Oxford determination. You are an Oxbridge man, I take it?"

Farraday shrugged and turned away from Froude towards Sunny and Kurtz.

"Well no matter, our Sunny is of that ilk, and you seem well on your way to initiation into the secrets of the local economy. And Edgar will pay you handsomely to write about them for the benefit of semiliterate tourists. You do *write*, don't you?"

"Now what would you be drivin' at, mate?" Farraday's attention, oily with truculence, was now entirely focused on Froude.

"Have you ever seen the inside of a Third World prison, *mate*?" Froude looked levelly at him. "No, I'm sure that wasn't in the brochure of the budget tour you came on, nor on the international studies curriculum of your polytechnic in Coventry..."

"Did you say you're the new credit manager for Barclays? Welcome," interposed Kurtz, as Farraday turned to him, less certain of himself in the face of Froude's unusual aggressiveness.

Kurtz shook his hand and led him off, saying, "I'm going to need to interview you in a few weeks..." Wegg, grimacing imperceptibly, followed them without a word. Wegg wore tinted glasses, had a brown, nondescript moustache, and the ability to seem not to be there. When he did break his unobtrusive silences, it was in a British accent that seemed rehearsed, its pattern coming from a stock character in a dinner theatre play in a small town in the Home Counties. I always felt that he was afraid of being discovered and sent back to his former life.

"Run along now, Sunny," said Froude. "Kurtz's appetites exceed even your own. He might well leave here tonight with your Mr Farraday."

"At least we haven't sunk so low as to Asiatics," smiled Sunny as she breezed off in a another whirl of yellow and blue tie-dye.

Her parting insult had taken me by surprise and I had no answer.

"Not to worry, old man, you need to come with some arrows prepared in advance. There'll be other days," Froude said, consolingly. "In the meantime, why not try to capture a little pigeon for the night?"

He was referring to the many glowing, copper-coloured,

young Asiatic and Mulatto women with wide, alluring red lips and sharply manicured eyebrows who flitted through the gatherings like riotously plumaged, fragrant birds, who would eventually come to rest on a pale, white-linen-sleeved arm. A lucky few would be installed, some months hence, in one of those wonderful houses in Cascade or St Ann's or Chancellor Hill, and be given a staff of black servants to ease the pains of their swollen bellies, and look after their incipient offspring.

After this incident, I was not at all surprised at Froude's piece the following week:

> I believe it was that idiot savant, Bert Gones, who cavilled in the 1930s about the linesmen from Yorkshire coming here to be made engineers on the national railway, and sadly, the traffic in third-rate imports continues. These birds of passage alight on our shores and, as they stand on the beach in their Crusoean daze, are rescued by our ardent ethnic nationalists and put into positions where they can do the most damage to our fragile economy. Indeed, the political economy of this traffic is at the heart of the continued failure of a sizeable part of the world. Perhaps some representation needs to be made to upgrade the standards for the issue of tourist visas, to discourage the butchers and bus conductors who, once they arrive, begin to see mirages in the heat and believe themselves to be engineers and surgeons, who are given the island as a theatre in which to enact their fantasies by our ardent patriots. These are the farsighted people who believe tourism to be our salvation, while they build houses and factories on agricultural land.

The inevitable Thomas rejoinder was brief:

> It is most amusing when the namesake of a bumbling tourist whose berth was in the upper deck of the steamers – I speak, of course, of the illustrious Froude of the 19th century, who came bearing the imprimatur of empire, and managed to be so dreadfully wrong about everything – now begrudges tourists from the lower berths the same privilege. Perhaps it is not that the quality of imports needs to be improved, perhaps they need to be stopped altogether, and local products cultivated. But no matter how Dr Froude raves against the quality of foreign imports, there is no question in his mind that they are superior to those of local manufacture.

It was true: Froude never tired of divining their antecedents and perversions, but his imprecations rarely went past a few verbal slashes. "You see that one," he would say, pointing to a pink-faced, portly man wearing a too-large khaki suit and a pink shirt, who lumbered sweatily around the room in squeaky loafers. "He's a plumber in Leeds, and they made him the head of engineering at the Port Authority. That one," thrusting his chin at a sharp-faced, twitchy young man wearing cream linen trousers and an open-necked silk shirt, "was a tout at a race track. He's an advertising executive down here."

But as much as Froude loathed those he considered interlopers and foreign exploiters, no one actually enraged him except for his nemesis, Johnny Leigh. I had met him one rainy night at the Nigerian embassy. As we waited at the gate for a green-turbaned servant with the large, white umbrella to escort us to our cars, a cherub-faced young man with blond curly hair and a giggly laugh stood behind us with one of the dark, white-teethed African dancers who had provided entertainment between the courses.

"Would you mind, mate?" I heard from behind me, "if we went first? Her carriage'll turn into a pumpkin."

I was about to gesture him ahead when Froude intervened.

"I do mind, *mate*," he said, grinding his teeth on the "mate". And pulled me under the umbrella that appeared in front of us, held by an impassive man in an African costume. As we walked off, he said over his shoulder: "Do say hello to your charming wife for me, won't you."

"Friend of yours?" I asked as the servant dropped him off at his car, and I continued on to mine.

I met Leigh a few weeks later, when I was out on the town with Rebah. Apparently Leigh knew her, and I returned to our table from the bar to find him engrossed in conversation with her. They looked up guiltily as I handed Rebah a drink.

"Hullo there, mate," he said, as Rebah made to introduce us.

"Yeah," I said. "Cinderella's date."

Rebah stiffened a little. "What? Whose date?"

Leigh did not bat an eyelid, smirked a little, but did not offer to explain. As I introduced myself, Rebah continued as if to cover her outburst.

"Johnny is an art historian," she said, as Leigh smiled. "Conducting research into, what was it, Johnny?"

" Nationalist narratives in ethnographic art," he said, his blue eyes flitting across my face, and then through the semi-dark room. We were in the *Pelican*, one of the places in the island where you were likely to see anyone at any time without it seeming strange or out of place. The *Pelican* sat at the foot of the Cascade hill. It was an old Victorian house which had been abandoned almost a century before by its planter owner, the result, it was rumoured, of a streak of madness induced by the infidelity of his wife with the field labourers. It was a stain the descendants had never quite managed to wash off, and as the estate was divided among successive legatees over the century, no one had claimed the house, and it had stood there, rotting, untouched and haughty, like a beggar certain of her aristocratic origins, until another of the decadent scions of the clan, who revelled in public and incessant miscegenation, had claimed it as his own.

Rather than tear it down, he had reinforced the rotting floors, and built an exoskeleton of rough, unpainted steel around the Victorian decay, and thrown open the doors of the old house to all who cared to come and pay for entrance. There was a dance floor on the upper floor, and smoky, dim rooms with comfortable chairs, old book cases, faded paintings, and ephemera of the 19th century – old clocks, yellowed maps, rusted sextants, barometers and telescopes – sitting on shelves out of reach, where you could drink and talk all night if you wanted to. There was even a dartboard to add to the atmosphere.

"It sounds interesting," I said, following his eyes as they lit lewdly upon the young women.

"Oh, it's much more than that," said Rebah. "He goes all over the island looking at old Orisa temples, Shouter shrines, and…".

"Oh, excuse me, my dear," said Leigh, "I see someone I have to talk to. But," he flashed a smile at her, "we'll talk later, alright?"

"Fucker," said Rebah, as the smile rearranged itself into a sneer as she watched him make his way across the room to meet a small Asiatic woman. "He has to eat out her pussy to pay his rent."

"Hmm," I said watching Leigh bear down on a young woman

with a pageboy hairdo, who looked like an burnished pixie. "Does she own an apartment building? Is she looking for tenants?"

"I'd like to see you trying to eat pussy without teeth," Rebah said, still looking at Leigh. "Do you know he had a wife when he came here? He was a friend of your new best buddy, Froude." I elected to let that pass, but I did not forget, and strangely, from that tiny seed, over the next few months, watered by the lazy, slow-running, meandering river of Froude's contempt for the expatriates, I found my curiosity to know the story slowly growing.

Froude would never divulge this information in normal circumstances, so I suppressed my desire through the thinning embassy evenings, whose charms were now fading for me, since I could see Mary whenever I wanted. The evenings had begun to resemble a huge blurry wheel, each spoke identical to the next, and which simply, through some external impetus, continued to spin. Looking at it all, I began to think of my life in a way I had never done before; I yearned to be at the point where I could pierce the circle, break free from its gravity, but I knew how much effort and violence such a challenge to things as they were would entail. My desire was sharp, but unspecific. I wanted the world, but could not settle upon a country, city, town, street, house, room. I wanted to be above it and everywhere in it at the same time. Froude's arrow pierced through the midst of this at just the right moment.

One day, after I had begun to go to the Queen's Fields most evenings and stroll across the grass, sit on the benches beneath the weepy trees, and look at cars and joggers, I walked into him on my way there from the office.

"Ah, there you are, old man. We haven't been seeing much of you these last weeks, have we? Why don't you bring your delightful trade attaché to my house on the coast?" He said it carelessly, almost in passing. But I stopped and stared at him apishly.

"You have a house on the coast?"

"I am quite rich, you know," he said, flashing his annoying grin. "Your inamorata knows where it is. I'll expect you on Friday evening for the weekend."

Rebah was incensed that Froude had invited me, though I could not tell why. Her sometimes on, sometimes off ardour for me had cooled considerably once she realized I had begun to see Mary regularly, but she'd never mentioned it directly. Our evenings out had dwindled into almost nothing, and our intimacy continued only because of our proximity in the office.

"His house? *His* house?" she asked several times. "Do you how his family got it? They stole it, that's how, that's how they are, stealing, oppressing, and smiling…"

"Come on, Rebee," I said placatingly. "Those days are over."

"You fucker. Fifty years ago, but go ahead. Go ahead. Enjoy." And she would say no more.

It turned out that Mary could not go with me on Friday, but promised to meet me the following day, and I went with Froude himself, travelling in his Land Rover from Porto Spano, setting off mid-morning. It was a longish drive to the northeastern coast of the island, and though I had made it many times before, on my own, this journey of a little over two hours diverged into layers of significance I had never seen before.

The drive through the smaller towns along the long highway, across the upper part of the island's torso was almost a drive through time. It began with the slums just outside the city, places of terrible poverty, without running water, with stolen electricity, and pot-holed streets that led up into a maze of rotting wooden shacks with rusted corrugated iron roofs, and littered with young black girls walking through the streets, trailed by half-naked, barefooted children. The only constant among all the colours, shapes, and sounds was the reiterated symbol of the national party, a heliconia flower – and its theme music: defiant, loud calypso music which followed the Land Rover like an aggressive flock of crows. The further away you got, the less elaborate the towns became: the billboards spoke to you in a way people no longer spoke; the street-light poles went from dull zinc to blackened, spiked wood. The houses on the outskirts of the small pungent towns were sullen and faded, the business drags bustling with poor people who looked as if they had stepped out of twenty years ago into the present – older cars, dingy street vendors, storefronts with grimy glass windows displaying clothes and wares no one would ever wear or use.

I closed my eyes to it all, but it was impossible to even entertain the fantasy of sleep in the rattling old Land Rover. Froude himself was attentive to the road and unusually quiet as I studied him. I noticed that he wore a thin gold ring on the ring finger, which I'd not seen before. I felt he was inviting me to think that the move away from the city would transform him somehow, and wondered why he had invited me there at all, and decided there was no reason for it. It was simply the next thing to do, with the entertainment provided by our work evenings so diminished. It wasn't a particularly incisive bit of reasoning, but I chewed on it like a rubbery piece of meat as the final few, straggling houses gave way to the farms along the highway, to green pastures where I glimpsed bored sheep and unblinking cows, and the occasional horse, still and unpicturesque in the bleaching liquid light of late-morning sun. I kept my eyes closed after seeing the animals, and opened them again only when I felt the air change temperature and sniffed something different in the breeze. On the right, was the aquamarine and emerald of the sea, just outside the car as it wound along the road that sketched the coastline.

After about a half-hour of this, the road began to curve inward, and a barrier of lazy green and yellow-leaved coconut palms on spindly trunks appeared between the sea and the road, and slowly, a village separated itself from the trees and bush. The village was remarkable only for its lack of remarkable features: old brown and grey plaster and wood houses, a decaying church in the middle, and a single-pump gas station, which Froude pulled into. The rocking and jolting of the Land Rover had been taxing. I kicked the door open and hopped out to stretch my legs as Froude got out and walked around to the pump. I stood, kicking my legs out and looking at the church. Its grounds were well-kept, though the yard was dirt rather than grass, with a few pruned azaleas and crotons lining the stone path leading up to the door. The path had obviously been swept, but the worn, wooden door was forbiddingly shut, the modest spire forlorn, and the old bell silent. An old black man wearing brown Texaco coveralls ambled out of the gas station's office and nodded to Froude, who was disengaging the hose from the pump.

"Hello Lester," he said, as he set the nozzle into the Land Rover's tank. "Is Jenny up at the house?"

Lester nodded and silently took over the pump from Froude, who came to join me in staring at the churchyard. "It is peaceful, isn't it?" he said, almost to himself, and then to me, "Two minutes up the road, old boy," and eased himself back into his seat.

"So do you attend church regularly, Froude?" I asked boredly, watching the church recede.

"The true faithful carry the church within them, old man," he said laconically, and flashed his ring finger at me; the gold ring was studded with nubs of gold on its circumference. I recognized it as a rosary ring that Catholics used to count Hail Maries.

The house was actually identical twin wooden houses, separated by a chain-link fence that contrasted oddly with the raw, unpainted stone and wood of the walls and roof. They stood a little way out of the village, built on a rock, with the sea at their back, and guarded by a wall of low, stout iron palings which bore the sign "Hau Hau House". We drove off the old road into a dirt yard that led to the houses' raised verandahs, which were connected by wide wooden steps. It was an odd arrangement; the positioning of the houses placed the verandahs close together – designed to converge on the yard – but the bodies of the houses were angled away from each other. Once inside, the consciousness of the sea roared up the rock through the house.

The houses were built along the natural slope of the rock, and held in place by steel girders which appeared to be bolted into the stone. The building Froude led me into broke into three levels: the first, a few steps down leading to the kitchen; the second leading off to the side into the bedrooms; and the third, down onto a wide verandah at the back, which overlooked the sea, and on which there were comfortable planters' chairs and old brown leather cushions. From the rear verandah, another set of wooden stairs, bolted firmly onto steps hewn out of the cliff-rock, led down to a white sand beach.

Froude motioned me into one of the bedrooms, and I went in and dropped onto the bed, and immediately closed my eyes to a last image of floury white sheets, doughy pillows, and the sound of gently creaking bedsprings. I woke in the late afternoon, thirsty and hungry, staring at a small crucifix with an effigy of Christ nailed to it, hanging over the door. In the kitchen, several pots covered with a white tablecloth sat on a sideboard shelf between an enormous, old-fashioned gas stove, and an ancient fridge. A sheet of white paper inscribed with the words "Help Yourself", in large capitals, rested on the tablecloth. Apart from the evidence of this note it seemed that I was quite alone. I lifted off the paper and the tablecloth and caught a faint, vaguely familiar smell as I did, but the scent of the food drowned it. There was home-made bread, a meat stew, fish, vegetables. The fridge was filled with beer, wine, and plentiful fruit.

I did as directed, and strolled outside onto the long, rectangular rear verandah, with a plate and two bottles of beer and sat in one of the planter's chairs, eating slowly and looking out over the sea. The sun set on the other side of the island, so there was no sight of the ocean devouring the light to look forward to, just a peaceful, imperceptible fading away into darkness. It was quite pleasant, lying there with my legs up, staring out at the now blue, now steel-grey plain, dead flat in patches, lightly rippled in others, discol-oured in yet others, the ragged clouds looking down upon it all like solemn tramps seeking a place to bed down for the night.

The wire fence that separated the houses ran down the slope of the rock, in its own steel track. You hardly noticed it at first, but once you did, it was so incongruous it kept drawing your eyes back to it. And it was during an involuntary gazes at the fence that I noticed signs of movement in the twin house. No one had appeared on the verandah, but I saw, through the windows, outlines shifting and moving, and imagined I heard the faint thuds of footfalls on the wood floors.

It didn't disturb the somnolence of the scene which I floated in for what must have been a few hours, until the back door opened and Froude walked out onto the verandah.

"Good job, old man," he said, settling himself into another of the planters' chairs, and slipped off his shoes and raised his rather thin, pink legs onto its arms. The darkness had just begun to take hold, but there was still a pleasant sensation of warmth and I was unwilling to drag myself out of my pleasant torpor, so I merely grunted, and he settled himself back, and sat quietly. I don't know how long we'd sat there before the music started, rock music, loud, violent and discordant, from the twin house.

"Oh, fuck," he said. I sat up in the chair to see him looking over the fence and sighing and shaking his head. It was a look I'd never seen on his face – of resignation rather than annoyance. I followed his eyes to the other verandah, and saw the dour, pale faces of two men and a woman staring back. Each side stared at the other silently, but whatever gravitas the scene might have possessed was deflated by the ridiculous music. Froude got up, walked to his edge of the verandah, reached behind one of the posts, and a tarpaulin close in colour to the wood dropped with a rasp, breaking the tableau. Then he turned and looked at me.

"Friends?" I asked.

"Family," he said. "We'd better go inside. It's going to get worse. More of them will come. They're going to have a party." I'd never heard anyone use the word "party" with such revulsion. "The music can be shut out from the inside. It'll be alright by morning."

I followed him inside, and saw, as we closed the door behind us, a slender brown young woman in the kitchen. I presumed she'd been there all the time I had, but been busy about the house. She looked up from the bowl she was stirring as we came in; her face was young, but she could have been anywhere between nineteen and twenty-nine – the prominent determined set of her jaw, the straight nose and her thick, brown hair, plaited in a French braid, suggested anything but youthful inexperience. And you only noticed this after you got over the leonine brown eyes, which instantly reminded me of Froude's, not in appearance, but in the way they managed to convey superiority and indifference in a glance, without help from any other feature.

"They've started," he said to her. She nodded and went back to the bowl, after a cursory nod at me. We went up to the first level, just inside the front yard, where there was a small sitting room which I hadn't noticed as I entered the house. There were two old brown leather easy-chairs with matching footstools and a leather sofa. A black piano sat next to the chairs and there were packed bookcases on either side of the window.

"Do you play, old man?" he asked, motioning me inside.

I didn't bother to answer because he'd already walked back down to the kitchen, and I idly scanned the bookshelves. The books had mainly black and brown cloth-bound covers, and seemed to have been there for decades. Their titles, such as *The Secrets of the Trobriand Islanders*; *Rounding the Cape*; *On a Camel Across the Kalahari Sands*; *The Cults of the Hindoo Goddess Kali*; recalled an earlier time, but they all seemed to circle the theme of discovery by restless men, travelling alone to the dark places of the earth. I pulled one out, half-expecting it to be covered in dust and flaking, but there was no dust. "We take them all out and wipe them every year," said Froude as he returned to the room. "And the wood is treated for termites, so the books are quite alright. You can look at one if you like." On the inside cover was a bookplate whose symbol was a cross within a circle with a Latin inscription: *Domini nos dirige*.

"Are they yours?" I asked, meaning where had he gotten them.

"They are now," he said. "But I don't know for how much longer."

I turned to him and raised my eyebrows, waiting for him to explain. The last few hours had left me feeling slightly out of equilibrium; it was the difference not merely in place, but in people: the Froude sitting before me was calm, gentle, and a little enigmatic. I found it a little discomfiting and displeasing. As my eyes met his, he pointed to a silver tray, on which sat a crystal decanter and two bulbous glasses.

"Brandy," he said, and sat, sipping meditatively, after he had passed me one. It was a strange scene. I wasn't sure what to do next. The room was warm and intimate, the sound of the waves outside was strangely comforting, and I sat with my feet up, a glass cradled in my palms and eyes half closed. I sensed him to be in a similar posture and I don't know how long we stayed like that before the ragged tinkling of smashed glass bit into the warmth of the room.

"Oh, fuck," I heard him say again. He was on his feet and I followed him outside and stood at the door as he rolled up the tarpaulin blocking the view of the other house.

"Jimmmmieeeee, *you focker*!" screamed a shrill female voice. It was immediately joined by a few other voices which ballooned into a cacophony from which occasionally an expletive – *cunt, focking nasty prick, dogshit* – would sharpen into audibility. The woman and two men were quite close enough to see – all young, all very drunk. The woman's blonde hair was limp and bedraggled and the men's hair was in various degrees of untidiness, but what struck was their faces: mouths open, teeth bared, and spittle flavouring their grunts as they bayed at Froude, who stared quietly at them. He let them scream at him for a few minutes, then, as they began to flag, he said: "Shall I get the hose, mongrels?"

This had a strange effect; it made them silent and they just stood there, staring hatefully at him. "Enough for tonight," he said. "Any more, you will upset Jenny and there will be action."

He dropped the canvas again and, as he walked past the door, said: "I suppose you deserve an explanation."

"Not really," I said. "I don't even know those people. I'd really much rather hear about Johnny Leigh." I hadn't planned to say this, or anything else; but there it was, and I wasn't particularly interested in why these obviously rich people had gone mad.

He laughed. "That's a long story, and your cultural attaché has plans for you tomorrow. Are you sure you wouldn't like to get some sleep?" I was intrigued that Mary should have plans which she seemed to have shared with Froude in advance of me, but he did not seem disposed to talk about it, so I did not pursue it.

I woke to find Mary sitting in my room the next morning, watching me sleep. We had fallen asleep together before, but it was the first time I'd ever woken up to see her sitting there, at the foot of the bed, staring at me from between two dormer windows looking out over the sea, with a cushioned stool between them. The bed lay off to the side, and the sun came up over the water, so the windows exploded with light until late in the morning.

"You look almost angelic when you sleep," she said, in a voice I never dreamed she had when I met her. Her pale skin, in this fissure of natural light, looked slightly unreal; her brown hair and grey eyes seemed almost on the verge of disappearing in the powerful stream of light. The only thing holding her to the reality of this world, I thought, was the purple sundress she wore, and the two large electric blue earrings.

"Uhm, alright," I said. I wasn't sure what else to say so I offered: "Interesting earrings." She smiled.

"Do you think so, really? I have wanted to wear them for so long, but the opportunity never seemed to be there…"

"Yes, I think you'd have to wait a long time for such an opportunity," I said.

"Let's go to the beach," she said. "It's not often I get this opportunity either."

An hour later, armed with the food basket Froude had left out for us, we went down the stairs and sat on a rug in the sand. The sea was calm in the morning, but the small beach was littered with the detritus of the night's roiling: leaves, mainly, and a few tree branches and coconuts gave the appearance of emeralds and rust-coloured trinkets on an untidy silver bed.

"So you have never taken me to meet your parents," she said after a staring out at the sea for about ten minutes. "Why is this?"

"I didn't know you'd want to meet them," I said, faintly surprised. "They're not very interesting or anything. And besides, the farm and ritually sacrificing goats and praying to Shiva every day keeps them very busy."

She pursed her lips for the barest moment. She said: "Well…" and seemed uncharacteristically indecisive, and I realised at that moment how little I really knew of her. We had known each other less than two years. She had told me her father taught Economics in Rotterdam, and her mother was a government bureaucrat; they were divorced and travelled a lot, and she saw them infrequently. She was, like me, an only child. Beyond this, I knew nothing about her life outside the island; where she lived, who she had loved first, who her friends were. We had spoken of the things of the moment, people we knew, but because the people we knew decided the future of the island, I suppose those conversations assumed an unusual and illusory importance. And of course there were the intimate things we spoke of as we lay together some nights, but these had no meaning outside those unreal moments.

Perhaps, I thought, the relationship had gone as far as it could. I had never really thought of a future with Mary. My time with her had been an interesting and pleasant diversion, a removal from the island that, I suddenly realized, I wanted more and more to be away from, from it all – though what "it" was, I had no clear idea.

"What if I wanted to meet them?"

"Then I'd take you to meet them," I said. "But I'd need to tell them a few days in advance so they could do the appropriate cleansing rituals and all that – you know, kill an ox, slaughter two kittens, and you could eat no meat, or sleep anywhere but the floor for nine nights."

She elbowed me in the ribs and ran into the sea. As I flopped back onto the sand to contemplate what this meant, I noticed her left foot, as the weight shifted onto the right, and her toes spat a little jet of sand: in that moment I caught the length of her leg from hip to ankle, the skin taut, the calf muscle bunched into a firm ellipse and the line of her shin tapering perfectly into her ankle. I took a transient fillip of satisfaction in the geometric perfection of it, and noted again that her ankles had not yet begun to thicken. I took a strange comfort in this, and I took her to meet my parents the following evening on the way home, before I had a chance to think about it.

Driving to the centre of the island with her was quite different from how I remembered it as ever being before, looking at it through her eyes. Unlike in the northern, upper parts of the island, the roads in the middle were straighter, but the pace was slower. The upper part of the island was comprised of remnants of a past of American films, soul and hip hop music, Black Power, the American occupation, and the port where hundreds of ships docked every year, leaving tourists, and even taking on some locals. There was a sense that the air breathed by the slaves of nearly two centuries ago still lingered somewhere deep in the lungs of the dark bodies that moved restlessly through its decrepit landscapes. It was there in the Levis, the basketball sneakers, the baseball caps, the bouncy yet uncertain way the people walked, the pastiche, plagiarized style of the billboards advertising local products, the frantic music.

Going to the centre of the island, you saw first the wide furrowed fields lying fallow, waiting for the caneroots to ratoon, then the dirty brown wooden shacks near the fields, then the plain, rectangular houses with bright red and yellow prayer flags on bamboo poles peeking from behind them, then the newer ones raised on thin concrete pillars, then the pastel yellow, sky-blue and orange suburban villas with stylishly broken rectangular shapes, porticoes and even a few gazebos sitting on the lawns, which could have come out a brochure for a Miami development. You saw, in between fields and houses, the green and white bulbs of Muslim mosques and Hindu temples sprouting from sleepy little towns still considering how modern they were, always, it seemed, with an eye cast back to days of wood and dirt. There were market sections in these towns: collections of drab, boxlike buildings with the facades decorated with streamers and hand-written signs selling things you would never dream existed in the other, upper parts of the island: Hindu substances like ghee, cloves, effigies of Hindu gods, bright gold, red, yellow and blue cloth, alongside garish lace, velvet and cheap silks rather than clothing. You could see balconies atop these stores, where on Sundays, when everything closed, you might see a few dark-eyed children with black hair and sad brown faces looking longingly onto the streets, but never up to the sky. You heard a different kind of music – whose lyrics were in a foreign language and whose rhythms came from different instruments and were more sensual, less frenetic than the music blaring in the towns on the way to Froude's place. You saw the people moving in time with the music from the cheap Bollywood films that played in the small movie houses here. And as in the north, there was a constant: here the symbol of the opposition party, a sunflower, made to look like the rising sun.

Passing through it all with Mary, I remembered that I had never particularly taken to it as a boy. I'd felt the towns too small, the music too loud, and the people too alien to the people I read about in books and saw on television. I suppose, though, it was because of this earlier life, that Rebah's and Froude's lives startled and interested me so much when I experienced them as an adult.

I had been briefing her on my parents. "My mother wears a veil," I said, "and is only allowed to speak five seconds after and in a tone lower than my father's."

"Is that correct?" she said absently, drinking in the fields, a few with bodies wearing large-brimmed hats, bent over in toil. Later, as I waxed inventively on the proper protocol of how to negotiate through the muddy fields to get to my parents' house, and cautioned her to be careful of the large snakes and frogs which were always about, and reassured her that the water would be safe for drinking, she stopped even murmuring.

My parents lived in a little cottage just outside the central town, in a suburb filled with quiet, contented people who worked in the oilfields in the south, and as nurses, teachers, or in the civil service. The black iron gates, wound up with creeping vines, were open as always and we drove in and met them sitting in the verandah, as they usually did on Sunday evenings, sipping tea and reading the papers. I had another jolt of surprise as I looked at my face doubled in my parents' faces, and remained struck by this for the rest of the evening.

My mother saw me first and smiled, as I smiled back into my own face. I had never realized how much like them I looked, and but for Mary's presence, I doubt I ever would have. My father pulled down his glasses over his nose to look at me and nod.

"Raju," she said. "You should have let us know you were coming."

"I wanted to surprise you," I said. "Someone wants to meet you."

I introduced them and she kissed my mother's cheek and shook my father's hand and we all sat there, with my parents looking at us expectantly. I turned to her and said: "Well, this is them. Here they are."

"Where are the oxen, the goats?" she said.

"Ah," said my father. "Has he been telling you the farm story? Or the religious cult story? Sorry to disappoint you."

"It's fine," she said. "Naturally I am disappointed, I would have loved to see animals being sacrificed. We see far too little of that in Holland. But perhaps we could discuss a little business."

They both settled in their chairs and looked at her with mild curiosity.

"Your son is a very strange man."

They nodded, looked at each other and nodded again.

"It's not like we didn't try with him," my mother said.

"But he just stayed like that," my father said.

"Well," continued Mary, "perhaps I can help."

"We are always willing to try something new," my father said.

173

"This is the situation," she said. "I would like to take him away with me. He is a great comfort to me. I have been in the government's service for ten years, and I am entitled to study-leave for three years. If he marries me, he is entitled to the same thing. The Dutch are very liberal like this."

My parents were surprisingly complicit with it, and we were married in a private civil ceremony a few days later, and in three months, we had gone. Mary's scholarship was to the London School of Economics. I managed to secure a place at the University of London. And it all might have ended there, if I hadn't seen Froude in London.

A few weeks after I'd left, Rebah sent me two clippings from the *Standard*. I assumed it was Rebah, since they came in a *Standard* envelope with no note. The first was an account of a legal battle, which Froude had apparently lost:

> History was made in the High Court today as the Froude family, who are among the largest landowners in the island, represented by James Anthony Froude, conceded and agreed to settle a suit brought by the villagers of Hau Hau Village. The villagers' claim was that the land in the village was improperly acquired by the Froude family some half-century ago, when an ambiguity in the wording of a government grant was exploited by then plantation owner, Adolphe Froude, who filed an application and with the help of the corrupt colonial judiciary, was able to annex the land granted to the villagers by the government for settlement...

But more striking than the story were the pictures that accompanied it: besides a likeness of Froude, were pictures of two men and a woman whom I recognized instantly: they were the ones who had screamed at him the night I saw them: they were his brothers and sister. The next clipping was a history of the village, but by this time, I was already enrapt in London, and memories of the island were now like dreams. Try as I might, I could not muster an interest in anything that happened there. I was stunned by the age of London, its monuments, its art, its orderliness, and besotted by the museums, the libraries, the reverence for learning. And I was stunned by the change that overcame Mary.

London's greyness seemed to encourage a sunniness in her that had been intimidated by the excessiveness of the island sun. She stitched patterns of flowers on her jeans, and bought bright voile sundresses, Grecian strap sandals, mules, and in the cooler weather peasant blouses and flowing Spanish skirts with high boots and knitted hats, and went around the city arm in arm with me, smiling and sometimes laughing like a little girl. I also realized, after seeing her for the first time in tight leather pants and a torso-hugging vest, why her suits always seemed half a size too large: it was because they were. Her bottom, coming from a civilization of flat Netherlands, protruded quite carnally.

It was the curve in the tight leather that made the impression. I'd long been accustomed to it naked, but at the sight of her ass in the sensuous, supple leather I exclaimed: "Oh my *god*! You've stolen a black girl's ass."

She turned red and spluttered, "I wish you could steal a black man's cock," and ran out of the room to return in a denim skirt.

It was on the walks through the city that I came to know her. It was discovering a country that I knew I could happily spend the rest of my life exploring. Being with her was finding a place to live at last, after a lifetime of feeling I had no country, but never quite realizing the profundity of the emptiness I felt.

So I had all but forgotten about Froude and the island when, a year later, one evening when I was alone, I opened the door of our apartment and he stood there. He had exchanged a couple of letters with Mary, he said, and that was how he had our address. He had actually been there for about three months, on a Press Association fellowship, studying parliamentary procedure and political reporting, spending time in the newsrooms of the large broadsheets, observing how they did things.

I invited him in to wait for Mary, but after a few minutes of sitting on our second-hand couch and staring moodily about the tiny apartment, he said he felt like going out to eat. He was unusually restless. He told me he liked to visit the old churches when it was cold, and sit in the middle of their centuries of reverence, and when it was warm, wander through the city when there were still people about, through Leicester Square and Covent Garden. As we walked through the cold November evening, I thought that the self-possession I remembered of him on the island was absent. Perhaps this perception came from my own distance and detachment from the island and the expansion of my own universe of concerns. I stole a look at him as we stopped for a moment to cross the street, and there, with his grey overcoat and scarf, the pale, narrow face, the unremarkable jaw and chin, there, everything but his eyes was indistinguishable amidst the black- and grey-clad unsmiling white faces, the clutch of the ordinary that stood blandly waiting for the lights to change. When the lights did change, and Froude moved off with the throng, for a moment, he disappeared. I pondered this as we walked to the tandoori place he favoured. My own penchant for invisibility was pointless here: where I had been ignored or discounted on the island, no one noticed me here: I now lived in imposed invisibility rather than the invisibility of cultivated indifference; I had not realized it till that moment.

"I chose this place in honour of you, you know," he said, smiling at me crookedly. "Your ancestors' greatest achievement: the tandoori house."

"Don't forget ganja," I said. "And child brides and dowries." I was wary of him, and myself. "But tell me about your ancestors. The village? The lawsuit?"

"Nothing to tell, old man. Didn't you get the clippings I sent?"

"You sent them?" I was surprised. "Why?"

"I thought you might be interested. The night you were there, you know, that was the last hurrah for my brothers and sister."

I remembered vaguely the first paragraph of the first clipping, but had no recollection of the second.

"That must have rankled, old boy," I said. "To turn over the spoils to the unwashed races."

"It always does," he said. "As you'll feel for yourself in a short time."

"What are you talking about?"

"Haven't you been following the news?"

"What news?"

"From home? Politics? The Asiatic party?"

"Home? I confess I haven't. But there's nothing much to follow, is there?"

"You'd be surprised," was all he would say, and I was happy to let it drop. My communication with my parents was sporadic and intimate; we spoke only of ourselves and things we knew. I would have been shocked if they'd mentioned politics to me in a letter.

"So what have you been about here?" I asked.

"Ah, the usual, feigning interest in the British Parliament and press. A bunch of public school geese, you know."

"Really?" I said. "Annoying to have to put up with these privileged pricks, innit?"

"Oh, I'm not saying they aren't capable, old man. It's just that they're boring. I doubt the other fellows would do any better. Inane rants against the upper classes, abolishing the peerage, socializing the state institutions. It's all been tried, you see. Orwell saw it. So does everyone who decides to grow up."

I was vaguely annoyed by this, because Mary was a committed socialist, and I was finding socialism attractive, if from a safe distance.

"So you suggest…?"

"Some are placed in a position to rule. You might say they're born to it. The best we can hope for in our present situation is to try to make sure they rule well. We all need to service our little part of the machine as well as we can. Have you noticed the street cleaners and waiters here? They do their jobs because it's what they do; there's no resentment of the people they serve, or those who drive or walk along the streets they clean. They understand their place in the world…"

"I'm sorry, I had no idea you were a Brahmin."

"Another excellent invention your people have left us, old man," he said. "It might be a bit unpleasant now, but it's grounded in inescapable human nature. Always, there are going to be those better and those worse; those more fit and those less so for power, privilege, and position. This is not to say the fellow sweeping the street could not go to school and get a degree and begin to sell real estate, or be a doctor. Nor should it be taken for granted that his son or daughter should have to be a street cleaner. Ideally those things should be determined on an individual basis, but that's been corrupted now, by the idea of birthright, an idea that your people have taken to its most absurd extreme. Birthright: it's a dangerous idea. It's what your friend St George and his people are so enamoured of: destiny, the right to rule and own, the right of inheritance as compensation for past suffering. It's a denial of the fact that we live in a time and place of randomness. My mother might have been a seamstress, but I, through determination, as much as by accident and chance, can be something more in this world."

It was a Froude I'd never seen or heard: the armour was off, and beneath it was no sarcasm, no irony. The grey eyes were clear and the brow slightly furrowed. I sat forward in my seat in anticipation, but the waiter bringing our curry interrupted him, and the moment was cracked.

After we'd eaten, there was no more talk of destiny and divine right. The food relaxed him, and he talked about the *Standard*, about Rebah and St George protesting when he had been given the fellowship to come to London, about Blake appealing to Kingsley Gardner, but to no avail. "It came from on high, old man," he said, smiling cynically. "There has to be some reward for enduring all those interminable evenings."

"But," and I'd wondered about this for some time, as the door to the room where I kept my memories of the island opened, and they flooded out, "why did you keep on going then?" It had taken me a year or two to begin to be invited, then a year or two to tire of those evenings. Froude must have been a habitué for at least fifteen years if my calculations were correct.

"It's… they…" he faltered. "Perhaps we're not all so lucky as you to find what we seek so soon."

It was the first time Froude had ever mentioned anything that vaguely hinted at romance.

"So is that it, Froude? You've been looking for love all this time?"

"Even if it were that," he said, "it sounds so sordid coming from the mouths of the lower orders. The very word becomes soiled in your mouth. This is why the lower orders have all these elaborate ideas about morality and god, which usually boil down to an armoury to combat the temptation of their animal natures to fornication and drink. They moralise because they lack the language to even express love, much less the emotional capacity to experience it."

"Oh, my god, Froude," I said, looking at him in horror as the realization struck. "You're gay. You're a queer, an ass-muncher, a fudge-packer, a sausage…" And it struck me; obviously Mary would have known and, given that disgusting Dutch liberalism – which I made a note to repudiate as soon as possible – would have sympathized with Froude.

"Hence my attraction to Asiatic men," he said, acidly, not denying it. "Homosexuality being built into their nature."

I burst out laughing, because I did not know what to say, and did not want to say anything, and we left soon after that. His hotel was nearby, he said, and he would take his leave that night, as he was leaving in the morning. As we walked along the curving, narrow streets, our breaths wafting from our mouths in small, smoky puffs, I clambered over the memories that had begun to rise, provoked by this revelation. Unwilling to broach it further with him, I groped and dredged for something that would take us safely away from this new and dangerous terrain. "But what about Leigh, Froude? You've never told me about him." And in the half-hour it took to walk to his hotel, he told me all about Leigh.

Leigh's Story

"Leigh began life in Sheffield, you know. Up north, they say here, with more than a bit of contempt. His father was a lowly civil servant and they moved him to London when Leigh was in his early teens. Coming from that early poverty, he was hit hard by London. Everything here was so bright, clean, the people so happy and rich. He had only two suits of clothes: one for the summer and one for the winter. He resented it. Who could blame him? This was around the time the government began encouraging people to go to university here, and his father advised him that he should be the first in his family to go. He was very lucky; he got into the University of London, and rather than Economics, as his father advised, surprised everyone by turning to art history.

"I suspect Leigh did this to prove that, because he came from a poor background, he would not automatically choose a career that would lead to affluence. The figure of the Romantic aesthete – Byron, Pater, Ruskin, you know – attracted him. Men who had been what he dreamed of becoming: brilliant, revered; not of

179

aristocratic stock, but comfortable in aristocratic circles. A lot of the life-choices he made were about responding to his background.

"But after he'd performed brilliantly at his undergraduate work, he found himself little better off than before. He was stuck in a cold room, working his way through an advanced degree at the University of London, each day hating it a little more. As luck would have it, around that time, Mokombo Cojo arrived at his University with a stack of awful paintings of beaches, markets with black peasants handling grotesque-looking produce, and, uhm, *vegetation*.

"Cojo, you know him, don't you? His real name is Marcel Peters. A thug who thinks that he's the first person to ever teach himself how to scrawl on paper. Apparently he'd gotten the government to think so and they sent him over here on a sponsored cultural exchange to do art things. He sexually assaults the minister of culture regularly – I believe they are said to have a *relationship*. So he ended up on the notice board of Leigh's department: an island artist would speak to the students about his work, with a little picture of Cojo wearing some sort of African costume.

"And here is where Leigh proved himself to be a man with at least one trait of the man he wanted to be. His fellow students saw a joke, but he saw an opportunity. He went to the talk, along with a few others, and noted the black louts in ill-fitting suits who came into the seminar hall and sat, watching the exchange, their anvil-like heads and thick lips bobbing in approval as the students asked Cojo polite, pointless questions about technique and form, about which he knew nothing, and replied that his African ancestors guided his hand. These were the petty thieves sent to infest the embassies under the title *attachés*, but who spend all their time looking for poor white unfortunates to copulate with. After the talk, Leigh went to his professor, who looked like he wanted to die of embarrassment, and offered to take Cojo on a tour of art galleries.

"Leigh started him at the National Portrait Gallery, but his guest, though awed by the surroundings, was not awed by the renditions of aristocrats, peers, and the royal corpses. Nor was he moved, and seemed quite put off by the modernist imprecations of the newer galleries. He was scandalized by Duchamp's urinal and everything that came after it. What really affected the oaf were the religious renderings of Titian and the pre-Raphaelites. His primitive religious instincts were aroused by the Biblical scenes, and the Italian landscapes and portraits of the reclining courtesans and peasant wenches. But it was not till he saw some of the early Picasso, when he was experimenting with Cubism and African art and all that, that he turned to Leigh in satisfaction and said: 'Thank you. This is what I was meant to see.'

"Cojo was superstitious, like they all are, you know, and considered Leigh his deliverer into a new life. He adopted him and began to take him to lavish dinners at the embassy and introduced him to those drooling imbeciles who might have provided a sister or daughter as a whore to a government official and who were sent abroad as a reward. Leigh warmed to the luxury; this childish, vulgarly excessive Third World version of it found harmony with his own fantasies. He was led to believe something was coming to him. But then Cojo left, and no more was heard of the little island or from its embassy. After two years of waiting, and many letters and phone calls and cancelled interviews, Leigh gave up and married a plain-looking Polish girl, an undergraduate whom he tutored, who possessed a rich mother. Leigh was determined: one way or the other, he was leaving poverty behind.

"Then, just as he was awarded his MA, a letter came from the island's embassy. It was an invitation and he was made to understand that eyes had been on him, since an invitation and money to document the island's rich history could not be given to an unsuitable candidate. It was understood he was now about to submit proposals for his doctorate, and the government had authorized funding for him for five years to complete his documentation and writing, subject to the acceptance of his proposal by a recognized art school.

"The government made a great show of collaborating with the British Foreign Office and the British Council in making its award to Leigh. I believe a small notice appeared in the arts section of one of the broadsheets here, and the idiots were ecstatic. Naturally, the British Council consulted me, and asked me whether I would be his unofficial supervisor down there, and whether I would put him up, keep him close, keep him safe.

"Leigh left London in rain and fog and arrived on the island on a warm, breezy afternoon with his wife, Sofia; a delicate, plain little thing, but smart as a whip, much smarter than he was, though she did not allow him to see it until it was too late. I quite enjoyed her company. It was she who told me that the change in him started as soon as he stepped off the plane, and into the hands of the smiling hostess waiting for him.

"Leigh looked around, breathed the air in, and decided he was never leaving. 'It was right then,' Sofia said to me a few months later, 'that I began to fade from his eyes. The girl they sent to meet him was tall, glowing like new bronze, with long curly hair, red lips, large breasts, a huge bottom, and with a smile a foot wide. And as she walked, it seemed she threw her legs open a little bit with each step inviting him, and every other man within sniffing distance, to fuck her.'

"But I didn't know any of this then. I took them home, to my place in the city, you know. Up on Chancellor Hill. Delightful place. An old plantation mansion, with a ballroom and porticoes at the front and back, an old crystal chandelier, made in Paris in 1878, in the main room, and a view of the city at the back. Sofia was only here for a few days to see him installed. But once she left, he and I started to work into each other. I was interested in him, naturally, in the manner of a protégé. We talked a lot, I let him into my library, I told him about the island, the people he would meet. I got the impression he was like a sponge; he sat there with his blue eyes attentive, and those curls of his. Many times I looked over at him in my living room and thought I'd been sent a delectable choirboy.

"But, of course, he was of interest to other people too. I began to take him out with me, to the evenings, to introduce him round. Some of the people we met at parties – the local carnivores, always on the lookout for fresh foreignness to devour – were enamoured of him and began to appear at my door at obscene hours to 'take him round'. The government people who controlled his money and who were interested in his research were not happy that he was staying with me, and after a week, they took him in to meetings about what they expected. Of course, he came back and repeated it all to me: they expected he would explore the island's rich artistic heritage, placing Cojo at the centre of an indigenous emerging tradition. He would submit drafts of his work to them before sending them on to supervisors.

"I was more outraged than he was when he told me this. 'And what did you say to that?' I asked. I wasn't worried, of course, merely offended; even if he did submit his work, who in there could read it?

"'Oh, I told them, of course,' he said smiling in that engaging way. The boy had lovely teeth, I thought. 'But what's that worth down here?'

"Maybe that was the moment I should have seen it, but, foolishly, I used it as a reason to pull him even closer to me. I was not so naïve to believe that my interest in him was confined to my finer impulses; the animal instincts were stirred, you know. Like when you Asiatics have drunk your rum and go at your miserable women like depraved goats. But this was his charm, you see, he made you feel protective, he made himself seem vulnerable.

"I took him to the university, put him in Corinne Rajah's care. At least I knew she was incorruptible, and I watched him go with some pride, and not without some passion. And then one night, I think we were at some embassy or the other, and we were talking to a British diplomat, and I introduced him to Leigh. And I saw it in a flash.

"Standing in the presence of the British fellow – he was one of those aristocratic types, nephew of Lord Something or Other, fourth generation in the diplomatic service. I saw Leigh's face change. It was a mixture of awe and resentment. And his voice, his voice.

"'So how is your little sojourn in the colonies,' the British fellow said.

"'Oh, quite agreeable,' said Leigh. 'They're showing me the local colour. Most amusing, I have to tell you.'

"'You're looking at their art, I believe?'

"'Oh, yes, their art,' said Leigh, with his pleasant smile. 'I am looking at their art quite closely. Primitive, powerful, expressive. It's as if all they cannot and daren't say or think about themselves is in there. It should make an interesting study.'

"But it was that phrase: *their art*. I don't know, perhaps I saw something that was not there. But I heard a mixture of contempt, derision, amusement; it was the one place Leigh could stand on equal terms with those who were his betters at home: their shared superiority over here. And it hit me: the rules did not matter here; here, he was free in a way people at home could never understand.

"From that moment, I began to look at him differently. His intentness, instead of interest, was, I saw, mere rapacity. Other things began to happen. Others began to take an interest in him. He began to be taken away for weekends to the coast. Those delightful little birds from the embassy parties began alighting upon him, and I began to see him less and less, except for our meetings at the house.

"One day, after about three months, he came in a little drunk from one of his evenings, the contents of which I had not yet begun to suspect. I sat on the porch, you know, drinking brandy and looking out over the city. He walked up to me and stood next to me, and I saw, for the first and last time, the hunger in his eyes: raw, naked, carnivorous. He sat and looked at me.

"'So I see you've been out and about, John,' I said, averting my eyes. The intensity of that hunger, you know. And he stood there and looked at me. It was evening, my balcony is of white plaster, old and wide, cracked and faded, but I like it that way. It's shaded by some fig trees, with thick lianas linking the spreading branches, where parrots sleep at night, and iguanas crawl around during the day. He was wearing a white linen shirt, open at the neck, and he looked down at me, and then sat on the arm of my chair, and his fingers brushed my arm. The meaning was unmistakable.

"'No,' I said. 'No.' He moved out the next day. But it wasn't over. There had been murmurs before, but there always are. I began to see his picture in the papers, at government functions, at receptions I wasn't invited to, at artistic events I wouldn't go to. But it wasn't until his wife came a few months later that I got the full story. She appeared at my door one morning. She had come to visit him, as arranged, and met someone she barely knew. His appetites had increased, and changed, she said. He was like a man possessed, deranged. And after a few days, she realized, she couldn't satisfy them. He left her in the night and went out, and came back with the face of a satiated predator. She knew, as I now did, what went on, and did not need to know, as I didn't, the details. She left a few days later, and that was my last direct contact with anything to do with Leigh. I did see him from time to time. I suppose I was hoping that the island's heat and friction would wither him. But it didn't. He remained the same. He didn't age, he merely fed and fed on everything the island produced, but did not change. I wondered more than once if there was a picture of him somewhere that became more and more ravaged every day. I was, I admit, terrified of him."

That last conversation with Froude stayed with me. His relationship with Leigh echoed disquietingly his relationship with me. I unwillingly began re-examining our association, the possibility of gestures I had misread or not seen. During the course of my studies, I'd encountered his namesake as a major Victorian literary figure. I'd known of his claim to infamy in the island's history, but now, locating it in another, more urbane and sane context, I looked up his other works. His major histories, I discovered, were admired for their literary style and fastidious scholarship, but criticized for their moral subjectivity – which sometimes went against the currents of his time. He was no reactionary; in his youth he'd written anti-establishment religious polemic and fiction which had scandalized his Oxford tutors, but he was a friend and confidant of Carlyle, Tennyson and Arnold. He was a man who wrestled with the great ideas of his time, which he had helped to shape; his twelve-volume history of the Reformation had reshaped an age's views of the Tudors and tempered his countrymen's harsh views of their Roman Catholic monarchs. His history of Ireland had been sympathetic to the Irish.

Froude's impression of our island was contained in a brief section in a minor book, which had entailed his visiting all the West Indian islands. Thomas's response to it, titled *Froudacity*, was a sedulous refutation of inconsequential fact – mistaking hyperbole and irony for learned exposition – and had missed what lay at Froude's and his book's common heart: a meditation on the inevitable decline of empire. The luxuriation in drawing attention to the primitive, and the derision expressed towards the local aspirants to civilization were minor themes. In refuting Froude, Thomas had almost vindicated him. The tragedy was that Thomas was a man of circumscribed genius. He had been cruelly treated by fate with debilitating illness for most of his adult life, and his genius could never flower in an isolated country town at the bottom of the island, in the way Froude's had been able to at Oxford, despite the tragedy of his mother's and siblings' early deaths, and his distant, strict father's disapproval. This striking paradox of the ridiculous mingled with tragic irony seemed to write a conclusion to my island experience, and I put away the books, and both Froudes, into receding memory. I looked to my new life. And there it might have ended, but, like fate, it did not.

II

The black women look with envy at the straight hair of Asia and twist their unhappy wool into knots and ropes in the vain hope of being mistaken for the purer race; but this is all. The African and the Asiatic will not mix, and the African being the stronger will and must prevail...

Three years after Froude knocked on my door, we had both finished our higher degrees, and had become quite at home in London. Mary had another year of accumulated leave left, and I was lecturing part-time at my university college, and our life had entered that kind of pleasant timelessness of ripened youth, comfort, and love.

As the fourth year drew in around us, Mary began unwillingly to look back at her career. She could leave or stay in it. Either way, she had to work for her government for two years. We discussed it endlessly for months, lulled into a kind of security by her government salary, and the comfort we artificially enjoyed. As it turned out, the decision was made for us. Six months before the end of our final year, she was informed that a position had opened in the island; the ambassador had decided to resign and she could have the position of head of the mission for two years, the time remaining in her predecessor's tenure.

It was through Mary's re-entry into the island that I confronted the reality that the government in the island had changed. The Asiatic party had managed to win a surprise election about two years after we left. This should have been enormous news, but its significance to me was muted by distance, apathy, and relief that I was no longer there. We returned early one morning, tired and a little fed up after the long flight; the winds made any flight to England relatively short and pleasant, but the return journey was always turbulent, tiring and fraught with delay. Mary's new status, and mine, by extension, made our arrival considerably different from our departure. We were taken through immigration into a waiting car before anything had time to register. For me, it was more than a little unreal – I stayed at Mary's side, and the officials all addressed themselves to her, the embassy security officers, the immigration officers, and the diplomatic staff.

But I didn't have the time to reflect on the sensation of being the silent partner, which, though strange, was not without its satisfactions. Almost as soon as we arrived, I found myself deluged by the island. A reception had been planned in honour of the departing ambassador and it had been decided to use it to welcome his successor as well. I'd barely had time to collapse onto the huge, soft bed of the Hilton's ambassador's suite, and wake up, than we were dressing for the evening. I had been thinking of the inversion in our roles, mainly that it was not really an inversion, since I had always been led by Mary.

"So," I said as I sat on the bed watching her before her mirror, "do you realize it's even more apparent now?"

"What is that, sweetie?" she asked, daubing the pale pink lipstick she wore with a tissue, and looking back at me through the mirror.

"Well, my dear, I seem to be your bitch. Have you noticed?"

"Hmm," she said, finishing off her lips. "I was going to buy you a short, frilly maid's dress. But then I thought of your hairy legs. You wouldn't shave them, I suppose? And your back?"

"Only if I got to wear the penis at least once a week," I said.

But more had changed than the dissolution of whatever claim

to manly authority I had, and as we stepped out of the car and onto the lawns of the large Georgian-styled house on Chancellor Hill (which we would inhabit in a few days), the island rushed up to meet us. We met the outgoing ambassador and his wife. He was of medium height with silver-white hair and a crooked nose, and a look of perpetual patriarchal discomfort on his lined face. His wife, Els, looked younger, though her blonde hair seemed to glisten just a little too much to be real, and the glow it threw over her features, which had only just begun to relinquish their tautness to wrinkles, was somewhat overpowering. She was still attractive, but it was evident that the heat had withered her a little, and she'd had enough of the island. Her smile was plastered in place, and remained there when she spoke. She wore a regal grey skirt-suit, which blended nicely with her husband's navy blue, as she stood next to him and I next to Mary as the new ministers wound up the path to the main tent on the lawns, past neat rows of white cloth-covered tables with red and yellow floral arrangements on them, to pay their respects. Despite myself, I found myself paying attention to how Els greeted the people who were presented to her, and how she adapted herself to her husband's movements and gestures.

But distracted as I was, it was something of a shock to see the Asiatics as they came to be presented. There were more Asiatics present than I remembered ever seeing at these affairs. They were either light-skinned and fine-featured, comfortable in their expensive suits, or jowly, dark, heavyset men with enormous bellies pushing their jackets open. They were obsequious to Mary and her patrician predecessor, leered at Els and ignored me. Yet again, I was invisible. But it left me time to observe that their attempts at smoothness seemed undermined by the too-calculating slickness of men too used to getting around rules to care about ceremony overmuch.

Once the more eminent of the personages were dispensed with, I left Mary surrounded by a group of diplomatic people and wandered around, peering into many familiar faces I did not care to recognize, and who, with a surprising amount of animus, did not care to recognize me. I did take note, though, the distinctive Asiatic presence: women in saris, with ornate gold jewellery, sensually shaped eyebrows, heavily powdered brown faces and silky long hair; men whose faces, so unused to being recognized and acknowledged, simply refused to present an outstanding feature, standing uncomfortably in dark suits with the air of not being quite sure of what was coming next, and being a little tired of the meaningless rituals. And, of course, there were the usual denizens – the civil servants, the business people, the press, the other diplomats – who stood apart from them, nursing glasses and muttering to each other, as the banal chords of the obligatory calypsonian warbled across their heads.

As I stood, contemplating whether Mary's diplomatic immunity would get me freed for killing the calypsonian (who was droning an inane song about watering a garden, as far as I could tell), I felt a hand on my shoulder.

"Look who's back. It's the great white pussy hunter."

"Sweetheart," I said, turning to Rebah. "It's only because the dark meat was going off." But I stopped short. The voice was Rebah's but the person before me I barely recognized. Her hair, once shiny, straightened tresses, was now matted in dreadlocks and dropped mutinously down her back. But that was nothing compared to her clothes. She wore a plain white blouse with a kente pattern stitched into the neckline and cuffs, and her skirt was of the rough, rich, colourful material you saw sometimes in London worn by Ghanaian women at street fairs and on Sunday when they went to church. On her left hand was a large silver ring with the crest of a black circle, and her own face was much more defiant than I remembered it.

"Love the hair," I said.

"The new me," she said, but smiled as she kissed me. "Come and say hello to Uncle."

St George was his usual effusive self as he greeted me, and asked me how I'd enjoyed London, whether I'd gone to the theatre, and whether I'd been to Buckingham Palace. As I chatted, I began to look around for Froude, and made a mental note to ask after him. Just then, the calypsonian finished droning, and I let go a small sigh of relief, and turned to Rebah to ask whether she wanted a drink. It was by the merest chance that several things happened at the same time: the music changed, and instead of the inane calypso chords, I heard a different melody, one I'd heard before, but never at these functions. It was the music I'd heard only when I visited my parents, in the town I grew up in, but even from the first few bars, it was evidently faster and raunchier than the music I knew. My surprise at hearing it was nothing compared to the change in the look on Rebah's face. Her lips had pressed into a line, jaw clenched, brow crinkled and her eyes flashed. St George hid his distaste a little better, confining himself to a slight pursing of the lips. Rebah quickly schooled her features as I turned back to her. But as I walked away, I noticed that every Asiatic suddenly became a little more Asiatic; at the sound of the music they stood out a little more, looked a little more alien in that landscape.

As I was contemplating the meaning of all this, the music stopped altogether, and the crowd parted. I thought the new Prime Minister had arrived, but no, it was a man and woman wearing floor-length, purple-and-black robes, which wouldn't have looked out of place in a Biblical epic film. As they walked through the crowd, some people were nodding their heads, and others, with various degrees of overtness, were genuflecting. The man looked vaguely familiar, but the hauteur of his heavy, bearded, thuggish face was a little disconcerting. Rebah's breath caught, and she ran over to him and touched his arm and bowed a little. The woman with him, dark-skinned, with slightly bulging eyes, large breasts and a round stomach – a little reminiscent of the African woodcarvings you saw for sale on the pavements in Notting Hill – stood a little way behind, and looked on impassively as he patted Rebah's head gently with a dark, thick-fingered hand. As the pair walked past me on their way to be presented to Mary, I remembered who he was: Cojo. His coming changed the mood of the place – it was more tense and an imperceptible mood of hostility came from the black waiters, which I had not noticed before.

As I stood there looking at Cojo's entrance in some amazement, I felt an arm brush mine and stop. "They're fucking crazy, you know. First the bowing and kissing, then the hymns, then they start handing out the machetes." It was Els, with a glass of scotch in her hand and her smile finally gone, replaced by the pensive, ruthless look you might see on the face of a huge jungle cat contemplating a herd of zebras. From her breath, and the slight trembling of her forearm as it touched mine, it was evident that the glass of scotch was not her first.

"I was wondering," I said. "No one else seems to think so."

"Look at the Asiatics," she said. "They look disgusted and frightened. This is how it starts. The educated ones form a cult, then it spreads down. Be thankful you don't have many radio stations."

"Radio stations?" I asked, looking down at her.

"You are a sweet looking boy," she said. "I'm leaving tomorrow. Would you like to fuck?"

"I'm sorry, I'm gay," I said.

"So is my husband," she said, with some annoyance, walking off.

Later, when Mary and I were alone, she told me what her predecessor had relayed to her. The national party's loss of the election had come out of nowhere, and it had caused a great deal of upset among those who had considered their ownership of the island to be god-given. They had been so complacent that they had hardly noticed the Asiatics spreading into communities they hadn't been before – and tilting the voting balance, or the poor blacks' disaffection becoming so pointed, they had begun to listen to the Asiatic lawyers and unionizers who formed the Asiatic party. And because the newspapers were so focused on their own concerns in the city, and barely registered the existence of anyone outside it, no one had noticed that black faces had begun to appear in the ranks and in the masses of the Asiatic party.

When the election results were announced, people like St George felt as if a limb had been suddenly removed. There was much talk, at first in private, then occasionally in the pages of the papers, about destiny and historical rights as they watched the Asiatics scramble over the spoils of office. The new movement which had formed around Cojo was at first small, just a few people, but soon, those released from sinecures – made extraneous by the Asiatics placing their own people in such positions – who had become satellites detached from their orbit, gravitated towards it. Cojo's childish ideas about the destiny of his people, and their ancestral entitlement, had the virtue of being simplistic enough to become dogma, which the displaced began to swallow like men in the desert falling into a trough of none-too-clean water.

It seemed a little ridiculous to me, but Mary said some of the older diplomats were shaking their heads with a foreboding they did not wish to put into words. I did not have time to dwell on it because immediately after the reception, we moved into the ambassador's residence.

The house was set back on a green, well-barbered lawn, its straightforward rectangular façade and latticed windows staring out expressionlessly into the hills. Its Georgian plainness was a relief from the lavish plantation porticoes and pillars the old planters favoured. At its back, overlooking the city, was an ice-blue swimming pool and tennis court. The house was furnished in a rich but restrained style; no chandeliers and extravagant sofas, but discreet embedded lights, sleek, tantalizingly curved metal and black leather chairs, glass and pewter tables, zinc bar-tops, stainless-steel stools, silent sliding doors everywhere, tasteful reproductions of Dutch artists' paintings in the inner rooms, and a few originals from local artists in the dining room. It seemed that the previous ambassador had either elected to leave all his personal memorabilia, or the decoration came with the house. There was a library, but the books were mainly in Dutch. I found a little room which looked out over the back of the house and placed my books in there.

Safe in there, inside this ruthless order and austerity, the import of what I had seen at the reception faded. When I began to read the papers, Froude's name was nowhere to be found. Mary said she'd not kept in touch with him, and did not know where he was. But Froude's absence, and mine, had seen the flowering of startling changes in the *Standard* and the *Guardian*. Then the papers were laid back, completely in agreement with the status quo, and the one television station and three radio stations, all owned by the government, were almost comic in their obliviousness to other views.

Now, the papers were angry, vituperative, bristling with barbs aimed at the government. And there was another feature: as if their existence had suddenly been discovered, several Asiatics were now prominently displayed on the opinion pages. Their presence alone was remarkable, but more remarkable was the anger they displayed, and how utterly opposed they were to what had been assumed to be normal, right-thinking positions on just about everything. They objected to everything from state funding of carnival to the process of senatorial appointments. But most of all, the virtual absence of any Asiatic presence in all state institutions, long accepted as all but inevitable, enraged them, as did the new rigour with which the governance of the Asiatic party was being examined.

On the first day I looked at the papers, I saw a photo of a fierce-looking St George above an article headlined: *Don't they know it's democracy?* He wrote:

> The desire of this new government for privilege at the expense of the less fortunate – notice their frequent foreign trips, their new cars, the renovations to their residences – is nothing short of scandalous. Do these men understand the principles of democracy – that the people come first…?

Next to him was a column headed by a picture of a fleshy, bilious-looking Asiatic, Sathi Narayana, headlined: *Black dreams, brown nightmares*:

> So now they are interested in institutions and the Westminster tradition, as if these things have recently been discovered, and asking all these nonsense questions of the government. Where were these questions before, when the black government was destroying the country…?

I stopped reading. It was all too unreal for me. I had never encountered this kind of naked anger in the pages of the paper before, or anywhere else that I could remember. I thumbed through, and noticed that many of the articles and advertisements contained a word I had never heard before used in any serious way in the island, and hardly at all in conversation. The word was "African". It was everywhere in the *Standard*: announcing lectures on African history, a meeting of the African association, African celebrations, and African fashion and beauty shows.

I looked at the *Guardian*, and saw, to my relief, that the phenomenon seemed to be confined to the *Standard*. But the articles in the *Guardian*, once a compliant echo chamber for government press releases, now seemed to comprise rigorous analyses of government projects, mobilizing project financing details, technical expertise and eloquence which I could hardly believe they were willing to pay for. I thumbed through till I found an article by Sunny Cheval, a review of a South African play:

> Art inevitably returns to its moral function, and in this play, the story of a poor African man seeking redress from the injustice of a dictatorial regime, that moral function is beautifully vindicated. The struggles of the African for justice echo loudly in our own corridors of power, which are now thronged by new oppressors…

I visited my parents on the first Sunday we were there, but they took the strangeness as normal. They knew nothing of the African association. They had never taken the papers seriously anyway, but, they pointed out, their lives and the lives of the people they knew were beginning to change for the better. The roads were a little smoother, the water supplied a little more regularly, the electricity outages fewer, government offices a little more efficient, and new schools and hospitals were being built. These changes were small; away from the capital, the pace and rhythms of lives were not much changed. You noted change only when you looked and realized the difference in the roads, the houses, the schools, the service you now expected in government offices.

But living in the capital, and seeing versions of the first pantomime I'd seen at Mary's reception played out every night, this change in atmosphere took on a more insidious aspect and, I confess, I was stunned, paralysed – not out of fear, particularly, but by my own moral inanition, my fundamental apathy toward the island, and my desire simply not to be there. I had lived for four years in a place where all these questions had been settled, and people were free to live in ways motivated by desires other than primal, gut-driven instincts born of living in one or other ethnic corral. I realized that I, and many people, had unconsciously hidden from this ugliness all our lives, and this hiding had allowed the national party to spread itself like a weed, which was in time mistaken for a flower. Looking at it now, I also felt the inevitable end of this open hostility before I saw it. I hid in the house on the hill for months. I swam in the pool for about an hour each day; I read the foreign papers, listened to music, read books and drank, and blanked out the island.

I realized then that this was the very complacency that would allow the evil to flourish – this inertia, this slow-motion slide into decadence. I lived among a staff of black servants who were managed by an embassy official named Helga. They were uniformed, respectful, and efficient, mainly because they were briefed every morning, in military style, standing in a line, while Helga, large, efficient, unsmiling, directed them and quickly reprimanded them for any shortcomings. I did not learn their names, and I did as much as possible to avoid them, but in the midst of the comfort they provided, it was impossible to sustain any sense of urgency. My knowledge, instincts, and experience were going in different directions, leaving me feeling sad and a little ridiculous, a little ashamed of being kept, and becoming so shamelessly what I'd always despised when I'd looked at it from the outside.

So I was usually by the pool, or in my study room when Mary came home. I rarely accompanied her to the functions she was obliged to attend. Instead, I began to get the staff to set the table for dinner when she came home early, and we talked, sometimes for hours. I felt it was the last I would ever see of my manhood, but the happiness of these hours kept me whole and reassured me. Like all shallow, self-involved people, I did not realize how obvious my decay was. One evening, three months after we'd moved into the house, Mary came home early and said: "Let's go out."

"Where are we going?" I asked.

"To see an old friend," she said. But we used the official car and driver, and it drove us out of the city and through the hills into the small town of St Frederick, to the university campus. We were met by two smartly dressed young women who led us to an auditorium, where I saw a poster announcing the event: "Dr John Leigh Talks about Nationalism and Art: A Formula for Salvation."

"No," I said.

"Yes," she said.

The auditorium was packed with a few hundred people many of whom, I realised, I knew. They were from the papers, from the embassy parties, and many of them were former politicians who had coalesced into a new institution: "civil society" groups, whose purpose seemed to be describing the enormity of the very existence of the Asiatic government. They specialised in scrutinising its procedures for procurement, for appointments, its attempts to hamstring that most sacred of instruments, Press Freedom (because they refused to talk to reporters who called them thieves and liars).

The emergence of these groups had been a natural consequence of the order of things. When it had taken power nearly thirty years ago, the national party had begun to plant its seeds everywhere: relatives of party officials were given national scholarships, placed inside low, but upwardly mobile echelons of the civil service, placed in the United Nations, and UN agencies; and into the judiciary, the university, the police force. In time, the party's control of government was the least of its powers: it also controlled, informally but tightly, the police, education, culture, civil service and links with international organizations and the outside world. From tourist brochures to academic books, every image and idea came from the bowels of the ruling party. And this had been made possible by people like Leigh and St George.

At the lecture, I noticed, were a few Asiatics looking sombre and collected. Many more people wore variations of the African costumes Cojo and his partner had worn, in varying degrees of completeness. Some merely wore dashiki tops over normal trousers and skirts, some merely wore a fez-like hat, others a small, but prominent and signifying piece of jewellery, often with the symbol I'd seen on Rebah's ring. It emerged on lockets, rings, and stitched onto clothing. On closer inspection, it appeared to be a black snake devouring its own tail.

Mary and I sat at the back, well outside it all with the principal of the university, who was our host, and a few professors and officials. About five minutes before the lecture was scheduled to start, a hush fell over the crowd, and they all stood. Cojo had arrived, dressed in the same manner as before, but the veneration in the greetings was more overt now. Many people touched his feet, and he stood, in the middle of it, with his heavy features frozen in an expression of crude aristocratic indulgence. Once he was seated, in the centre of the front row, Leigh entered from the back of the stage, walked down to Cojo, put his hand on his heart, and bowed. The crowd applauded his gesture, and by the time the applause had died down, he had made his way back to the podium and had begun talking. The years had added to Leigh. He wore a black suit with a white shirt open at the neck, and he looked impressive and powerful. His hair had been barbered and carefully combed back, and his blue eyes looked penetrating, even from the distance.

"Nations are not formed from wars or treaties, or won by elections," he said. "They are formed from ideas. Ideas form their soul. Anyone may take a piece of land and build a fence round it; its intrinsic nature will remain unaffected except perhaps by a paltry claim of legalistic ownership, which is unenforceable without artificial force; armies you must pay for, and which die once physical sustenance ends. Enduring nations are formed when people who are propelled by the same beliefs, who feel, think and breathe in unison, coalesce. The question before us this evening is this: how do people – a people – who have been torn from their natural place, oppressed and alienated from their language, cut off from their culture, and forced into another set of beliefs and values which are not rooted in their intrinsic selves, recover that intrinsic self? The ideas exist, but how are they rediscovered? I am proposing here, that in this place, those ideas emerge in creativity, in art, in music. All the things a civilization wishes to say but cannot are embedded in its unconscious, where it waits until a deliverer comes, to dredge those images up, give the nation a body and a face, and give it the template of its character…"

At first, I listened with a mild, amused scepticism, which grew into something more disturbed as Leigh continued to speak. Cojo was that deliverer, his copied images, puerile ideas and utterances of ethnocentric nonsense were the body, organs and mind of the state. But this was only his starting point; familiar ground which had been covered some time before. From there, Leigh moved to various other things I vaguely remembered from my days at the *Standard* – the old dances which people claimed were African in origin, songs and games children in the country played, bands that paraded at the (as I remembered it) anaemic, ragged touristic

Carnival. Finally, he arrived at his conclusion: it was Carnival, calypso and steelpan, those things which had been most abused, degraded and devalued, that contained the seeds of the nation's soul. Here was where the truth about the island lay, and anything else was a foreign distraction.

At the end of the lecture, we were led to the principal's residence, a sprawling colonial house in white and grey, with a gable roof and windows, jalousies, and a wooden porch with high-backed, cushioned rattan chairs which looked out over lawns sentried by the solitary, voluptuous shapes of citrus and pomegranate trees in the darkness. Only a few people were invited – the mass of Cojo's devotees had taken him somewhere – and within an hour most of the guests, mainly academics and university committee people, had gone, leaving just five of us on the cool patio, sipping coconut water and scotch.

Mary and I sat with the principal, Corinne Rajah and an Asiatic man. The principal was a pleasant, urbane man, of slight build, balding, with spectacles, and dressed like a senior civil servant – a short-sleeved tastefully checkered shirt, grey trousers and Hush Puppies. The Asiatic man, Professor Poonwa Chamaran, wore a garish long-sleeved gold and green shirt (through the undone top buttons of which a gold medallion peered out, held by a ropy chain), brown pants and zip-up boots with noticeably elevated heels. He was balding, and his dark hair was combed in a hopelessly vain fashion to conceal this. He spoke in an obsequious, singsong voice.

"So, Cassius," Corinne was saying to the principal, as we sat in the warm evening, breathing in the pleasant scent of the fruit trees, "what do you think of this latest oratorical masterpiece?"

"Most amusing, my dear. I had no idea the fellow had such a feeling for… what does my granddaughter call it? Ah, 'stand up comedy'," he said lightly.

"Oh, I don't know," said Chamaran in his singsong voice. "It's an interesting thesis; we should hear it out. How harmful could it be?"

"Interesting and harmless if you haven't read *Mein Kampf*," snapped Corinne. "Stop it Poon, you're annoying me. Save your pretensions of open-mindedness for the promotions board."

"We wouldn't want to annoy you," said Chamaran, with an oily smile.

"See that you don't," she said. "You lower castes seem to be attracted to fascism, even when it's turned against you. Let's ask the young fellow, he looks as if he could pass for a Brahmin. He's even married to a white woman."

"I'm not sure where this stuff came from," I said. "I went away for a few years, and now I come back and I land in the middle of the Fascist Fantasy Island."

"There you are," she said. "He can see it."

"Surely you're giving them more credit than they deserve, my dear," said Cassius. "How much harm can they do? What we saw tonight was the whole movement. A few hundred, no more, and many of those are just hangers on. He has fifty followers, if that many."

"You're not an historian, Cassius," said Corinne. "Ideas are like fuel; throw them on ashes, you might get nothing. Throw them onto smouldering remains, you might get an explosion. The right idea at the right time entertains no moral considerations. I've been watching them for these last couple of years. They still cannot get over the Asiatics taking power from them. Well, who could blame them? They weren't Brahmins. But they're grasping at straws. The steelpan and calypso – students are starting to write papers and propose theses, and the theses are not about studying these things, they're to prove their belonging to one group, and to outline the rights that come with that ownership… And the articles in the papers."

"That might be our saving grace, my dear," said Cassius, "No one can read, and no one takes the papers seriously."

Then Els's statement made sense to me. "But if they got their hands on a radio station…" I said, half to myself, and the possibilities unfurled with the speed and momentum of an avalanche.

"Oh, dear lord, don't even suggest that," said Corinne.

"As you said, moments and their ideas… Anti-Semitism had been around for centuries, and Hitler was a foot soldier with no rank or authority in WWI, but 20 years later…" I said lamely.

"Actually he was a corporal," said Corinne. "And he was

decorated several times for bravery. But your point is not fundamentally inaccurate. Though, clearly, you are not an historian?"

That was directed at me. "No," I said. "I'm... My work was on Romantic poetry."

"Oh, how interesting," said Chamaran, glad for the opportunity to slip by Corinne. "What did you do?"

"I looked at the themes of nature and industrialization in the earlier and later Romantics," I said, glad to be off the topic, and we spent the rest of the evening discussing Byron's and Shelley's sexual appetites and Coleridge's opium addiction, and whether he nurtured a homosexual attraction for Wordsworth.

Later, as Mary and I sat in the back seat of the car, she moved closer to me, draped her legs over mine and put her head on my shoulder and left it there for a long time. Then she said: "So when would you like to start?"

"Start what?" I asked.

"Lecturing at the university," she said.

"They put you in charge of that now?" I asked.

"No, you bobo. You just had your interview. Why do you think I took you there?"

"Not to hear Leigh's lecture?"

"Well, I'm glad you did hear it, but no."

"What do you have to give in return for this?" I asked.

"The principal is retiring soon, and would like to enjoy his pension and gratuity. A scholarship for his granddaughter to go to the ISS would let him do that."

"Is that all?"

"Well, I had to promise to sleep with the minister of education and the commander of the regiment."

"That sounds reasonable," I said. "Should I make some notes for them?"

"I haven't told you what you have to do yet."

By this time we'd gotten home and she'd lapsed into silence.

"What's wrong?" I asked.

"Nothing," she said. "It's just..."

"Just what?"

"The government is being encouraged by the EU to expand access to media, to grant new radio and television licenses.

They're willing; they want to be seen as progressive and liberal. They're planning to give out the first set of licenses within a year, before they call the election."

The university was a huge, Kafkaesque bureaucracy, designed by British colonial administrators intent on creating Xanadu in the tropical reaches of the empire: paradise for anyone lucky enough to find his way there. It was run by governing boards and committees, nominally free from government control. Once locals had penetrated, and the masters were safely away, they mastered the byzantine complex of rules, regulations, and inter-pretations, making the institution into a curious hybrid of intel-lectual freedom – lecturers could not easily be interfered with – and intellectual enormity when some of the locals, elevated by obsequiousness and political manoeuvring, promptly became decadent, tyrannical, and determined to stay in their positions for life and pass them on to their kin and protégés.

Into this semi-independent republic I was gently set down, after a farrago of advertisements in the newspapers, applications, interviews, and letters back and forth, to initiate the island's youth into the mysteries of Romantic poetry and Victorian literature. And there I began to understand how easy it is to come to terms with evil. Because, after a very short time, it became evident that many lecturers were incompetent, misguiding students, and shamelessly using their posts to do everything from coercing students to have sex with them to securing board appointments in private industry. However, like everyone else I met, the princely salary, lordly perquisites, and freedom from conse-quences created a bog which trapped my every moral impulse. Thus, over decades, the university became a breeding ground for lunatics, frauds, one or two of certifiable psychotics and at least one functional illiterate who ambulated, flourished, died and were ossified in their positions in the citadel.

The work itself presented its own formidable perversity – trapping the pilgrim between the soul-crushing indifference of undergraduates who stared blankly at their books and reproduced almost word-for-word what you said in class in their essays, and the hydra-headed university bureaucracy. I was, as a matter of course, placed on committees for academic advisement, scholarships, research, oversight, quality control. The committees, I quickly realized, were designed to give only the appearance of work. The meetings were ritualistic and all decisions were made well in advance; appointments, grants, exceptions, titles, dispensations – these were all ratified by an arcane system of voting, and everyone, except me, seemed to know how it all worked.

In short, the university was a simulacrum of the society except that, given its predilections, some features were exaggerated. On the campus, for example, the African movement was quite in vogue. Some lecturers had taken to wearing the costume to class, preaching Cojo's dogma, and encouraging students to produce extrapolations, extensions and pseudo-analyses. For all the enthusiasm, though, I thought, watching it all, it was not likely to go very far. The lecture I had attended was, it seemed, an anomaly. Other events that attempted to stir and stimulate an African essentialism attracted only handfuls of students and staff. A few lecturers were evidently true believers, but many were attentive in public to the movement but patronizing in private. In my own classes I was particularly well-insulated, since, apart from the occasional question about why it could possibly be important to study the works of dead white men, the students mainly droned on dutifully, plagiarized where they could, and with the greatest unwillingness stirred themselves to make the most banal observations about Byron, Coleridge, Dickens and George Eliot.

After a few months, I felt myself sinking into that seductive, milky pool of decadent comfort without any struggle. But the security of knowing my tenure was brief, and that I did not need the job the way the others did, encouraged a few sallies I could not always control, and whose effects I invariably miscalculated. Affected by the perversity of the place, I decided for no reason, except the pleasure of seeing the students' looks of horror that they could not plagiarize from the essays of previous years, to change the set books on the Victorian literature course. One of the authors I wanted to introduce was Anthony Trollope, who had, mystifyingly, been absent from the list.

Naturally, this change had to be approved by a committee I was on – a formality, but like everything else at the university, it was one that had to be observed. The meetings were usually bland, brief affairs with the agenda being read off, assents being asked for, given without thought, and all members signing the memos later in the week. The committee comprised eight people, but usually only four, the quorum, appeared. I understood that members rotated responsibility for attendance. Being the most junior, I was not consulted or informed, so I had to go to each one. On the fateful day I attended the meeting in Corinne's office, only four people were present: Chamaran, Corinne, and a Cojo disciple, Eric Williamson. As the meeting was winding up, I cleared my throat and said: "Could we deal with just one thing before we close?"

"What is it?" said Corinne. "You know you should have asked for it to be put in the agenda."

"Sorry, it's just a change of books for my course," I said.

"What books do you want?" she said, with a martyred sigh. Chamaran and Williamson had risen to go, but stood in identical positions, fingertips on the desk, waiting to nod in approval and be gone.

I rattled off my list: Dickens, Gaskell, Collins, Hardy, the Brontes. They all nodded, dutifully, but as I came to the last one, and said: "Trollope's *Barchester Towers*", the mood in the room changed.

"What?" said Williamson. "Did I hear you correctly?" He was a tall, florid, red-faced man with a bald head and an impatient demeanour, who wore his spectacles low on the bridge of his nose, and was noted for his aggressiveness with his students and co-workers alike. He was very light brown in colour, which made him a visual anomaly among the Cojo disciples – the movement was impatient with those of mixed race, preferring the wholly black, and the rare, token white.

"If you heard 'Trollope's *Barchester Towers'*…" I said, catching sight, too late, of Chamaran's almost imperceptible negative shake of the head and Corinne's biting of her lower lip, looking uncharacteristically disturbed. Before I realised it, Williamson was onto me.

"What the fuck is wrong with you people?" he shouted, lunging across the table.

"What… what the fuck…?" I said, pulling back instinctively, taken completely by surprise, and grabbing at the first thing my hand fell upon. As it turned out it was glass pyramid paperweight, and seeing him close to me, his eyes inches from mine and feeling the heat of his breath, I saw I was in an almost completely submissive position, and the tension which had built in me these last few months (and years, I realized), about my disappearing manhood, chose this moment to explode.

"You people? You stupid fucker," I said, to my own surprise, and butted him in the face. As luck would have it I struck him in the nose, where his spectacles rested, and they cut my forehead. He was taken as much by surprise as I was, by the few drops of my blood which wet his forehead. I held the point of the pyramid up to his eye and said: "What if the last thing you saw on earth was one of *we fucking people*?"

We stood frozen like that for several seconds. Then he pulled back and walked out of the room without a word. Chamaran and Corinne exchanged glances, and Chamaran went after him, as I dropped the pyramid, and felt my forehead.

"Well," said Corinne, reaching into her bag and producing a box of tissues. "I didn't think you had it in you. Have a seat. These are antiseptic. I use them to wipe my hands after I handle old documents."

I took the damp tissue, put it to my forehead and sat down, looking up at her, and waited for her to explain. She told me about Trollope's visit to the island, which had preceded Froude's by about two decades, and his account which was equally contemptuous. Williamson was especially annoyed about it because, apparently, Trollope's hosts, then prosperous planters, had later miscegenated, and the Williamsons were one of the brown roots of that miscegenated tree.

"And that's why he attacked me?" I asked in disbelief. "For something that happened more than a century ago?"

"Oh, he's attacked people for much less," said Corinne. "And you can be sure he won't attack you again. But they're sensitive about that kind of thing these days. They're stirred up, you see. Like the Black Power days. Anything that can be perceived as an insult, and that includes things that happened hundreds of years ago. Especially things hundreds of years old. Thank goodness you didn't mention Froude."

And it was then that we had our conversation about Froude and J.J. Thomas, and that moment spurred my curiosity to find my old acquaintance again, to find why, when the war he had been spoiling for seemed about to erupt, he was silent. Corinne had never been close to him, and Mary had lost touch with him. I called the newspapers, but no one knew about him; many of the younger reporters didn't even recognize the name. His house in the city was shut up. Mary asked some of the people who knew him from the embassies, but no one knew where he was. Several weeks passed. It was then I recalled the house on the coast.

I had not been to that end of the island since I went with Froude the last time, and the road was different from how I remembered it. It wasn't just being in a comfortable, air-conditioned car instead of a rattling old jeep – if anything the rolled-up windows and the air-conditioning insulated you from the outside – but I noticed the differences in the towns, the new billboards, the changed facades of the shops, and in the people, who seemed to walk more purposefully, with more energy and, it seemed, with a little defiance, but to what, it wasn't clear. The clothing suggested an even more intimate involvement with the cinema, American music, and a new, violent genre of local music that had found inspiration in the maniacal Jamaican songs threatening unspeakable violence and sexual violation that had succeeded reggae. All this I noticed in passing, because the journey seemed to go by much quicker than I recalled.

Even the little town seemed a little more alive, with a few large shops, new buildings. The church was as I remembered: clean, genteel, and destined to soon fade away. The old gas station where Froude had stopped had a new pump, and a truculent young black man operating it. I drove past, up the hill, along the narrow road, and through the gates. If it had not been for the car parked at the side of Froude's house, I would have turned back. The front porches took the full heat of the afternoon sun and the front door was closed. I sounded my horn and got out and walked around the other car. It was almost new, a sleek, modern version of Froude's Land

Rover. I inspected it desultorily and stood contemplating what to do, and decided that as I had gone that far, it made sense to knock on the door at least. As I was walking up the steps to do that, the door opened and a woman came out. I recognized the eyes instantly; it was the young girl whom I had seen briefly in the kitchen the last time I was here. The skin had the complexion of very light coffee, her bronze-streaked hair was pulled back into a pony tail and the face had fleshed into an enigmatic allure, not quite finished with its youth, but beyond it. Overall the effect was quite stunning.

"Yes," she said inquiringly, and looked at me for a moment before the recognition sparked her features.

"Hello," I said "I'm…"

"Jimmy's friend," she said, smiling. "Of course. I remember you from the last time."

"Ah," I said, surprised. I had seen her for a few minutes at most. "I'm, well, that's surprising… but I suppose I remember you as well…" I finished uncertainly. "Actually I'm looking for…"

"You're looking for Jimmy…" She finished my sentence and stood aside and beckoned me into the house with a graceful, long-fingered hand. I walked in and waited as she closed the door and led me down past the kitchen. It was clear she wasn't a servant. She wore a pair of old, loose, white linen pants with a drawstring, and an armless vest, under which the top of her red bathing suit was visible. I followed her out to the back, my eyes sliding along the perfection of her neck, to the points of her collarbones where they connected at the shoulders, the mesmerizing swirl of the linen around her bare feet. On the porch were the planters' chairs as I remembered them, a small table with sandwiches, a frosty jug of pale liquid I took to be lemonade, and a large, hard-backed book, about the size of a ledger, with a plain black cover. I just managed to see that the pages were filled with sketches rather than text before she closed it and gestured me to the other chair.

"I'm only here for a little while," she said. "You're actually quite lucky to catch me. I thought about leaving yesterday."

"Ah," I said, still a little off balance. "So you're…"

"Jenny," she said, "I'm Jimmy's sister."

"Oh," I said. "I didn't realize you were…"

"Thought I was the maid?" she said, grinning as she offered me a glass of lemonade. "Or would you prefer a beer?"

"Maid... no, I didn't think that," I said. "But I didn't even know he had a sister. Another sister."

"Yes," she said. "Jimmy likes to let people think I'm the help. Or his girlfriend. It's our little joke."

"I can't imagine Froude sharing a joke with anyone that didn't border on mortal offence," I said, relaxing a little, and trying to stop staring at her. She really was breathtaking.

"Oh, Jimmy shares everything with me," she said. "I know all about you, for instance."

"Oh, really? What? I mean what would there be to know?"

She laughed again, showing perfect, strong teeth. "You'd be surprised how many weekends he came here and talked about nothing but you."

"About me?" I asked in surprise.

"You didn't know, then?"

"Know what?"

She smiled gently and tilted her head to look at me with a slightly bemused curiosity.

"That he..."

"Ah," I said. Well, I know now, but back then, I... we never..."

"Jimmy was very taken by you. He thought you were gay for a long time, and was trying to devise ways to lure you up here. But then you started seeing the Dutch girl, and, you know," she said, "he became determined to do everything he could to help you find love. Or something like that.

"Ah," I said, the mention of Mary bringing me back to my mission, and I seized the opportunity to steer the conversation away from my apparent homosexuality, which, with many other things had escaped my notice. "He wouldn't be about, would he?"

"No," she said. "He's away, travelling. He's been gone for a few years."

I contemplated this, and the disappointment must have shown in my face, because she said, "When he's not moving around he stays in our house in London, though. I could give you the address."

I nodded, and she reached for the book on the table, flipped through, tore out a blank page and scribbled on it, and handed it to me.

As I held the page up to read it, I caught a faint scent of the paper I could not quite place. And as I looked at the handwriting – the flourishing, ornate script had become more economical and confident than the last time I'd seen it – I remembered where I had seen it before, and looked at her.

"Please don't think me rude, but what's your name again?"

"Jenny," she said.

"And your last name?"

"Thomas."

"You're J.J. Thomas?" I asked slowly. "But you must have been a child when the letters were written."

"Oh, I'm a little older than I look," she said, blushing a little. "I was a teenager, and it's GJ, actually; Genevieve Jeanne Thomas, but the other J was for James. Another one of our little jokes. At first, Jimmy dictated them as a way of making me practice penmanship, and later, he made notes, and I would write them out."

"But why?" I was perplexed. "Why the whole fiasco?"

"You really don't know him very well, do you?" The beautiful face for the first time betrayed a hint of its own perplexity.

"I think I know him less the more I hear about him," I said, feeling more than a little foolish. "Please, tell me."

J.J. Thomas's Story

"Jimmy's and my mother, Eloise, was born in the village. She was one of those treasures that wash up in wild places, you know, like the diamond the size of a fist the African tribesman finds sitting on a river bank, or the rare, beautiful plant which can cure any ailment that grows in the middle of the jungle. Everyone in the village knew she was special almost from the moment she was born. Her voice had the most wonderful effect on everyone around. From the moment she could talk, she sang, and people would stop working to listen to her. That was decades ago, when this place was still lit by candles and oil lamps.

"She grew up in the church, the school, and the fields. It was hoped she would be the schoolteacher, but it didn't work out that

208

way. Nowadays she would be a savant. She didn't discover this until much later in life, but she had a remarkable gift for languages and music. She spoke ten languages when she died, and began to play the clarinet at fifty-eight. But all there was here back then was the church organ and the old school with a teacher who wasn't much smarter than his pupils. The priest, Father James, taught her music and French, but she was poor and dark, so there was no chance for her to go any further than that, and when old Adolphe Froude saw her, at age fourteen, her fate was sealed in other ways as well.

"Old Froude was at least decent enough to wait until she was sixteen. Father James still maintained some level of control, and Froude had to scheme and wait and manipulate. He owned the village, you know, and had brought his wife here. I think she was suffering from depression, and he didn't want questions asked in Porto Spano. He brought Eloise to the house, to work as a seamstress for his wife, and be her companion, play music for her, read to her. Adolphe and his wife didn't have any children when Eloise's first child for Froude, Jimmy, was born. Father James gave him his name, and the patron saint of the village, St Anthony, as a middle name, and he threatened Adolphe with excommunication if he ever touched Eloise again or refused to support her and Jimmy. That's what made Father James different. Other priests knew, like everyone else, what was going on everywhere in the island. They'd always known, and still white men could do anything, even at that time. If it had been another village, where someone like Eloise was not so well-loved, and protected by someone like Father James, the young girl would just have been sent away, sent to live in shame with her child. It happened a lot, you know.

But Father James needn't have worried. Adolphe was worried that his wife would never have children, and once he saw Jimmy's colour, he was smitten by him, and built a house for Eloise, but left Jimmy with her, because back then he couldn't take him to the city, and his wife made sure the family never came here again. So Adolphe came when he could, to see Eloise and Jimmy, and I was born ten years later, a year after Father James died. Those books in the study room were Father James's, and he left them to

Jimmy. He's read each one at least ten times, and knew all about the Kalahari, the Trobriand Islands, New Guinea, snake cults in India, before he was eleven. When I was little, he used to tell me stories from the books, and promised to take me there, but I never wanted to go.

"Jimmy was as bright as Eloise and Father James took him in and tutored him, and by the time he was eleven, he'd won an exhibition to go to the Catholic College in Porto Spano. It was Father James who first told him that Adolphe had stolen the villagers' land, and from then planted in him the conviction that it should be returned. I think Father James was an forerunner of what we'd call a liberation theologist; he was a Jesuit, and had a strong sense of justice so he fell out many times with the Catholic hierarchy. He was sent here as punishment. But he loved it, and Jimmy was like a seed he planted.

"When it was time for Jimmy to go to school in the city, I was a year old and, as you can see, I took more of my mother than my father's appearance. Froude came and told my mother he had arranged for Jimmy to stay with the priests at the school in the city. But Jimmy refused to go. He told Adolphe he wasn't leaving Eloise or me. Adolphe beat him and took him to the city. He ran away and came back. Adolphe came back again and beat him and took him again, but he came back. So in the end, Adolphe moved us all to the city. He bought us a little cottage, and gave us a little allowance.

"By the time Jimmy had finished school, he'd won every prize there was, and a scholarship to go to Cambridge. Adolphe was by this time bursting with pride. His wife had had children some years after Jimmy was born, but none of his other children had done so well, and he wanted to claim Jimmy as his own. He began telling everyone Jimmy was his son and insisted Jimmy take his name, and took him home and told his wife. Things were changing, and it wasn't uncommon for someone like Adolphe to bring in an outside child. But Adolphe was so struck by Jimmy that he told his children Jimmy would be their boss. I think the boys tried to attack Jimmy once when they were teenagers and old Adolphe beat them with a garden hose.

"I can't remember myself what Jimmy's relations with Adolphe were like. All I know is what Jimmy told me, and he told me that he agreed to take his name, and come back and take over the family business when he'd finished his scholarship – on the condition that he go to the University of London, and not Cambridge, and that he could take Eloise and me with him. I think Jimmy quite hated this place by then, because Adolphe's other children and their mother were so shallow and foolish, and so privileged, and Eloise was so gifted but could do nothing but bear children for the master. That enraged him, and he was determined to take Eloise and me to England with him. Adolphe would have been quite happy to forget about Eloise and me; his interest in her had died once she entered her late twenties – there were always other young girls in other villages.

"Adolphe bought us a house in London, and we all went to live there. For me and Eloise it was like a fairy tale, but Jimmy would tell her no, this was real life, she had just left an awful fairy tale. He took us to concerts, the opera, the theatre, art galleries, and he encouraged her and me to play the piano, the clarinet, to make our lives joyful. Jimmy finished university and then came back to keep his promise. But it wasn't a good time. Independence had come and the new government had run the country down, and it was bad for business. Adolphe died soon after and Jimmy sold off most of the businesses, gave Adolphe's wife and children half of everything, and bid them goodbye. The only contact he shared with them was the house in the village, and he had it split in two so they could have their share. Eloise never came back from London, and while she was alive, I would come back to spend the summers with Jimmy, and after she died, I came back to live with him here during the breaks in college. Then, I just shuttled for a while, trying to decide what to do with myself. Jimmy was like a father – he's always been that to me, and he encouraged me to do nothing but travel, draw, paint, make music. But it was Eloise who got me a job; I'd got her knack for languages, and I'd picked up Greek, Arabic, and Cantonese by the time I finished college, and I was lucky enough to get a job as a translator at the UN in New York, and I'd come back here every other month to go to the beach, draw, and think.

"The year you came was just at the time he'd managed to get the village land transferred back to the owners; he'd had to get them a lawyer, and have them sue him to do it. That appealed to him – suing himself. He wanted me to be here, to take the house from him. He told me that after that he'd done everything he could for the island, and he wanted to go away, and after you left, he did."

Along with what I had seen happen to the island in the few years of my absence, Jenny's story simply added to my accumulation of experiences – which I could not fuse into any coherence. I told Mary about it, and was relieved that she had not known about Froude's origins. I wrote to him the next week, at the address Jenny had provided, to inquire how he was and what he was doing. But even as I wrote the letter, I realized I was unsure about what Froude could have provided me with, what information I really wanted from him, and how unimportant it now seemed. I had lapsed into an uneasy wait for our tenure in the island to expire. About three months before the end of Mary's term, the first radio station licenses were awarded. The African radio station came on air almost immediately, and Cojo began preaching four times a week, about the Africans' destiny to rule, the Asiatics' visitor status, and Africans' entitlement to use force – this sandwiched between litanies of the Asiatics' corruption that passed as news reports – and gospel and evangelical Christian programmes. Cojo quickly generated imitators on other stations, and the rhetoric began to build in intensity. These radio stations became a fetish in those communities lining the northern part of the island; they were everywhere and always on. The Asiatics had launched stations as well, and these flowed with their own demagoguery and bile, but, quite simply, no one listened to them, and theirs was not the rhetoric of mayhem, but of anger and persecution. Everyone who mattered listened to the African stations – the masses who were willing to march, riot, and threaten violence to their enemies. The rage of the small band of former national party sinecures was slowly fed into these people by Cojo and his kind, and from being in an unstable state between despairing apathy and formless anger, their violence became focused by the slogans they heard incessantly on the radio.

The Asiatic government, Mary told me, was furious and they

attempted to shut down the offending stations, but St George was ready for them. Kingsley Gardener, advised by St George, began to speak about the virtues of the press, and the Asiatic government's inherent inability to appreciate the subtleties of concepts like freedom of the press, which further proved their unfitness to rule. Several international organizations, hearing of this struggle for freedom, lent their support. The newspapers concluded that the Asiatic government constituted a threat to democracy, and this occupied the newspapers and the radio stations for months: there were marches for press freedom, front-page editorials, and calls for an election date.

By the time the election was called, we were a month from the end of Mary's term and, we had decided, our departure. There was little doubt now as to what was coming, and more and more of the diplomatic community were quietly sending wives, children, and money home. I visited my parents a few weeks before we left to ask them to come with me.

"Come where?" my mother asked. "With you? To England? What would we do there?"

"Well, not be killed, for one thing," I said.

"And then what?" my father asked. "After not being killed. What about our friends, our home?"

"You can get a new home, and your friends really don't like you that much," I said, getting desperate, but they just looked at each other, and the issue was closed.

On the plane, I saw an article in the latest *Economy* magazine, by Kurtz, which described the difficulty the Asiatic government had in handling democratic necessities like press freedom, for which Gardener and others were courageously struggling. The airline magazine, published by Edgar Wegg, devoted the whole issue to the theme of Caribbean Freedom which, apparently, was found in Carnival, steelpan, Pan Africanism, and in every corner of the Caribbean but the island governed by the Asiatics. I put the magazine aside, leaned on Mary and fell asleep.

At the end of her term, Mary was entitled to two months' vacation, and we decided to stay in London. About two weeks after we arrived, a letter from Froude was forwarded from the island. He was in London, he said, and would be there for some time, and it was a pity I was not there; there were many things he wished to talk to me about.

The house was one of an aristocratic looking line of stylish post-War houses in a genteel suburb in North London. As I walked along the unusually broad street, lined with trees growing out of carefully measured gaps in the pavement, I noticed the Volvos and Saabs, and the other expensive cars, and idly wondered who lived here, and its difference from the places where the new immigrants were found. The pavement was empty; there was no traffic, no school children, no old ladies with shopping trundling home, no young couples out for the evening, walking hand in hand.

Froude answered the door wearing a grey cardigan and dark trousers, and looking much the same as I remembered him, though as I looked at him more closely he was clearly more physically fit. His features were paler but sharper, his posture more erect, his shoulders held more squarely. When he shook my hand, his grip was firmer and the veins on his hand pressed turgidly against the skin. He still had a moustache, and his eyes remained as before, reserved, but alert. I followed him into the wide living room, which was furnished with the same Victorian restraint as Hau Hau House, with rich leather couches, matching footstools, oaken bookshelves, but with a few touches I did not recognize: a metallic coffee table with an intricate leaf pattern on its face and elaborate curved legs; a loveseat in black velvet; modern, cartoon-like drawings framed on the walls; wall-hangings of solid coloured fabric with abstract patterns; theatrical masks that looked as if they were from Restoration court masques.

"Would you like some tea?" he asked.

"No brandy?" I asked.

"It's a bit early in the day, old man," he said, but with a faint smile.

"Since when? Alright," I said. "Tea then."

A few magazines and newspapers sat on the coffee table. I looked through them and saw the *Economy* magazine I'd seen on the plane. I flicked through it, and thought for a moment about what I hoped to find out here: it was to close the mystery of Froude, but I already knew the answers; all I had were a few inconsequential questions which I doubted he would entertain. But as I glanced around the room, I began to discern two different personalities at play. The masks, the hangings, the paintings were new, and did not match with the bourgeois complacency of the brown leather, the creamy walls, the oak bookshelves, the plain rug, and the discreetly yawning black-painted fireplace.

I mentioned this to him when he came back in with the tea.

"Two personalities?" he said. "Interesting observation."

"Hm," I said. "So what did you want to talk about, Froude?"

"What?"

"Your letter, you said there were things you wanted to talk about."

He looked at me, unsmilingly. I had not seen him for years, and our ease and familiarity had not survived the period.

"You've just come back from home?" he asked.

"Yes."

"And what do you think of it all now?"

"What do you think?" I said. "You haven't been there for a while."

"No," he sighed. "I haven't, but I saw what was going to happen. The radio stations have started going, haven't they?"

I nodded, and picked up the *Economy* magazine. "Your dear friend has been keeping you informed, I see."

He scowled and said: "You mean you haven't seen the rest?"

I shook my head but he was already on his feet; he disappeared up the stairs, and returned with a file. They were clippings from the London press, not many, but the names were surprising: Wegg, mostly, and a couple by St George. They were all about the corruption and anti-democratic tendencies of the Asiatics.

"They've been laying the groundwork for the last couple of years," he said. "Talking about threats to democracy and injustice, so when it explodes, the sympathy of the international community will have been prepared. Not that anyone here really cares, but the foreign office collects things like these, and the fellows down there, fellows like Leigh, are sympathetic to the nationalists. The black-white thing you see. No matter how much they beat their chests, they still crave the approval of the whites. It's hard to resist that power and the privileges that come with it."

215

I digested this silently and said, weakly, "Where's J.J. Thomas when we need him…"

He stopped at this, and sat there with the folder on his lap and smiled, then sighed. "Jenny told me you'd caught on," he said. "Good job. I always knew you were a smart one."

"Years late, old man. I'd hardly call that smart. But tell me why…"

But even as I asked I knew why: his unique position to see into both sides of the equation, his divided sympathies allowed him to make arguments no one else was capable of making. And he would have thought it was funny.

"Oh, you know why," he said, and smiled that cynical smile. "And it doesn't matter now, does it? You Asiatics have really done yourselves in."

"Yes, I suppose we have," I said. "But where did you go those years you were away?" But I knew the answer to this, too. "To the dark places of the earth?"

He smiled again. "I started to, you know. I thought I'd trek through Asia, maybe East Africa for a while, but then… then I…"

"You what? Caught a scurrilous disease? Found love? Discovered a new sea route to the Indies? What?

"Yes," he said.

"Yes?"

"Yes," he said, looking at the masks on the wall.

"You mean…?"

"Yes."

"Well, Froude, I suppose congratulations are in order. Where is the dear fellow?

"He's out. He didn't want to meet you, you know."

This was too uncomfortably close to topics I had no desire to probe, so I just nodded, and sipped my tea.

"I thought what I was doing, with the papers and all that, might be useful," he said, "but now, you know, I see it wasn't. I didn't think anyone noticed those Thomas letters, or even knew or cared who he was or what he was about. I misinterpreted history; I misinterpreted how it works. People, and ideas, have a time. I don't know the reason. I don't know who decides what time. But I do know I have never been in the right time. I do know, from what I have seen, now is the time for people like Cojo and Leigh, and I suppose all we can do is either let history work or work against it and be crushed by it. I like the vantage I've got here, and I know Mary has given you such a vantage, on the edge of the whirlpool, as it were. It doesn't sound noble, or heroic. But you can take some comfort from the fact that, in the end, nobility and heroism are indistinguishable from cruelty and luck. And someone has to leave some sign that what happened was not inevitable, that at least, we tried to turn it around, to steer it, to make it better."

"At least you're not losing your faith, old boy," I said.

"I don't know whether it's better to be angry with god, or to ignore him," he said. "I've been angry with him all my life. Now I think I'm going to ignore him for the rest of it."

I smiled a little as I listened to him, and as I was leaving, he said: "Are you staying in the city? Come back, meet the dear fellow. We exiles have to stick together."

I said that I would, and left him. As I walked down the line of white houses to the tube station, two Arab girls who looked like sisters came out of one of the houses that looked identical to Froude's. One wore tight jeans, calf-high leather boots and a short, fitted red leather jacket. Her raven black hair played off her pale skin and red lipstick quite dramatically. The other one wore a Muslim headscarf and long gown which left only the oval of her face uncovered, but beneath it, I saw, she wore the same boots as her sister. I watched them go by in the quickly fading British afternoon, along the clean, empty avenue. I wasn't an exile. I was something far less noble. Something a little despicable.

The END

217

American Fall
ISBN: 9781845230432; pp. 72; 2007; Price: £7.99

Raymond Ramcharitar's sophisticated and formally ambitious poems have Trinidad as their centre but are global in scope. This is reflected both in their subject matter and their form. The regular movement between the Caribbean, Europe and North America that several of the poems chart is seen both as a contemporary reality, and as no more than a continuation of history's patterns: of, for instance, Indo-Trinidadians who are the 'scions of waylaid Brahmins and pariahs'. This particular migration is placed in the context of a wider world of human movement and 'new theologies springing from old longings'. In form, too, the poems refuse to be confined by any limiting sense of the contemporary and the Caribbean. Use of the archetypes of classical mythology, traditional verse patterns (such as the villanelle) and the careful, confident use of rhythm and rhyme are the most evident outward features of Ramcharitar's concern with form. There are homages to Derek Walcott and Wallace Stevens, but the closer one's acquaintance with the poems, the more evident that Ramcharitar's post-modern voice is a thoroughly individual one, with a capacity for writing verse narratives that are condensed but reverberate like the best short stories, dramatic monologues that skilfully create other voices, and lyric poems that get inside the less obvious byways of emotion.

David Dabydeen
Our Lady of Demerara
ISBN: 9781845230692; pp. 288; August 2008; £9.99

The ritual murder of a mysterious Indian girl and the flight of seedy drama critic from his haunts in the back street of Coventry to the Guyana wilds to find out more about the fragmented journals of an Irish missionary in Demerara are brought together in a hugely imaginative exploration of spiritual malaise and redemption.

Brenda Flanagan
Allah in the Islands
ISBN: 9781845231064; pp. 216, August 2009; £8.99

When Beatrice Salandy, first met in Flanagan's novel, *You Alone are Dancing*, is acquitted in a trial that divides the sympathies of the people of Santabella between rulers and ruled, she attracts the attention of the Haji, the charismatic leader of a radical Muslim group. Against her judgement, Beatrice is drawn into his orbit.

Curdella Forbes
A Permanent Freedom
ISBN: 9781845230616; pp. 210; July 2008, £8.99

Crossing the space between the novel and short fiction, this collection weaves nine individual stories about love, sex, death and migration into a single compelling narrative that seizes the imagination with all the courage, integrity and folly of which the human spirit is capable.

Earl Long
Leaves in a River
ISBN: 9781845230081; pp. 208; November 2008; £8.99

What brings Charlo Pardie, a peasant farmer on an island not unlike St. Lucia, on the edge of old age, to leave his wife, family and land and take himself to the house of Ismene L'Aube, known to all as a prostitute? And what, three years later, takes him home again?

Anton Nimblett
Sections of an Orange
ISBN: 9781845230746; pp.152, June 2009; £8.99

In this collection, characters migrate between stories, (just as they migrate between Trinidad and New York), being sometimes at the fringes, sometimes at the centre. Writing with equal empathy about the lives of gay men, heterosexuals, young and old, country folk and urbanites, Anton Nimblett is a singularly attractive new voice in Caribbean writing.

Geoffrey Philp
Who's Your Daddy? and Other Stories
ISBN: 9781845230777; pp. 160; April 2009; £7.99

Whether set in the Jamaican past or the Miami present, whether dealing with sexual errantry, skin-shade and culture wars, with manifestations of the uncanny, or with teenage homophobia, Geoffrey Philp's second collection confirms his status as a born storyteller.

Patricia Powell
The Fullness of Everything
ISBN: 9781845231132; pp. 240; May 2009; £8.99

When Winston receives a telegram informing him of his father's imminent death, his return to Jamaica is very reluctant. 25 years in the USA without contact with his family has allowed mutual resentments to mature. Told through the perspectives of Winston and his estranged brother, the novel explores the power of past hurts and the possibilities of transcending them.

Ed. Courttia Newland & Monique Roffey
Tell-Tales Four: The Global Village
ISBN: 9781845230791; pp. 212; March 2009; £8.99

With contributions from Olive Senior, Matt Thorne, Sophie Woolley, Adam Thorpe, Catherine Smith and twenty others, this collection of stories from the UK-based Tell-Tales literary collective touches on love, sex, death, war, global warming, immigration and crime in sometimes dark and sometimes funny ways.

CARIBBEAN MODERN CLASSICS
Spring 2009 titles

Jan R. Carew
Black Midas
Introduction: Kwame Dawes
ISBN: 9781845230951; pp. 272; 23 May 2009; £8.99

This is the bawdy, Eldoradean epic of the legendary 'Ocean Shark', first published in 1958, who makes and loses fortunes as a pork-knocker in the gold and diamond fields of Guyana, discovering that there are sharks with far sharper teeth in the city.

Jan R. Carew
The Wild Coast
Introduction: Jeremy Poynting
ISBN: 9781845231101; pp. 240; 23 May 2009; £8.99

A sickly city child is sent away to the remote Berbice village of Tarlogie. Here he must find himself, make sense of Guyana's diverse cultural inheritances and come to terms with a wild nature disturbingly red in tooth and claw.

Neville Dawes
The Last Enchantment
Introduction: Kwame Dawes
ISBN: 9781845231170; pp. 332; 27 April 2009; £9.99

This penetrating and often satirical exploration of the search for self in a world divided by colour and class is set in the context of the radical hopes of Jamaican nationalist politics in the early 1950s. First published in 1960, the novel asks many pertinent questions about the Jamaica of today.

Wilson Harris
Heartland
Introduction: David Dabydeen
ISBN: 9781845230968; pp. 104; 23 May 2009; £7.99

First published in 1964, this visionary novel tracks a man's psychic disintegration in the aloneness of the forests of the Guyanese interior, making a powerful ecological statement about man's place in the 'invisible chain of being', in which nature is a no less active presence.

Edgar Mittelholzer
Corentyne Thunder
Introduction: Juanita Cox
ISBN: 9781845231118; pp. 242; 27 April 2009; £8.99

This pioneering work of West Indian fiction is not merely an acute portrayal of the rural Indo-Guyanese world, but a work of literary ambition that creates a symphonic relationship between its characters and the vast openness of the Corentyne coast.

Andrew Salkey
Escape to an Autumn Pavement
Introduction: Thomas Glave
ISBN: 9781845230982; pp. 220; 23 May 2009; £8.99

This brave and remarkable novel, set in London at the end of the 1950s catches its 'brown' Jamaican narrator on the cusp between black and white, between exiled Jamaican and an incipent black Londoner, and between heterosexual and homosexual desires.

Denis Williams
Other Leopards
Introduction: Victor Ramraj
ISBN: 9781845230678; pp. 216; 23 May 2009; £8.99

Lionel Froad is a Guyanese working on an archeological survey in the mythical Jokhara in the horn of Africa. There he hopes to rediscover the self he calls 'Lobo', his alter ego from 'ancestral times', which he thinks slumbers behind his cultivated mask.
Denis Williams

The Third Temptation
Introduction: Victor Ramraj
ISBN: 9781845231163; pp. 108; 23 May 2009; £7.99

A young man is killed in a traffic accident at a Welsh seaside resort. Around this incident, Williams, drawing inspiration from the *Nouveau Roman*, creates a reality that is both rich and problematic. Whilst he brings to the novel a Caribbean eye, Williams refuses any restrictive boundaries for Caribbean fiction.

Visit www.peepaltreepress.com for safe on-line ordering and a wealth of information about Caribbean writing.